Here Be Monsters

Jamie Sheffield

2013

To my wife Gail –
without your endless help and support,
this book would have stayed forever in my head

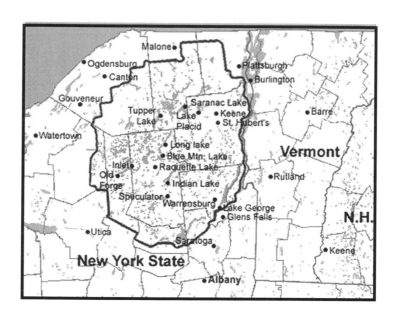

CONTENTS

FOREWORD

When I was a boy, we lived in New York City, in the middle of an orderly and boring gridlike neighborhood, within/abutting a squad of similar neighborhoods; but my dad had maps, lots of maps... they intrigued and seduced me. There were maps of wild places and vast oceans and endless forests and towering mountains and featureless deserts. Some of his oldest maps, from before satellites and airplanes, had empty spaces beyond which nobody had explored. These spaces sometimes had drawings of horrible beasts, and warnings that, "Here be Monsters". I loved the idea of living at the edge of the map, at the rim of uncharted and unknown territories. I promised myself that someday I would live at the edge of the civilized world; I do. The trouble with living at the edge of the map is that the uncharted and unknown territories scare me, and sometimes there are monsters living beyond the light of humanity. Without a good map, you can get lost in the wilderness beyond the edges of maps.

T.C.

BEGINNINGS

Jacob and Sadie, 9/4/2012

There was a gentle glow coming on in the sky to my right as I drove north through the cold and empty beauty of the Adirondack Park. I would have pointed the impending dawn out to the girl in the back of my Element if she wasn't unconscious and bleeding on the easy-to-clean floor. I crossed the northern border of the Park at the same time that the sun crept over the white pines on the side of road. I don't know if that first ray of morning caught her eye, but my passenger groaned, cleared her throat a bit to try and speak, then clacked her teeth hard together again to hold back whatever she was starting to say. I consulted the map in my head, determined that I wouldn't make it to the house before she started acting up, thought about Murphy's Law and the prevalence of state troopers on backcountry roads for only a moment, and then pulled over to deal with Sadie Hostetler.

"Sadie, my name is Tyler Cunningham. I'm a friend of your father, Jacob, and I'm taking you home, unless you'd prefer to go to a hospital." I spoke in the same low tone I use with the skittish dogs I walk at the shelter. I'd talked with Dorothy about this very moment, what I should say if I did manage to find Sadie, and how I should say it. Dorothy runs the animal shelter in Saranac Lake, and if I had friends, she would be one of them.

Based on a lifetime of reading everything within reach on every subject that caught my eye, my opening statement to Sadie should have been reassuring. It should have started to build some trust between us; it didn't. I'd pulled over and opened the door to the back of the car, so when she hit me with her shoe, we didn't crash, but that was the only good news. She raked for my eyes with significant talons that I hadn't noticed when loading her into the car at a little before 5 a.m. that morning. I grabbed her in a bear hug to try and still her; it didn't work. When she started trying to butt me with the back of her head, I pushed her away from me.

"STOP IT!" I yelled, in a much less sympathetic tone than Dorothy might have used in the same situation, but my ear hurt (*from the shoe*) and my cheek stung (*from her nails*).

"I'm not going to hurt you, we're only about ten miles from your home, your family likely already has breakfast on the table, and that's where I'll take you if you will stop hitting and screaming." We were actually closer to 9.2 road miles from Sadie's home, but I've found that people without maps (*and brains*) like mine don't want or need that level of exactitude.

"Who the fuck are you, what's going on, and why on Earth would you think that I want to go to my father's house?" she asked in a tone that I believed signaled anger and fear and frustration, but not imminent violence.

"My name is Tyler Cunningham, owner and operator

of SmartPig Thneedery. I'm bringing you back home at the request of Jacob Hostetler, your father. I'm not at all certain that you want to go home, but I'm very nearly certain that it's a better option than the place you were until a couple of hours ago." Again, 108 minutes is more precise than people generally look for in conversations.

"Your dad ... father, asked for my help when he heard from a friend of yours, Hannah, that you had gotten in some trouble, and subsequently disappeared, while on your Amish version of Walkabout ... Rumspringa." This next bit wasn't true, but it was close enough for a girl that had my right ear ringing and blood running down my face and into the collar of a reasonably new shirt. "I owed him a favor, and he asked. Finding you in my world is the sort of thing I'm better at than he would be, or he would have done it himself."

"How did you find me?" she asked, now with some interest and a hint of trust in her voice ... at least no open hostility.

"The same way I do everything else, I read and I research and I ask questions ... I throw stones in the water, watch the ripples, and adjust my aim until something happens." I could tell that my answer didn't satisfy her, but also that she wasn't going to ask again, which worked just fine for me.

"What are you going to tell my father about how and where you found me?" she asked, noticing for the first time, perhaps, that she had on a too-big man's shirt (*mine, from the get-home-bag I keep in the car*) and a pair of panties that wouldn't be out of place in a dirty laundry-bag.

"He asked me to bring you home, and that's what I plan to do. What you decide to tell Jacob about the last week of your Rumspringa is your business. Will those men in Placid know how and where to find you, if they decide to look?"

"N-no," she stammered, paling and clenching all over with the memory. "They only knew my first name, unless ... my purse!"

"It was on your barstool when you vanished from the bar two nights ago. Your friend Hannah grabbed it and gave it to me when I talked to her yesterday. It's on the front seat, where you can ride now if you want. So we ... you should be clear."

She nodded and looked up into my face from the back of my car, and giggled unexpectedly (*to me, at least*), "You're not what I expected."

"What did you expect, the Marines?"

"No, I had this fantasy that my father and uncles would come in whacking those guys with ax handles, or something. I didn't figure on a skinny guy who would cry because of a scratch from a girl."

"I'm tearing, not crying ... and for your information, the scratch really hurts. It could get infected."

Sadie smiled and moved into the front seat. We headed down the road again through the thinning woods and into the farmland of far-northern New York, towards home.

Jacob's dog heard my car long before I got to their house, and they both were waiting by a pole-fence when I crunched into the circle in front of the Hostetler home. The Amish dress and the lack of pickup trucks in the farm's yard made me feel as though I was driving out of the present day (*where girls got snatched as playthings for monsters masquerading as boys*) and into something that Norman Rockwell (*or his father*) might have drawn.

Jacob nodded at Sadie and waved her up onto the porch where her mother Mary was waiting. He spoke to me only after the women had embraced and gone inside with arms around each other. "You'll come inside for coffee."

It was a statement, not a question, and so even though I would have preferred a CCoke, or to be home in bed, I climbed the stairs into Jacob's house, nearly tripping on one that was taller than the others. We sat at a heavy kitchen table made from slabs of maple wood that was probably chopped to clear the land for this farm a hundred years ago. A younger model of Sadie put steaming cups of black coffee in front of us and closed the door behind her as she left us alone in the hot and pleasantly yeasty kitchen.

Before I made the drive up here to meet Jacob two days earlier, I had (*as always*) done some research, in this case on the Amish, and particularly the Amish of Northern New York. Each small community has their own "Ordnung", or set of rules relating to the "Demut" (*humility*) and "Gelassenheit" (*calmness*). Jacob was the leader of the community in Madrid Springs, which included eighteen families. His interpretation/ understanding of the rules was law in their valley. Coming to me, an outsider, for help with his daughter had cost him ... might end up costing him the position of leadership he held in his community. I had asked him about it when we met on the second, and he dismissed it with a wave, either assuming that I wouldn't understand because I was an outsider, or that I took it for granted that people took care of family, regardless of cost.

"Tyler Cunningham, I can never thank you in any meaningful way for what you have done for me and for my family." While he was verbally sneaking up on what was, for him, an uncomfortable subject, I studied ... him, his clothes, his kitchen (*most of the room was taken up by a wood-cooking stove and this huge table*), the faucets at his sink,

7

gas and kerosene lanterns on the wall and overhead, and the lack of outlets along the walls. I was mapping this place and the way that it felt and smelled and sounded. I could feel my brain sucking it all in, and the maps that I have inside my head of people and places and ways of being, growing, extending. My interest in Jacob's world was the reason I had allowed myself to be roped into this mess in the first place; not the money he was going to awkwardly offer me in a minute or five.

"My friend Gregory Simmons told me that you helped him a few years ago," (*it was actually seventeen months ago*) "and that you would help me, but in my rush and upset of the other day, we did not discuss your fee. We can pay any fair price that you name and will count ourselves blessed by God to do it."

"I'm not a detective. I'm just a guy who does favors for friends with problems or situations that interest me." There was no upside that I could envision in telling him that his daughter didn't interest me nearly so much as the plumbing in their house, or the presence of a gas-powered tractor with wooden wheels on a farm with no trucks.

Jacob seemed flustered by a response different than what he had anticipated, "Is your coffee all right?" I hadn't touched the mug in front of me, while through some magic of timing or signals, as soon as he had finished his, the younger daughter had come in, refilled it, and left again without being asked or summoned.

"It smells wonderful, but I don't enjoy hot drinks." Jacob took this in, looked as though the words hadn't come together in a configuration that he was used to, and pressed ahead.

"I have paid my way in this world since I was fifteen."

"Gregory bought one of my photographs after the

favor that I was able to do him," I suggested.

He seemed to understand this quid pro quo, and followed up on it. "I saw this photograph when I went to seek Gregory's help in the matter of Sadie, and it's a little ... showy for my taste."

"Last spring I painted a series of watercolors twenty miles east of here ... fields and barns and streams and sky. I used a soft color palette that might go nicely with both your beliefs and with the colors in your house. The last painting I sold in that series went for five-hundred dollars."

Jacob seemed relieved to have a number, and excused himself for a minute, returning with five one-hundred dollar bills. He put them in my hand with some ceremony, and intoned, "For the rest of my life, when I look at the painting, I will remember the service that you did me and my Sadie. Still though, I hope that you will call upon me if you ever have need. It would be a blessing to help you if it is within my power."

I told Jacob that I'd bring the painting around within the week. We talked for a few minutes more, about Rumspringa and having to explore the world in order to know it, and the possibility of beauty without the sting of evil. We were talking about Sadie, but also about Jacob and about me. We shook hands and I walked out and down and into my car (*adjusting my stride to avoid tripping over the single uneven step on my way off of the porch*).

I left the Hostetler Farm at 8:14 a.m., and headed south, headed home to Saranac Lake, New York. I had expanded my world and maps a little, and seen but not learned (*again*) the lesson that a simple life in a simple place is not talisman against bad things or bad people. The next ten days would teach me this lesson once and for all, at great cost, and in ways that I couldn't imagine as

I navigated my mental map of the world I had built. Everything would be new and unfamiliar, and for people like me, the unfamiliar (*even good, if unfamiliar*), is worse than an anticipated bad thing.

About halfway down to Saranac Lake, at 9:03, I celebrated the twenty-ninth anniversary of my birth, as always, in silence and with a hollow awareness of my movement through time and space.

DISRUPTION

Beginnings and Beyond, still 9/4/2012
(*with some background in sidebar form*)

I pulled into my parking space behind SmartPig, grabbed the small bag of garbage (*and medical waste*) from the back, and headed up the back stairs to really start my day. I grabbed a Coke from the Coke-fridge, a banana from the fruit bowl, got my laptop going, and stole some Wi-Fi from my downstairs neighbor to check my email (*I have my own internet connection, but stolen Wi-Fi is in some ways more satisfying when it will suffice to the need*). I weeded out the spam that made it past Gmail's algorithms, and was left with one email from Frank, one from Cynthia, one from Dorothy, one from Mickey, and seventeen articles from various sources in PDF or .doc format. Eleven years later, I still catch myself looking for birthday messages from my parents, especially my mom.

—sidebar—

I was born on September 4, 1983, a day made famous by my birth and by a group of crazies walking across the bottom of Sydney Harbor in Australia; my dad had an article that he ripped out of a newspaper (*and saved forever*) while waiting for me to "arrive". For the first eighteen years of my life, I was homeschooled, which to many people suggests kooks or hippies, but in my case meant a consortium of "Masters of the Universe" (*MUs*) who, like my parents, had somehow ended up with children, and took turns teaching each other's kids whatever they were good at (*or interested in*) and organizing fieldtrips to museums or zoos or businesses or concerts or libraries in and around New York City (*where I grew up*). The MUs considered this to be superior to either the public or private schools available at the time ... (*an opinion that I shared ... I wouldn't have functioned well in either of the other two educational settings*).

On my eighteenth birthday, at 9:03 a.m. exactly (*because we made great ceremony of time in our family*), my parents and I had a discussion about where my education was going. They argued for college, I countered with reading (*always a strength of mine*) and shifting from student to teacher in our homeschooling collective. The topic was tabled forever a week later when they were killed at their offices during the attack on the World Trade Center (*Dad worked for Wexler Insurance in Tower 1, Mom worked for Xerox in Tower 2*). The 9/11 attacks changed the physical, and my personal, map of New York City (*which was my whole world until that Tuesday*) completely. We had gone to the Adirondacks one summer for a week; the difference and the wildness called to me ... so I went.

/sidebar

I worked my way through the emails, top to bottom based on their arrival. Frank wanted to meet with me, and suggested the neutral ground of his son's afternoon football practice. Cynthia had some ideas for some research I was doing, reminded me that some books that I had wanted through inter-library loan had arrived, and mentioned something interesting had come up that she wanted my help with when I was free again. Dorothy sent pictures of a new dog at the shelter, and wanted to know when I'd be out to visit. None of the ones from people up in the Adirondacks mentioned, or had reason to know about, my birthday, which was a relief. I haven't celebrated a birthday since my eighteenth, and could happily die that way. Mickey, who was one of the parents from my childhood teaching and learning consortium in NYC, wished me a happy birthday, asked about what had happened since we last talked (*his birthday on June 9th, the same date as Henry Dale and Les Paul*), and asked me to give him a call when I got a chance. He is one of the few remnants of my old life that has stuck with me through the years, and communication with him is awkward for me ... both anticipated and avoided. His contact reminds me of being loved and being a part of a circle/group, and highlights (*to me, if not him*) my inability to return love, or even friendship, in any of the ways that other people seem to do so easily. I answered the emails: sounds good, thanks, later today, and I will ... and then read the articles.

I read everything that I can get my hands on covering a variety of subjects ranging (*this morning*) from: insect predation in the Amazon, to mountain erosion and deposition rates around the world, to trends in violent crime around the US (*looked at both geographically and from a population density standpoint*). The PDF articles were a mix of inter-library loans (*ILL*), some from Cynthia or other library/research geeks that I know, and some from me; I either found/sent them, or emailed the authors for copies based on references I found to the articles in other stuff that I read. While I took notes, other lines of research/interest occurred to me, and by the time I had finished the last article, I was ready for the library. I grabbed another Coke from the Coke-fridge, fed the fish in my saltwater tank, and headed down the stairs to the almost invisible door that led onto Main Street.

I like to think that the world is my classroom, but my local base of operations is the Saranac Lake Free Public Library (*SLFPL*). Primarily they keep me in paper books, fiction and non-fiction of all sorts. While I love learning online, I'll never lose my bias for printed paper. For a small town library, they maintain a wonderful collection, and seem to exist solely to order what books they don't have for me through ILL. I discovered the Adirondack Research Center, housed in their basement, a few years ago, and found that the more I learn about the Adirondack Park, the more I want to know about the place and the people. Besides the physical books and journals that they have on-hand, or can acquire for me, the SLFPL gives me access to all sorts of databases as well as help from my personal (*and unpaid*) research assistant, Cynthia.

I first met Cynthia Windmere on December 9, of 2001, a few days after I had decided on Saranac Lake as my new base of operations; and, if I was the kind of person who had friends, she would be my friend. I walked into the SLFPL with a few bizarrely diverse topics of interest/research, and she cleared her desk and invited me to join her behind the counter. Three and half hours later, I walked out with my library card, twenty-six articles printed from various databases, eleven books (*two pleasure reading, nine 'schoolwork'*), and an appointment with the curator of the Adirondack Research Center for the following day (*to start my immersion in their collection*). I know, and am known by, all of the people working in the library, but it is most often Cynthia that I work with, especially when trying to explore new or tricky research sources or materials.

On the too-dark afternoon of March 26, 2002, Cynthia told me to ask her out for coffee at the end of a particularly long session digging through some databases for information on drug use in the U.S. and abroad. She invested herself more than usual in her work whenever we were looking at anything having to do with the world of illicit drugs, and this day was no exception. I now think that she perceived a growing common bond between us, beyond my studies, and wanted to expand on it outside of her workplace; a perfectly reasonable thing to do, but that's exactly the sort of social nuance that I don't understand. "I don't drink coffee or other hot beverages," was my standard response, and it initially worked, but then she suggested an early supper. I mentioned that I had some leftover pizza up in the SmartPig office fridge that I planned to nuke; and at that point she left it, and me, alone.

I was reading a murder mystery later that night, and came across a passage strangely reminiscent of the scene that Cynthia and I had played out in the library that afternoon, and I had a twenty-watt revelation. I stayed away from Cynthia and the library for weeks out of a combination of shame and fear and lack of understanding. I relied on the information that I could harvest for myself online, buying books at a used bookstore in Lake Placid, and twice sneaking into the library when I knew that Cynthia wasn't working. Growing up in New York City, it was relatively easy to avoid or ignore people, based on the size and impermanence of the population, but the same was not true of Saranac Lake.

She tracked me down one evening upstairs in SmartPig, saying, "I saw the light on, and hoped that I could catch you." I just looked at her, until after an interval of eleven seconds she spoke again. "I don't want you to avoid me or the library anymore. I don't know if you've got a girlfriend or are gay or just aren't interested, but I miss you and your 'studies', and the way you jump from topic to topic. I was going to leave it alone for a while longer, but one of the database admins got in touch with me to find out why our traffic has halved in the last month, and it pushed me into coming here tonight," she admitted with a slight grin.

I looked at a spot on the wall behind her. "I'm not gay, and I don't have a girlfriend. I'm interested in you, but not in the way you mean, or maybe want. I like working with you at the library, and was comfortable knowing the way you think and sit and talk and type, and access information and guess related subjects that I might want to check out next, but I don't really have friends, and I don't kiss, and I'm not interested in sex." I got this last bit out as a wheeze, my breath running out with the final syllable. "I don't know what I did, or how I broke our relationship, how we relate, but I want it to be like it was before, and I don't want you to be gone from my life, or be sad or be angry with me." The final thought was a drop-in at the last moment, based on a memory of previous relationships that had changed for reasons that I didn't understand, and how the people looked like they felt when it happened.

"Oh ..." she said, and took a half step forward, stopped, and cocked her head as if she could see me better at an angle. "Ok ... well ... I've got some good stuff to show you, based on what we were working on last time, and what you've been working on in the Adirondack Research Center with Tim. I hope to see you tomorrow," she said and then left.

I was in the library when it opened at 10 a.m. the next morning, with a coffee for her and my usual Coke. We took turns feeling awkward for a couple of days until we got our work back on track, and we even got together for a separate-check dinner at the Chinese place on Main Street a week later, something that grew into a weekly event over the years. Sometimes she has a boyfriend, sometimes she doesn't; but to the extent that I relate to/with other people, we have each other for work and talk and weekly dumplings and orange chicken with broccoli.

The background on our relationship was so that you would understand my state when a newish library intern handed me a stack of books and printed articles from a shelf behind the desk that they added for me thirty-eight months ago, and mentioned casually that Cynthia hadn't been in so far this morning or yesterday; and hadn't answered her phone when Beth, the intern, had called with questions about a book club that they were in together. I asked Beth to get Ben, the director of the library, for me, and I sat down to wait.

"She spoke to me last week about some personal stuff that she was dealing with. She said that she needed to take Friday and Monday off and might need to take some more time off or work a reduced schedule for a while if things got complicated." Ben said to me, by way of explanation for his state of calm with Cynthia being absent from work. I'm not great with facial or tonal expressiveness, so I asked Ben if 'complicated' was his word or Cynthia's; it was hers.

"I expect that someone in her family is sick or dying or dead, and she had to leave in a hurry. I'm assuming that whatever took her away for Friday and yesterday stretched into today ... we can cover her time and duties. She's never missed much work before, so it's no big deal. I expect that she'll answer my email in a day or so, with an update and explanation ... you know ... family," he ended with an expressive shrug of his shoulders that conveyed nothing of use to me.

I had no response to his statement, or shrug, and no reason to talk anymore with Ben. So, I grabbed my books and articles, went back to SmartPig to drop them off, and headed over to Cynthia's home to see if she was in.

Whispers, still 9/4/2012

As a boy, I wandered the streets in our neighborhood on the Upper West Side in concentric circles with our apartment as the point of origin. I wasn't comfortable/ happy until I had a map in my head a mile on each side with our home as the center. From there, I worked my way out through Manhattan and the boroughs, enlarging my 'familiarity map' along lines of customary travel and utility. I knew where there were movie theaters, and branches of the New York Public Library, and playgrounds/parks. The map extended for miles in every direction along the easy to access subway lines and bus routes, but there were blank spots in places that were difficult to reach or that held no appeal to me. My map essentially ended at 96th street on both sides of Central Park, except for an island of known territory near Columbia University. I crossed an ocean of "empty space" on a regular basis to get to that area known both for their spectacular library, and for the best barbeque place in New York.

When I lost New York City, I drove north until I found a sizable trio of towns in a boundless ocean of trees—Tupper Lake, Saranac Lake, and Lake Placid. The wilderness, and its lack of definition, kept me awake and on edge for weeks after I moved to Saranac Lake; then I started over the same procedures that I had used as a boy to find my place in the world. I walked, and then drove, in circles, exploring Saranac Lake and Lake Placid and Tupper Lake. I got to know the main streets, and the back streets, and the places in between the towns where houses became scarce, and the roads on the way to nowhere where houses hid.

Once I had a map in my head of my new world, I looked at physical maps of the "empty" spaces between the towns and outposts; the Adirondack Park covers more than six million acres, some of it little towns and roads and such, but much of it simply trees and lakes and mountains and swamps and bugs and beasts. Early on, I found that people up here all had maps of the Adirondacks in their heads, most of them entirely devoid of detail for the majority of the Park; the space between Saranac Lake and Lake Placid is, to most people, made up of a road going from the former to the latter, with trees by the side of the road, but nothing else.

The map in my head reminded me a model of a carbon atom, a moderately densely packed nucleus (*Saranac Lake*) with clusters of electrons (*Lake Placid or Tupper Lake*) orbiting at a distance along tiny paths; with vast amounts of empty space between each component. The difference being that some cool forests and lakes and mountains and swamps actually took up the space between the towns (*and to an even greater extent between my three towns and the rest of the world*).

I made it my goal to learn about the Adirondack

wilderness, to find the great places and add them to my mental map. I added great walks and mountain climbs, and camping spots, and canoe trips. Then a few years into my discovery and mapping project, I discovered that the map of the woods was entirely different in the winter; I redrew the map with parenthetical winter notes as I learned to enjoy the wilderness in the cold months (*skiing, snowshoeing, camping, ice-climbing, and so on*). The mapping process allowed me to familiarize myself with the place I was living without ever having to get to know (*or map*) the people living around me (*a deficit that I was both used to, and untroubled by*).

I found myself thinking of the unfamiliar ocean of people that I swam in every day as another unmapped wilderness. Once I had processed that, and tried to knock it apart, I grudgingly started to map a few of the people in my world. I've never been very good with people, I don't understand why they do the things they do, and why they cannot spend time alone or quiet. My people-mapping project is going slowly, and the map is still limited to those I have to interact with most frequently, with vast emptiness all around these lines radiating out from me to those few that I know, like Frank and Gregory and Dorothy and Mickey and ... Cynthia.

Cynthia's house is, as is too often the case to be coincidence, very much its occupant—Cynthia ... small, neat and businesslike. This occurs to me every time I pull into the driveway (*and every time it makes me wonder what that truism says about me*). I heard someone else describe her house as a red brick shoebox, with a too-flat roof and too many windows. But, they likely never hid from a Nor'easter in it, watching Cynthia gleefully run between front and back windows at the sound of snow dumping off of the metal roofing (*I don't emote much myself, but learning human emotions has been a lifelong pursuit, and Cynthia is a superb subject).* I stepped up onto the big fieldstone by the front door, and squashed the bell with my thumb for five seconds before listening for a response.

I moved my head closer to the left side of the entry, where I had helped Cynthia replace a broken security inset with a piece of single pane glass after we had to break in one cold night. Turning my ear in towards the house, I looked back up the street to see if anyone had noted my time on the entry porch. I could hear nothing but the grandfather clock just inside the door and that generic hum that electrical current seems to give a house. I couldn't see anyone on the street or in windows of any of the houses facing me, so I grabbed the key from Cynthia's hide-a-key stone, and let myself in. I was a bit surprised that the bolt was engaged, but figured that maybe she locked up more seriously when going away for a death in the family, went inside and closed the door behind me.

People have secrets. People trust in their houses to keep all sorts secrets, but a house is just a box to keep the rain out; the secrets are still there, and everyone hides them in the same places. I'm really good at getting people, and houses, to give up their secrets; but I wasn't going to give Cynthia's a truly thorough going over ... I had neither the time, nor did I wish to invade her personal space to that degree.

I checked the front hall closet and noted that Cynthia's raincoat was gone, but her running shoes weren't. There was an odd smell in the kitchen, so I looked under the sink and found she hadn't taken a day or two's worth of garbage with her when/if she went. She had washed, but not put away the last meal's dishes, looked like supper. Her bathroom held no surprises (*I look in other peoples' cabinets/drawers whenever I get a chance, and also read the P.D.R. whenever a new edition comes out).* It looked as though she had taken a couple of prescription bottles *(from the empty space on that shelf in her cabinet),* but not her contact lens stuff. There was a hamper full of clean clothes on the bed, but that doesn't mean much *(I have two hampers, one for clean clothes that gets emptier as time passes, and one for dirty clothes that gets more full as time passes ... when clean is empty, dirty full, I go to the laundry place).*

She hadn't put a vacation feeder *(which I am certain are a scam, but she fervently believes keep her fish happy and healthy)* in the ten gallon tank in her living room. I felt odd doing it, but I unwrapped and dropped one of the things into the tank, because she'd want it for her fish. Her car was not in the garage. I found 850 dollars in the freezer, a loaded pump-action shotgun in the front hall closet *(a Remington 870 in twelve gauge),* some items I won't discuss in a bedside table, and a picture of me and Cynthia that I don't remember anyone taking. I found the picture about halfway down through a stack of pictures that included shots of old people that might have been grandparents, a very young Cynthia with a nearly identical sister, a succession of boyfriends posing with Cynthia, and a picture of Cynthia and two people that must have been her parents at what I assume was Cynthia's college graduation. None of what I found helped me decide where she was, but the picture made me feel nervous/uncomfortable ... I hadn't thought that anybody had pictures of me, and wondered if it implied/represented some social contract between Cynthia and me.

I was certain that Cynthia was out of town, but found myself oddly uncomfortable with some of the findings of my search *(running shoes, garbage, dishes, contacts, and the unfed fish*). Cynthia had gone out of town before in a rush, and forgotten things, but I have learned over the years to trust the grumblings of my sub-conscious, as it generally takes more information into account than is available to my forebrain. Determined to both push a bit, and give the lizard bits in the back of my head time to figure things out, I backed my car out of the driveway and drove back to my parking spot behind SmartPig. I went upstairs to try and think and take a nap before I had to meet Frank in a couple of hours.

SmartPig, still 9/4/2012

SmartPig Thneedery is my base of operations, my office,
my bat-cave, my studio, my bolt-hole, and my place from
which to watch the Winter Carnival Parade on Main
Street each February. I can walk to almost everything I
ever need in town, and sometimes go a week without
seeing my Honda Element in the parking lot behind the
building. "SmartPig" is from a play-on-words game that
my dad used to play with me about our last name,
Cunningham. He would come up with variations on the
theme in different languages as I grew older, but SmartPig
(*from when I was four*) was always our favorite. The concept
of a Thneed, an item that can be anything to anyone,
came from a duck-squeezer book my mom read to me
when I was a kid. I loved the idea of a Thneed, if not the
transparent agenda of a children's' ecologist with
questionable credentials. I am seldom whimsical, but
when the landlord asked me what should go on the
nameplate and mailbox, I told him, "SmartPig
Thneedery".

As the name suggests, I provide all sorts of things to all sorts of people; most of it entirely legal, some of it a bit less so. I do charcoal drawings, carve wooden decoys and fishing lures, mess around with digital photography, make a few bits of camping gear, investigate and solve mysteries, work at watercolor landscapes (*I use more cerulean blue than I should, but it's coming along*), split and stack wood, deliver Adirondack/regional documents, and also make dog and cat treats.

Your eye likely skipped through the list, and then jumped back to the one in the middle about investigations and mysteries; mine does also, but it's the one that's most problematic and that I understand the least. All of the other things, along with a dozen more that take up the majority of my time as a thneed-tician, I learned by reading about and reverse-engineering samples and talking to experts in the field; the only explanation that I have for the sleuthing is that I read a lot.

I used to love to read detective/crime novels: Block, Burke, Chandler, Child, Christie, Crichton, Deaver, Doyle, Hamilton, Hammett, Hiassen, Leonard, MacDonald, Parker, Sandford, Stark, Stout, Thomas, and lots of others to a lesser degree (*the ones that I listed above have been read completely, with other authors I read only selected works*). Starting at about eight years old, I started mixing these books in with the other things my "teachers" had me read as a part of my education, like spices in a nutritional but sometimes boring stew. They kept me reading when the other kids in the homeschool collective wanted to get together after school hours ... I couldn't relate to them in the ways that they (*and I?*) wanted. Mysteries provided relief and escape from the pressures of being different (*in my own different way*). I have a list of sixty-seven books that I've worn out with repeated reading, they got me through the months after 9/11, and carried me through to my new life here (*I have multiple copies of each of these books cached in a couple of spots in case of zombocalypse, Ebola, or some other extinction level event that miraculously spares me*). I think that reading detective/crime fiction would be my guilty pleasure, if I understood or felt guilt.

Mysteries, along with reading books in other fields of interest that I've data-mined over the years, combines with the way that my brain works and allows me, from time to time, when the mood (*or subject matter related to the mystery*) inspires me to do so, to dabble in private investigations. Most of the time though, I find other things that I'm more interested in than other peoples' problems, such as camping and/or exploring the Park to expand my mental world map.

I felt a nagging concern for Cynthia that I couldn't shake or get to solidify into reasoned thought; it just lurked at the edge of my consciousness bothering me (*like a mosquito inside your tent can do*). I had been thinking about her a bit while breaking into and exploring her house, chewing it over in my back-brain while rifling through her things, wondering if she had in fact lost a parent during my brief absence (*to the best of my knowledge, she has no other close family*). She had talked with me briefly the previous Thursday about something that she needed my help with (*more specifically, she had said "your kind of help"*); something having to do with drugs (*a boogeyman topic perennially lurking under the bed or in the closet for her*). She had started talking about it in the library, and then shut down at some point, while describing the information/proof that she had gathered, and asked if she could meet with me after her work to discuss a "field-trip" to see what we could find out and prove.

Later that afternoon, I got a call from my acquaintance Gregory, and tumbled headlong into my Amish adventures for a long weekend of research and driving, six minutes of agonizing stress, followed by more driving. I had begged off on the meeting with Cynthia, and promised to look her up when I got back, but now she wasn't ... here. I had a feeling of dislocation and anxiety that reminded me in some ways of the days and weeks following 9/11.

I grabbed a Coke from the Coke-fridge and sat down at the kitchen table by the big window overlooking Main Street. I don't have a kitchen, but the table is nice for working or reading or thinking ... for thneeding. I sat down prepared to think about tracking down Cynthia in an orderly manner, using a sharpie and my big pad of newsprint paper; and before I even got started, I knew, without much room for doubt, that Cynthia had been taken while messing around with stuff with which I should have been helping her ... the stuff that she had asked me to help her with.

I can't explain the process or even the leaps that my mind takes from observation to conclusion any more than a dog could explain to me why one stick is better than another, or a fisherman can explain catching fish to a novice. Knowledge and observation and experience mix together with wiring in our brains and miraculous things happen. Regardless of how it happened, I was now in a place where I no longer thought about finding so much as rescuing or possibly recovering Cynthia. The trouble was that I had no idea how to do that; while the initial stages of my investigation may have been a closed book, the next step was a blank page.

I felt a driving and personal need to find her and fix this ... I had allowed her to place herself at risk, and I had to undo the damage that I had done. I had wasted four days getting a complete stranger out of an admittedly nasty situation of her own making, at Cynthia's expense (*to what degree I still had no idea*). I had found the Amish and "Rumspringa" aspects, contrasting with the "club-kid" and date-rape slick-nastiness of Jacob's (*and Sadie's*) problem more interesting than Cynthia's long-term hang-up on the drug trade. Now, though, I wanted those days back; would have traded Sadie back to the boys that took her for Cynthia in a second. A part of me wanted to bring the police in now, this very second; but I knew that they wouldn't be particularly interested or motivated to find her without more concrete reasons to worry.

I needed to think, but it felt as though that was the one thing on Earth that I was incapable of at that moment; my anger at myself for getting seduced by the plain but mysterious ways of the Amish, and at Cynthia for potentially jumping into harm's way by herself without waiting for me, was interfering with the normal functioning of my thought-process. I found it slightly interesting and very scary, as I do most new things in my life.

When I investigate things, I don't do what police do, because the police are good at what they do, have more men and time and equipment than I do, and are trained to think and act in a logical and straightforward manner that solves the vast majority of crimes that are going to be solved quickly and efficiently. If Cynthia could be found through those means, then the police would do it; so I had to find other means. In other investigations that generally means reading everything that I can find on the matter and/or pushing on everyone even remotely involved, and watching for reactions or mistakes that lead me to a next stage, and eventually to the subject of my investigation. I needed to think about how to proceed with Cynthia as the object of my investigation, mindful of the ever-present possibility that I was wrong, and that she was at her Aunt Mo's funeral, and would be angry and hurt by my intrusion both into her house and into her affairs.

I lay down on the couch that often serves as my bed, balancing the half-empty Coke can on my forehead, and focusing on keeping it balanced to avoid a sticky mess until the conflicting opinions/feelings/worries about Cynthia quieted down a bit (*thus hopefully avoiding another kind of sticky mess*); then I moved it to the floor and went to sleep for a bit.

I woke up nearly four hours later. I keep trying to program a clock in my head, as some characters in books I've read seem able to do. Admittedly, my brain seems as though it should be well-suited to this sort of thing, but no luck so far, so I try to come up with interesting facts about my nap lengths. I splashed my face and thought about 233 minutes of sleep ... not only is it a prime number, but it's also the thirteenth number in the Fibonacci sequence ... and a sexy prime. I was determined to try and sleep 239 minutes after getting some work done (*I don't sleep for more than two to four hours at a time, unless I'm sick*). The face-bath and numerical nerdery had me awake enough to face Frank for our informal meeting at his son's football practice. (*I've never been to an actual informal meeting that needed to identify itself as such, so I had my doubts about this one*). I grabbed a Coke from the Coke-fridge and a handful of jerky from the cupboard on my way out.

Frank, still 9/4/2012

I walked over to the football field outside of Petrova Middle School. I would have been able to pick Frank out of the crowd even if I didn't know him, he was wearing his uniform. The juxtaposition of the informal setting and official costume balanced the tenor of our meeting with a reminder (*implicit threat*) about the way the meeting could go if everyone (*me*) wasn't smart. Frank Gibson is a police officer working for the Saranac Lake Police Department, and we've been playing a careful game of cat and bigger cat since I arrived in the Adirondacks. He probably could have been chief by now, if he was more interested in doing the correct thing (*as opposed to the right thing*) and less interested in knowing the answers to questions he shouldn't ask. I was willing to bet a fridge full of Coke that today's meeting was going to be all about Sadie and Jacob and the car fire unless I could derail him with something he would find more interesting.

"A state trooper, friend of mine, saw you driving a few under the speed limit on Route 56, a bit south of

Potsdam, early this morning." Frank's opener set the tone a bit ... no question as such, so I did my quiet thing.

"Coming back from a birthday party?" he added, to give my comfortable silence a nudge towards worry.

"I had to give a friend's kid a ride home," I replied, hoping that a half-truth was better, in this case, than a full-on lie.

"How on Earth do you know Jacob Hostetler?" Frank dropped the bomb, short-circuiting some clever back and forth that I had already scripted.

"He purchased one of my watercolors recently." Very recently.

"So his daughter just happened to call you and ask for a ride home?"

I nodded in response to this, not wanting to give tongue to the lie, when a gesture would do as well.

"You pick her up in Saranac Lake?" This was a trap, but Frank had the courtesy to smile and let me know that he knew it was an easy one.

"No, I picked her up sometime around 3 a.m. (*more like 2:25, but precision never improves the early drafts of a story*), at the gas station near Despo's." This last detail was a lie, but I had stopped at that station on the way out of town for a Coke and some other stuff for the drive up to Madrid Springs; I even had a receipt if it came to that (*I find that precise details/evidence that don't really mean much can nonetheless be useful in persuading Frank to move on to harder targets*).

"So you weren't at the Olympic Motor Inn last night for the excitement?" Frank asked.

"Nope, what happened, and what's it got to do with Sadie." We could both play at the faux show of our cards game.

"Probably nothing ... I hope nothing. I got an earful

from a friend of hers two days ago about Sadie going missing after dancing with some boys, said they were from North Country."

"North Country School?" It's always worth dodging the easy traps.

"North Country Community College. Sadie's friend thought that the boys might have doped her drink and taken her for a private party back at their place; and late last night two boys from NCCC had some car trouble ... their car, what kind was it again?"

"I don't know, you tell me." I've been trapped by Frank before, but the day he gets me on a lob like that, I'll pack my bags and move to Detroit.

"It was a Honda, if that matters." I couldn't imagine how it could, but didn't want to stop Frank's flow; he continued, "It burned to the exterior metal, and melted the tires so it was resting on rims by the time the fire department finished foaming it down."

"Sounds nasty, was anyone hurt?" I already knew the answer to this one, but I liked serving it up to Frank to remind him that I'm as careful as I can be.

"Lucky break ... nope, nobody hurt ... the boys had asked for a room way off to one end, so there weren't any other cars nearby. Interesting thing about the fire and the boys though ..." He left that hanging there, so I stepped up, reasonably sure that I could see the path this conversation was taking.

"What's that? Did they know Sadie? Now that would be a coincidence." Luckily I don't do much in the way of facial expressions, or I might have let a smirk slip at this point.

"Well, at first they were really pissed about the car, and who wouldn't be? They were yelling at each other when the LPPD rolled up after the fire trucks were pretty much done hosing their car down. But once they started talking to the police, they got quiet and stupid and obsequious with the LPPD."

"Nice word," I nodded at Frank.

"Thanks ... anyway once they started talking to the responding officers in LP, they backtracked a bit from an earlier version that sounded as though they blamed 'some bitch' or 'that bitch's friends'. Instead, they decided that the fire must have been their fault."

"Huh ... well there you go, nothing to do with me or Sadie, just some dumb kids." I'm not a physical guy, and once I had found Sadie, I couldn't think of a way to get her out of the room, past the two big guys, that didn't involve Frank's type of solution, or me bleeding in the gutter ... neither option appealed to me, so I went with plan C. A nice parking lot fire is easy to start (*HEET gas line cleaner, works well*). It gets peoples' attention, makes lots of noise, throws lots of pretty colors and shadows, and generally provides great cover for a daring rescue. Once the boys went out to watch their car burning, I let myself into their room with my key (*a wrecking bar*) and took Sadie out and away in the confusion.

"Must be that's the way it happened ... anyway ... they signed a statement to that effect." Frank kept eye-contact longer than I was able to, but I covered by slapping a non-existent mosquito off of my calf.

One of the beautiful things about Frank Gibson, cop and sometime dinner-host to yours truly, is that he didn't feel the need to call me on my activities of last night (*or arrest me for arson and whatever other laws I broke getting Sadie home*). He knew, and I knew that he knew, and he knew that I knew that he knew; but he was glad that Sadie got home and away from the monsters-in-training and that nobody got hurt any more than could be avoided. He had busted my chops a couple of times over the years about my investigations without benefit of license from New York State, but since they really are arguably favors for friends, and not services for cash, he is mostly interested in keeping an eye on me (*and in letting me know that he's keeping an eye on me*). Official business out of the way for the afternoon, he relaxed a bit, and started into the small talk.

"Meg wanted me to ask you when you're coming over for supper again." Frank and I fell sideways into the bizarre relationship that we have because I knew his wife from my dealings with the Tri-Lakes Animal Shelter. Despite what television, and lots of books, would have you believe, cops and detectives don't work on the same side, same team, or for the same reasons. Most of the time, the police (*rightly*) view detectives as window peepers, ambulance chasers, bounty hunters, or criminals hiding behind a lightweight badge; Frank initially felt that way about me (*and to some extent still does*). Dealing with Frank had been like porcupine sex for the first few years, but we now had some ground rules established, and made it work by building/mending fences where/when needed. He had become the "go to guy" among the Tri-Lakes law enforcement community whenever my name came up or I was connected to a case somehow, so we had meetings like this one from time to time.

"Next Monday, the tenth, would be great, if that works for you guys." Really any night, including tonight, would work for me, but I like to give him some time so he doesn't feel like I'm rushing him ... also, a bit of time might allow any remaining questions about Sadie to occur to Frank and then recede again. A fly on the wall during one of these dinners might think that Frank and I are friends, we talk about a variety of non-crime-related subjects centering mostly on a shared interest in camping. I met Meg, Frank's wife, a school psychologist, while walking dogs for the local animal shelter ... we both walk dogs a few times a week, and our paths crossed enough times that she found out who I was. One day she came by SmartPig to check me out; saying that I rang enough weird bells to interest but not scare her, which is better than scaring her, but can sometimes lead to more sharing and self-reflection than I want. We had spent that day talking about our childhoods in big towns, and living in a small town; in combination with our love for homeless dogs and Friehofer's chocolate chip cookies, it was enough to build an initial bridge that led to friendship over the years.

"Fine. Same time as usual, and you can bring Cynthia, or someone else, if you want," said Frank. I've never come to his house with anyone else, but he keeps asking; I think that it's a combination of three things:

1) He has some level of discomfort with my relationship with his wife, which covers ground and emotional content that theirs does not,

2) He wants to put me in a box, straight/gay/ single/dating, so that he can get a better handle on me,

3) He wants to make me squirm a bit (*as I always do*) for the reasons above.

"No, thanks, just me; don't actually know what Cynthia's up to right now, but can I bring dessert? I make a mean tiramisu." I'm not one hundred percent certain what tiramisu is, but am sure that I could make one if pressed. I blurted my offer out to cover my slip about Cynthia. Mentioning that she was missing and presumed (*by me*) to have been taken, crossed the line between small talk and shop-talk, which was something that Frank and I don't do, for all sorts of very good reasons. Frank stopped watching the football practice to turn and look in my direction for the first time since I had walked up to join him by the practice field. I got a small chill as the benign, bumbling facade slipped for a second while Frank replayed my words and partial recovery, and examined me for guilt or anxiety.

"Funny ... I brought her up because she's been on my mind. She called me the other day to ask me some questions about the way drugs move to and through the Tri-Lakes and Northern New York in general. I went to the library this morning to follow-up and see if there was a reason behind her inquiry, but Ben hasn't seen her; doesn't seem worried though, death in the family or some such ... sister maybe ... illness." Cynthia lost her sister to drugs while they were both in college, and had strong opinions on the subject; I had found this out during the early years of our working together.

I wanted to get Frank off the topic of Cynthia, because if we were both looking for her, we would inevitably find each other first; with complications for me guaranteed. "It's always seemed that there's as much drug use here as anywhere ... maybe a bit more over in Placid ... ski-town and all ... and at the colleges, of course, but no opium dens on Main Street, so far as I know." I was hopeful that useless platitudes and generalities might prime the pump, and get him talking about something besides Cynthia.

"There actually used to be more drugs sold in the Tri-Lakes then we have today, if arrests and related crimes are anything to go by," Frank said. "Things seem to have settled down from a few years ago, although George somehow finds enough to keep himself in nice rides." He pointed with his chin down to the end of the field where a big grey-haired sloppy-looking man in a fancy sweat suit was leaning against a jet-black Range Rover.

"That guy's a drug dealer?" I asked Frank. "He looks so pedestrian."

"George stopped dealing ten years ago, nowadays he's management. He runs what passes for organized crime up here since chasing away all of his contemporaries; he gets a piece of most everything illegal that happens in the Tri-Lakes."

"If you know who he is and what he does, why isn't he up in Dannamora?" Dannamora is a maximum security prison not too far away, one side of their Main Street is literally lined with bars and pawn shops, and the other side is a sixty foot high concrete wall with gun towers every one hundred feet; it is both reality and metaphor for those of us living in the North Country.

"He's clever, he's careful, he keeps clean, and he gives us a steady stream of little fish and little busts to keep the system happily chugging along. In some ways, things are better since he took over; he's actually clamped down on the drugs in the schools a bit since his son", Frank pointed to the hulking center squirting the ball to the quarterback, "got into middle and then high school. Less drugs for kids than there were five years ago, but he still seems to do okay."

"Are you a fan?"

I got a cold look from Frank, "He's a stain, but the pragmatist in me sees that my kids are safer with one in-control person running things than with fifty assholes competing for the souls of seventh graders."

"That's an interesting thought ... a cop using a big word like 'pragmatist' ... kidding, I meant the lesser of two evils in a practical situation." I felt as though I/we were coming out of the dangerous segment of the conversation essentially intact, and that poking him a bit might close the deal.

"Fuck you", Frank said pleasantly enough. "If he ever falls in my path in a way that allows me to take him off the streets and put him inside forever, I'll jump at it. But in the meantime, rich ski-bums will always smoke and snort their fun and my kids are in less danger than they used to be."

We had transitioned away from Cynthia, I had some ideas of where to start looking and poking and I made a mental note to do some research on tiramisu ... and George ... and drugs.

SmartPig, astoundingly still 9/4/2012

I left before the football practice ended, somewhat unsure which of the helmeted brutes was Frank and Meg's son, Austin. There is a number schema (*normally my kind of thing*) at play on the football jerseys, but it didn't help me in this instance, so I just waved and inserted a generic, "He's looking good out there!" into the space created by my standing up to leave. I walked back down to SmartPig, stopping at the gas station across from the town hall for an ice-cream sandwich on my way. My office seemed dark and quiet after the football practice, which suited my needs and mood perfectly. I grabbed a Coke from the Coke-fridge and settled down to work through a couple of ideas.

I did some light-duty data-mining in various state and federal databases, using access given to me by my SL and NYC public library accounts. I wanted to see if Frank had known what he was talking about in terms of the drug trade. I didn't think that he was lying, but we all run the risk of preferentially finding, organizing and internalizing the results that we desire. Rather than accurately assessing what is really out there, we tend to edit out or avoid the information/conclusion that doesn't fit our world-view or the tracks that our thoughts are moving in at a given point in time/space. The size and number of arrests for drug-related crimes had indeed dropped in our immediate area. However the far north end of Franklin County, up near Malone, had seen a spike in drug related crimes that seemed to outweigh our improvements. Moreover, our local arrests tended towards marijuana and cocaine, while outside of our safe-ish haven, much of the money and criminal activities (*and violence*) in the drug industry was focused on methamphetamine production, distribution and consumption.

My drug of choice is caffeine (*administered freezing cold, in combination with sugar, in the form of Coca-Cola*), which is as mind-altering as I get. I have never understood why people drink alcohol or smoke cigarettes, much less use illegal drugs; there's no judgment involved with my stance based on the morality of drug-use, I just don't see how the cost-benefit analysis works out for people who use them. The world of people is filled with things that I don't understand, but I can still study and learn from these things by looking at them as "Black Box Systems"; lots can be learned about a system by watching the input and output, to see how it functions, and how it affects the people and environment and other systems that interact with it. Using this method, I have concluded that drug use seems to be an empty expression of self-hate, that is expensive and dangerous and illegal to boot; it remains a mystery to me.

I didn't have sixty plus days to wait for the IRS to get back to me about a form 4506 (*FOIA tax return request*) having to do with George Roebuck, so I would have to find other ways to learn more about him. Google didn't have much to say, he owned a couple of sandwich shops in Northern New York, he lived in a big house with his family (*or so it appeared from satellite imagery*), and he was (*as Frank had opined*) apparently the lesser of two possible evils. I had stopped at one of his sandwich places a couple of times ... it was dirty and empty at noon and the bread was stale. On the upside, it was quick and cheap (*which worked for me ... as you may have guessed, I'm not much of a foodie*). There were a couple of articles in various local papers mentioning him in passing, but nothing very informative. I finished the Coke that I was working on, debated grabbing another, and decided to call it a day ... when the going gets tough (*or boring*), the tough (*or bored*) quit for the day.

I checked the weather outlook for the next sixteen hours, saw a nice/dry/cool night ahead, grabbed my Kindle Fire e-reader from the shelf where I charge stuff, filled a Nalgene bottle at the sink and headed out to my car. I keep the Honda Element packed with a breakdown kit, get-home-bag, some food/water, and a basic sleeping setup, so I didn't need anything else for an overnight. I headed for a quiet place to read and think and sleep. Given the structure of the Adirondack Park, this is easy; there are more great places to spend a night than I have nights left in my life, especially with the freedom that my hammock grants me. I need two trees, twelve to sixteen feet apart, preferably with a nice view of sky or woods or water; I had a spot in mind a few miles out of town to the southwest on Lower Saranac Lake, a spot near Lonesome Bay. I found a dirt track to pull off onto, parked, grabbed my stuff and walked away from the road, and towards the smell of water.

I found a perfect spot 150 feet back from the water,

looking out at the tiny islands that dot the surface of that end of Lower Saranac Lake, and hung my hammock. I ate a bit of jerky and some GORP, drank most of the Nalgene, hung my food (*more from squirrels than bears, although both frequent these woods*), and climbed into the hammock to read for a bit before bed. There's nothing like gently swinging in a hammock, warm in a sleeping bag and fleece-hat, reading a good book, smelling the woods and water all around you, and fighting sleep because everything else is better than sleep ... and you know sleep is going to be pretty great too. I read for almost two hours before I started dropping the book on my chest, so I got up to pee and stretch, drank a sip of water, and climbed back in to go to sleep, exhausted by a long day, with the promise of more like it to come.

Homeless? 9/5/2012 (*finally*), 3:18 a.m.

I slept more than the desired 239 minutes, blamed it on
the sound of waves from the lake down the hill along
with the wind in the white pine needles above me,
decided that I didn't care about oversleeping, and thought
about leaving the hammock in place for a couple of days.
Sometimes I move to a different spot every night for
weeks, and sometimes I've stayed for as much as ten days
in one spot depending on the location, the weather, my
mood, my workload, and sometimes ... laziness. In theory,
I need a permit from the area ranger for stays of more
than three days, but I keep a low profile, and it hasn't
been a problem. In winter, I tend to stay in one place for
a couple of days at each spot, because the setup takes a
bit longer (*tarp and a slick piece of kit called a hammock-sock
which is just what it sounds like—keeps me warm as can be, even
below zero*). Sometimes in the spring or fall, I get tired of
unremitting rain and sleep on the couch at SmartPig (*even
though my lease forbids occupancy*). I may be the first homeless
detective in history (*although to be fair, I don't advertise the fact,*

so it seems reasonable to assume that others in the same situation might also be keeping it on the down low).

I left NYC, after settling my parents' estate and selling their house, looking for a change. It sounds teen-drama and angst-ridden to say that my world had ended, but I was a teen, and that's how it felt. My map of the world, and my place in it, made no sense anymore; large chunks had been ripped out and burned down by hateful men crashing planes into my skyline, tearing my parents away from me. Being in the insurance industry, my father had over-insured both he and my mother, and both policies had paid off doubly through the good graces of a double-indemnity clause that hadn't foreseen something like what happened on 9/11. I sold their apartment, ill-advised after a major terrorist attack, but my wish nonetheless, made three piles of our belongings, a tiny one that fit in my first car, and a pair of huge piles that I left for goodwill and the garbage collectors.

Being socially retarded (*in the descriptive, not the offensive, meaning of the word*), I easily and effectively cut my ties to everyone and everything from my life in NYC on the sleety December day (*the twentieth, the solstice I believe*) when I drove across the George Washington Bridge for the last time. I found out, however, that some people won't let go; Mickey Schwarz being one of those people. He had been a frequent leader of outings and explorations in our learning circle. His daughters Mindy and Rebecca were both brilliant and thoroughly uninterested in any of the lessons and experiences that he could guide us in. Mickey used me as a foil when we explored the art and music and architecture of Manhattan. He spent the night of September 11th watching me watch the television, and the phone ... waiting. I never heard from my parents on the day of the attack, and no trace of their bodies was found in the weeks and months following. Despite strongly advising me against it, he helped me pack up my parents' home when the sale was complete. He brought his wife Anne and the two girls down for hugs and goodbyes when I had bought and packed my Element. He sent emails (*daily at first*), overcoming his dislike/mistrust of the technology when it became clear that I wasn't going to answer my cell-phone (*I had chucked the one he had the number for out the window while driving up the Henry Hudson Parkway after realizing that no matter who wanted to reach me, I wasn't interested*). He now sends an email once a week, early Monday morning normally, inquiring about my well-being (*financial, physical, and mental*) and sharing gossip about the other kids (*that's how I think of them, frozen in time since the last "class" I attended with them*) in the learning circle, and their parents; always asking when I planned to come down and visit him and Anne. I made a mental note to call him once I got back into cell-phone range.

I arrived in Saranac Lake a few days before the end of 2001, and made all sorts of resolutions for the New Year (*and my new life*). To rebuild my map (*both physical and social*), to continue my studies/schooling, to keep my life and my belongings as simple as possible, to do what I liked and avoid things that I didn't like, and so on ... homelessness was not one of my resolutions. I started out living in cheap college housing near North Country Community College, found/rented the SmartPig space, and bounced back and forth between "home" and "office" for a few months while experimenting with thneeding (*the money I had from my parents' deaths meant that I could live the rest of my life, if not in luxury, at least without starving or freezing to death, and doing whatever I felt like doing*). It was months later, once spring turned into summer and I had discovered how close and easy and friendly the Adirondack wilderness was, that I considered making the woods my home (*or no place my home, depending on how you look at it*). I liked the SmartPig office, and it felt extravagant keeping two spaces for just my use, so the little college apartment lease expired as painlessly as I drifted into homelessness. There's no shower in the SmartPig building, but when it's too cold (*or too far, or too much hassle*) to bath in the lake, I have a "community member" card which lets me use the gym and pool and showers at the North Country Community College athletics facility (*it's like a membership at a health club, but with smaller fees and smellier locker rooms*).

I got up and out of the hammock, had a drink and a pee and a stretch, and then grabbed some food and climbed back into the hammock to read until it got light. I had a bag of GORP with some jerky mixed in in a frontpocket of my hoodie, and grabbed a handful every few minutes; I don't think that a bear is going to assault me in my hammock/piñata, but I do worry about raccoons or mice or squirrels nibbling stuff while I'm asleep, so I don't generally sleep with food or other smelly stuff in my hammock. I was sufficiently engrossed in my book (*and thoughts/worry about Cynthia*) that I didn't really notice the gradual shift from night to morning, until a beaver-slap down on Lonesome Bay brought me back. I shut down the Kindle Fire to watch the sunlight creep over the tops of the mountains and roll down the trees on the far shore and then eventually the islands. I went for a swim, dried off, left my home in place for the day, and headed back to SmartPig, in town.

Early Morning, 9/5/2012

I took the long way through town, topped up my tank at the cheap gas place, and stopped in at Dunkin Donuts for a mixed dozen. They always seem hurt that I don't buy a coffee while I'm there. As I do every time, I looked at the array of donuts available, and then decided (*as always*) that you just can't beat four each of: regular glazed, chocolate glazed, and "not powdered sugar" jellies. The street was wet with dew and mostly quiet and empty, and there weren't any lights on as I ghosted into SmartPig for a couple of hours work.

My first order of business once I got inside was to call Mickey Schwarz; he always gets to his office by 6 a.m., and nobody else would think to call or visit him at that hour, so I almost always get him when I call at that hour. I was a bit early, but thought that I'd give it a shot anyway, and got lucky. On rainy days he often skips his jogged lap around the reservoir in Central Park, and it must have been raining down south, because he picked up sounding as though he was using coffee instead of exercise to start his day. He must have known that it was me, because he picked up the phone singing, "Happy Birthday!" with more enthusiasm than talent. When the dramatic warbling at the end finally finished, he drew a deep breath, and jumped (*as always*) right into our last conversation, exactly where we had left off.

"It'll be snowing up there soon; do you have enough warm clothes? Anne was worried about it, and has a box of stuff all set to mail to you." This was a lie, Anne had forgotten about me when my Element went around the first corner on the day that I left Manhattan, but it allowed him to both show and dislocate his concern for me. I told him to thank Anne.

"Great ... Great, she'll be happy to hear it. How are you set for money and work? Hopefully just enough of both ... heh, heh." His daughters had grown up with too much money and too little work, and they were beautiful and useless beings that embarrassed him; he joked/worried that the money my parents had left me would similarly 'ruin me'. Mickey loved his daughters loyally/absolutely, but had trouble finding anything to talk about with them when they returned home between boyfriends and husbands. I assured Mickey that I had just enough of work and money to keep me interested and interesting (*a callback to a discussion last month when he had said that Mindy and Becca were both bored and boring*).

"Funny you should say that," (*uh oh, I tried to look both ahead and back in the conversation for the other shoe, certain that it was either about to drop, or squash me*), "a friend of mine up in Albany" (*had to be someone in state government, Mickey knows legions of bureaucrats*) "said that your name came up recently in a particularly nasty bit of business up your way." He ended his sentence with an upturned near-questioning tone that was begging for a response on my part, but I ignored it, waiting him out.

"Yeah, someplace at the ass-end of the universe called Malone, or Mahoney." Mickey often talked like this on the phone with me, and I spent some time and energy trying to decide if he was slipping into a country accent or out of his Manhattan accent; he had grown up 'North of 90' (*Route 90 bisects New York State into "Upstate" and "Downstate"*) and moved down to the city as soon as he could.

"Malone," I answered, knowing where this was headed, but not understanding how he had gotten there, "What happened, and how did my name come into it?"

"My guy, we were in school together a million years ago, calls me from time to time with gossip out of the capital building that he thinks might interest me. Mostly stuff relating to my work." (*Mickey is a prominent oncologist who plays on both sides of the practical/research fence in the big leagues*), "but also occasionally other things that he thinks would grab my attention. He heard me mention you at some point, and when your name came up, he flagged the report and bounced a copy to me after giving me the gory details over the phone." He was stalling, playing with me a bit, to see how I'd take the news and the delay.

"Mickey, what happened, and how do I have anything to do with it?" I asked in my recently perfected tone of exasperation (*I don't emote particularly well, but find that it's necessary sometimes, so I've been working on it ... it's frustratingly slow-going, considering how easily most humans pick these things up*).

"Apparently some pedophile, or pervert anyway, in the county government up there, tripped over his dick with pictures and videos of who-knows-what on his home and work computers, and tried to invoke the 'some other guy' defense; he specifically named you as the guy."

"What's his name?" I asked, knowing that I was expected to, if innocent.

"Robert something ... Ward ... Warren ... Warren, I think. Anyway, they got him on about a million counts of this and that ... all of it nasty, so nobody took it too seriously when he reached out for someone else to blame ... dirt bag!" Mickey has no space in his heart for those who would victimize their fellow humans. If he knew the truth about what I had done to Robin Warner, our relationship would surely suffer, although he would understand my reasons for doing it by the end of one of his famous long lunches (*Mickey gets up before dawn, and goes to sleep very early, and as such the main family meal in the Schwarz household has always been around noon*).

"Never heard of him; Malone's about fifty miles north of here (*44.2 miles from the parking lot behind SmartPig, but Mickey doesn't value that sort of exactitude*); and as you know, I have no interest in that sort of thing." True enough, I see pornography a bit like looking at those odd shows that pop up from time to time on "Animal Planet" or the like; graphically biological, lacking in interesting factoids, and with the added queasiness I get from being reminded of a basic human interaction that I don't really understand, and won't ever participate in. Mickey once, wrongly, figured out that I was secretly dating his elder daughter, Mindy. The three of us had an awkward week trying to figure out how to communicate what none of us wanted to talk about with each of the others.

"Ah, well ... yes ... anyway ... hearing your name from my friend in connection with that business made me wonder again about how you fill your days up there on the rim of the planet." I'm six hours from Mickey's building, with stops for gas and food, and he talks as though I live in another country.

"As I told you last time, I sell some photographs and some watercolors, make some camping gear, go camping, read, and do research." He needs some, but doesn't want lots of, details.

"Fair enough, we loved the things that you sent Anne and I and the girls for Christmas." I sent them a bunch of my best photos of the Adirondacks, and a few of my watercolors for Christmas. Mickey is a Jewish oncologist who celebrates Christmas and snacks on pork rinds constantly ... he apologizes for nothing, doesn't see these (*or myriad other*) contradictions in his life, and gave me the gift early in life of achieving some level of comfort with what I was/am ... I loved my father, but Mickey might be my dad, if I can be allowed the distinction.

"Are you happy, up there Tyler?" Mickey asked.

"Yes, although I miss you guys." Neither assertion was strictly true; I don't think that I 'do' the emotion happy, nor do I miss people. I am familiar with the Adirondacks and my world up here, and that makes me comfortable (*which I translate for Mickey as being happy*). In other places beyond the edges of my mental map, I am uncomfortable, which might translate most closely in Mickey's terms to unhappy. I do miss Mickey and Anne and Mindy and Becca; because they are familiar, like New York City was, like Saranac Lake is now. Mickey knows and accepts this to the degree that he can; he once said, "Each human God puts on this Earth is unique, and of all the (*then*) five billion, you are the uniquest!" I'm not, just the "uniquest" that he knows.

"We miss you too Tyler, I hope you had a great birthday! I'll talk to you next week, maybe." He hung up, and I felt adrift for a moment, as though reaching for a human emotion that wasn't there; then I came back to myself, remembered the missing element of my social map up here, and settled into my morning's work.

Since I couldn't push anyone or anything about Cynthia until 10 a.m. (*when the library opened*) I grabbed a pair of Cokes from the Coke-fridge, booted up my computer and began to read a bit about the production of methamphetamine. I assumed that this may be the drug business Cynthia was digging into considering there were/are easier places to grow/refine pot or cocaine than the Adirondacks. Once I satisfied my curiosity, I then used up the extra time working on some other projects I've got going under the auspices of SmartPig. I'm working on some hiking and camping gear design and manufacture for a group of senior-hikers that want light and comfortable gear that doesn't cost a fortune. I make heavy-duty leashes/leads for the animal shelter; they use some and sell others. I've been doing watercolors all over the Park, expanding my personal map, looking for future "homesites", and trying to avoid the trap of always painting trees next to water (*unsuccessfully so far*). Digital photography has been great for me, freeing me from the smelly darkroom forever; I mess around with the image on my computer, and then send the finished product to interested parties through an online printing house. I do other things also, as well as favors for people from time to time, but I couldn't stay focused on any project this morning. So after noodling around with bits and pieces of these and other projects, cranking out a couple of nylon webbing dog-leashes, and finishing my Cokes before they got warm, I grabbed what I nowadays think of as a "bricks and mortar" or "actual" book, and read until it was almost 10 a.m. At that point I cleaned things up a bit and headed out and down the street towards the library.

The half hour when people are just getting their workday started is a great time to go in and push, prod, harass, and generally make a nuisance of yourself. I have found that at this time people are likely dealing with leftover things from the day before, as well as setting things up for the current day. They will likely be annoyed and won't want to help; but that's the perfect time to swoop in and deliver a swift karate chop to the base of their assumptions.

"I'm really sorry Ben, I know you're busy, especially without Cynthia." I had taken it as given that she wouldn't be there when I arrived. If she was somewhere in back, I'd be happy to try and feel embarrassed in exchange for her not being gone. "She has some papers and PDFs for me at her desk (*holding up a USB-drive and wiggling it at him*). If you're cool with it, I'd be happy to get things unlocked and lights-on downstairs before finding my stuff if it would help you guys get going." If I'd brought the box of donuts with me, it would have closed the deal, but since there were only six left, and they were re-packaged for my next stop, I had to try Smile #3, friendly/sincere/helpful.

I've been watching people smile my whole life, and didn't internalize that smiles were something people just "do" until midway through my twelfth year. Since then I've been studying and categorizing smiles; I have nineteen in my repertoire, and they're pretty solid until I get up into the newer ones in the mid-teens. Number three was likely to work with Ben, as he makes some assumptions about my relationship with Cynthia, and at the same time sees me as completely non-threatening to him personally or professionally. He paused only long enough to let me know that he was carefully considering the cost/benefit of taking my help, and then said, "Thanks Tyler, that would be fantastic, it's a mad house here today ... a mad house!" He had me categorized in the nerd/geek box, and used an appropriate set of quotes and references with me, many of which I had come across before, others I had to research (*which was easy as he didn't have much depth to his collection*).

I fumbled, then dropped, the keys that he tossed at my head, letting people feel superior never hurts in my experience, they tend to let their guards down ... plus the keys came straight at my eyes quite fast. I went down and unlocked the Adirondack Research Center, the study room, and the restricted collection space, and turned the lights on everywhere. I came back upstairs with a pile of books that would have to be re-shelved, and some documents and bound reports that had been left on one of the tables, and looked as though they needed tending; besides being helpful it eased my transition back behind the main desk and into the office in back, where Cynthia's desk/space/cubicle was located.

She had the usual layers and piles of crap on and around the desk in her area; I stuck a post-it from last week, with my name in her hand-writing, on a pile of stuff that wasn't obviously outside of my interest range (*no Justin Bieber biographies, or LOLcat pictures*) to give my presence a little credence. I stuck my USB drive into her computer as it started up, and entered the password I had seen from over her shoulder a few weeks ago, hoping that she hadn't changed it; she hadn't. I opened up a couple of screens and her browser, and dumped all documents modified within the last three months, the history and bookmarks from the browser, newish images from her cache, and everything from her computer desktop garbage can into the stick-drive. I moved the copy-progress window behind the browser and looked around a bit, while keeping my head aimed rigidly at her computer screen. She keeps a journal and notes about work and home project ideas in a series of those black marbled composition notebooks; I grabbed the five for May, June, July, August, and September and mixed them into the pile of books I had stuck the post-it note onto. I had been at her desk for four minutes and ten seconds, and it seemed long to me; I was nervous. I might have found more stuff if I stayed and hunted for another five minutes, but Ben might also decide to check and see what I was doing, and perhaps even hold the stuff until he checked with Cynthia. I put the USB drive into my pocket, put a bit of tape onto the post-it note (*to insure that it stayed in place*), and walked out of the library with an appropriately bored look on my face. I dropped off the stuff at SmartPig, took a Coke out of the Coke-fridge, grabbed the Tupperware full of leftover donuts, a box of finished leashes, and then headed to my car for the drive to the Tri-Lakes Animal Shelter.

Tri-Lakes Animal Shelter (TLAS), 9/5/2012, midday

Dogs like me. Cats do not like me. I don't understand the reasons behind it, but I like dogs too; maybe because I find them to be more interesting animals. Dorothy says it's because dogs like me preemptively, and cats look inside me; I don't know what cats see inside me (*maybe nothing?*), but they don't like it. Dorothy Bouchard runs the TLAS. She saw through my initial efforts at friendliness instantly and dealt with it in the only way she knows, honestly and straightforward, like tearing off a Band-Aid. "You're using us, you don't want a dog" were the first words that she ever said to me, which might have scared me off if she hadn't followed that up with, "That's okay, they know it and they're using you for walks." I nodded, smiled (*#2, friendly/gentle/clueless-ish*), handed her the leash of the dog I'd been exercising, and walked out; but I came back later that week, and every few days since then.

I mostly walk the big dogs that live in the back (*isolation*) room; the ones too big or aggressive or jumpy or crazy from long-term internment to be likely adoptees. Entropy is the tendency of systems to move towards homogeneity; in the TLAS entropy is illustrated by the various species of dogs present in the outside world homogenizing in the shelter toward a dark brown pit bull/lab/shepherd mix that weighs 125 pounds and is trained to digest babies whole by the drug dealers that breed, and then quickly get bored with them (*we call them Saranac Lake Specials*). I've yet to meet a dog incapable of being (*much*) better at loving other dogs and humans than I am, once they get a chance to run around a bit and get to know you. I come here to think and walk and watch and try to learn from the dogs; Dorothy was right, I'm using them and they're using me ... it's an honest and straightforward arrangement that benefits everyone involved.

"Hi, Tyler! Long time, no see ... since last week some time. Did you come to drop off leashes, walk dogs, or solve crime?" Dorothy's plainspoken, one of thirteen things that I like about her.

"A bit of each, if that's okay ... who needs a walk?" I ask handing her the box of leashes I'd finished along with the donuts hidden inside the box ... they brought a happy squeal form behind the desk ten seconds later. Dorothy teases that I consult with her dogs about the cases/jobs that I work on, which is at least partially true. I sometimes come by to walk a dog or two when I've input a metric crap-ton of data into my brain, and I need to give the forebrain a break, while the ancient lizard bits at the top of my spine figure things out; there's nothing like a walk in the woods at the other end of a chain from a Saranac Lake Special that hasn't seen sky or smelled squirrels in two weeks to clear complex thoughts from your head. I hadn't had time to digest the stuff I grabbed from

Cynthia's desk and computer at the library, so this was just a walk, no crime-fighting. Dorothy ran through her mental list of the dogs in the back, and came up with Peggy, a pit bull mix with black and white coloring that somebody had, in a dim or hopeful moment, described as a Dalmatian on the website. Peggy and I got along quite well after the first few minutes of excitement and jumping and "kisses with teeth". After a few well-timed treats, she calmed down and walked (*almost*) at heel along the trails behind the shelter for a while; we sat on the steps outside the shelter talking about Cynthia (*and my worries about her*), neither of us wanting to go back in.

I brought Peggy inside, with a promise to her (*and any people in the hall that assumed that I might be talking to them*) to take her out again soon. Dorothy trundled Peggy back into her dungeon in "isolation". The fact that the isolation room is so much better than the alternative says a lot about the world we live in; Dorothy was back behind her counter and at the computer a minute later. She gestured me back behind the counter, but as always, I leaned across the counter to talk with her; I'm a guy very much aware of which side of the counter I belong on, and I keep to the correct side. We talked a bit about the latest group of leashes, about an idea for a harness that I had, about the dogs (*the new dogs, the dogs that had found homes, and the dogs that had been there forever*), about the gigantic mastiff that Jacob Hostetler had at their farm up in Madrid Springs, about a trashy novel that she had loaned me (*and that I had enjoyed despite myself*), and about a few other areas in which we shared an interest ... but not my concerns about Cynthia (*they were still uninformed, maybe even unformed ... unfounded*).

In most cases, about most things, my trust-circle is very small, about the size of my belt. I sometimes talk with a limited number of people about some aspects of my work; even more rarely, about my personal and family life and history. Dorothy is one of those few people, Cynthia is another, Meg, Mickey (*to some extent, as he has known me longer than anyone on the planet*), Rick (*a guy that I connected with online, and who goes camping with me every month or two*), and ... oddly enough ... Frank. Frank was a surprise to me because he came as a package deal with Meg, and although we don't have a lot in common, I actually spend a significant amount of time/energy either misleading or outright lying to him, we do enjoy and trust each other (*within specific parameters*). I didn't mention Cynthia, either my concerns or my actions in support of those concerns, to Dorothy because I don't know enough yet, and also because I have concerns about how either/both of us will react if it turns out that Cynthia's disappearance is something more than a death in the family and unannounced leave.

Dorothy and Cynthia are two completely different types of human females, perhaps different species; I am the only thing that they have in common. Dorothy might be upset if Cyn was missing because she knows that I am fond of Cynthia, but she also might fake upset, for my benefit, which would be off-putting. I don't yet know what my actions or reactions might be to the information waiting for me at SmartPig, or to any information that I may gain in the coming days about Cynthia; by not talking with Dorothy about it now I am reserving the right to discuss the matter with this friend of mine whom I find to be interestingly amoral.

Dorothy is by no means an immoral person, but I have found that she operates her life based on attaining and preserving what she wants, or thinks is best, for herself and those nouns that she cares about. There are things that she cares about, and standards of behavior that she follows, but the moral compass by which normal society navigates day to day was not installed when Dorothy came from the factory. I've known her to accept dog food and toys that must have been stolen, along with venison and bear scraps from families that poach year round; and seen her dose dogs and unpaid/underpaid human TLAS volunteers and staff with the steroids and antibiotics on site without benefit of a vet or doctor. I once helped her break into a farm way out in the country to steal some twenty various animals that were starving and neglected; six were near death. We were too late to help three that we buried in the woods behind the farm, using time we couldn't spare (*but did anyway*). She works eighty-plus hours per week, stretches the lifespan of her work-shoes with duct-tape and gorilla-glue, and plows lots of cash (*some from her salary, some from less reputable sources*) back into the TLAS to keep things running. I like the way that she thinks, the way that dogs act around her, and I like to use her as a sounding board when the brain-trust at SmartPig is in the weeds on a sticky problem.

On my way out, I grab the Tupperware container (*which looks as though it has been finger-squeegeed clean*), promise to check back in a couple of days, and avoid the nasty cat guarding the front door as it hisses and swings a lazy claw in my direction as I walk by. On my way to SmartPig for an afternoon of reading and Coke and snacks, I stop at the good Chinese place (*as opposed to the shitty Chinese place*) for a to-go box of hot and spicy and greasy goodness. I'm ready to get serious about Cynthia, threading my way through the minefields of secrets and people to get my life back on track (*normalized*) again.

SmartPig Thneedery, 9/5/2012, 1:28 p.m.

I grabbed a pair of Cokes from the Coke-fridge, a fork from the clean-stuff mug on the counter, and sat down at the table to fuel up with the Chinese food. I could feel the spice and fat and protein and caffeine from this nearly perfect meal fine-tuning my mind and body for an afternoon of productive work. They know that I like my food hot, and by the time I was done and cleaning up, I was both sniffling and gently sweating, in spite of the cool breeze that ran from the window fronting Main Street to the one at the back of the building. I washed my hands and face, opened the Coke-fridge for one more to drink while I was working, saw the mocking sign that Cynthia had made for me, and sat down heavily with all of her stuff, determined to find something that would allow me to get a grip on her being gone; to help me find her.

It was the morning of October 17 of 2002 that I got the Coke-fridge. Cynthia was teasing me about it before we sat down to eat lunch up in SmartPig on that very same day. I had done a favor the previous month for a lab manager out at the Trudeau Institute, a biological lab in Saranac Lake most famous for their work on tuberculosis early in the twentieth century. In return, he hooked me up by bundling my order for a VWR lab-grade refrigerator (*with digital thermostat, thick insulation all around, and extra thermal mass to prevent temperature swings*) in with an order he was placing to upgrade one of the labs he worked with over there. I had been planning for months to combine Canadian Coke (*from a friend who makes frequent trips north of the border*) with the super-fridge (*set to 29°F, the perfect temperature for Coke*) to optimize my caffeine delivery system. Before the fridge had even cooled all the way down, Cynthia had stopped by to drop off her salad for lunch. For some reason known only to her, instead of using the dorm fridge we had been using for food since I moved into SmartPig, she chose to put the salad in the huge fridge sporting a blinking digital display showing 29°F (*target temp.*) and 37°F (*actual temp.*) despite the fact that it was filled to capacity with Coke. The salad was frozen and wilted long before she tried to eat it at lunchtime. So she made a sign with big PINK lettering warning the world of the folly of using my Coke-fridge for anything but Coke. Ten years later the sign was still there, but whereas it generally made me think of her, today it made me feel nervous and edgy.

I rummaged through the pile and started with the marbled journals for May through September 2012 first, and read through them three times: very fast the first time, looking for common or repeated names; carefully the second time, marking anything remotely interesting with tiny post-it notes and a highlighter; backwards the third time, in the hope of making connections that I missed the first two times. Most of what I read was personal or boring, lots of it was both. She kept track of what she ate throughout the day, work meetings, books and movies that she read/saw or wanted to read/see, dates and boyfriend prospects (*yes, those were two different things ... who knew*), weather, places that she wanted to vacation, programs that she wanted to offer through the library, weird stuff that I did and said and researched (*I think/hope that I come off more weird on paper than I do in the flesh, or that she was exaggerating*), and the results of constant people-watching and what she likes to call "impression-based, fact-free storytelling" (*she looks at people and makes up a story about them based on her first impression*). She noted the people who were making frequent use of the library, made up fanciful stories about them (*arranging sexual trysts, sharing roast squirrel recipes, plotting world domination, searching for lost treasures, etc.*), and expanded on their stories day by day in her journals; she loved the movie, "Rear Window", I remembered now, in passing. She noted when, and at which computers, the regulars generally did whatever they did, and that is how I think that she got into trouble; that is how she started paying attention to George Roebuck.

Once she took note of George, she started talking about the other people she kept an eye on less and less and him more and more. She was obsessed with (*and curious about*) the fact that a rich guy like him would have to have at least one computer at home, but came in almost daily to use a library computer. She knew by word of mouth that he had something to do with drugs, either now or in the past. That must have drawn her attention because of her fiery hatred for anyone involved in the drug trade at even the most casual level (*based, I believe, on her sister's death being related to drug use*).

The really interesting stuff happened about halfway through the July journal, she had torn out a couple of pages, a thing that hadn't happened in any of the other journals. She mentioned file dumping and software bought with a PayPal account (*which suggested this wasn't stuff bought for/by the library*). From here on through the first days of September 2012 (*the point at which she disappeared*), her entries got more and more cryptic but centered on a few sets of initials and towns in the portion of New York that lies north of Route 90. The towns (*Plattsburgh, Malone, Potsdam, Canton, Watertown, Syracuse, Utica, Albany, and Saratoga*) were all outside of the Adirondack Park and made a rough circle between 50 and 150 miles away from the Tri-Lakes region. Plugging in the USB drive, I was able to check files/documents/trash from her computer and found some files and documents and screenshots that helped me put together a picture of what she had suspected, where her research lead her, how she got into trouble, and who had likely taken her; the only problem (*and it wasn't actually a problem for me*) was that I couldn't prove any of it. Even if I'd wanted to dump it in his lap, Frank wouldn't have touched it with a pole of any length.

The woods near Lonesome Bay, 4:48 p.m., 9/5/2012

I gathered all of the relevant files and notebooks and the stick drive from my trip to Cynthia's desk at the library, and hid it all in the woods in a large ammo can that I had originally purchased for geocaching, but that worked equally well for hiding all sorts of stuff in the woods. Everything was double-bagged in gallon-sized Ziplocs, and then stuffed in the ammo-can. I have caches like this hidden way back in the woods all over the place; some with camping gear or food or money or books or other things that I don't want lying around at SmartPig where anyone could find it. For short term storage, I keep the coordinates on whatever GPS I'm currently using; for permanent storage, I send the coordinates embedded in lengthy text documents attached to, or as parts of emails to myself. I have found, in geocaching, and in establishing my other caches, that people in general stay on paths in the woods (*fear of unmapped places*), and if they do venture off-trail, will generally not go more than five hundred meters from the perceived safety of the road and/or their car without a very good reason.

After hiding the ammo-can, I walked back to my campsite, brushed myself clean of pine needles and twigs and spider webs, and climbed up into the hammock with a Coke, some GORP, and my Kindle Fire to rest my body and forebrain, and try to process what I had learned in the last few hours. I love Donald Westlake's Parker books for this very thing; Parker is a violent criminal who moves relentlessly forward through the problems he faces in the books like a shark or bull, actively charging towards/though the obstacles in his path. I wanted a clear path, and the drive to charge along it no matter the consequences (*sort of an anti-serenity prayer*), so I selected a Parker novel and let the casual, but ordered, violence wash over me; as always, I enjoy the simple plots with interesting variations and explorations running throughout ... like jazz with a brutal band of thugs playing their victims delicately with lead pipes. When I had finished the Coke and Ziploc bag of GORP, and the book, I had made some useful leaps, bridging gaps in my information with guesses and suppositions that I couldn't easily fault or poke holes in; nothing a jury would like, but most of it good enough for me. I put the can in the Ziploc, dropped them both on the ground beneath my hammock for retrieval later, tucked the Kindle back behind my head and closed my eyes to let my brain finish the puzzle while I took a nap.

I came back to the world in full dark and a damp coldness that let me know that it had rained; surprised that I had slept for more than five hours. I groped for my headlamp, stepped down onto the ground, found a tree to water, and then started my stove to make some oatmeal. I knew what had happened to Cynthia with as much surety as if I had watched it, and the enormity of what I knew made my head spin. I had spent a decade in Saranac Lake and the woods nearby, making it my home, remapping my world with people and places completely new to me after the upheaval of 9/11; it felt as though it had all been swept away ... again ... during the course of an afternoon. I focused on making my oatmeal, angry and scared and sad, and so bewildered by the presence of these emotions that I couldn't, for the moment, look beyond a snack in the dark to what lay ahead of me.

Fifty feet from shore in Upper Saranac Lake, 11:17 p.m., 9/5/2012

I floated on my back, feeling the water beneath me and the sky and stars above. After finishing my oatmeal and a drink of Gatorade, I noted that I felt more than a little grimy and stiff, and so made my way down to the water's edge, stripped to my boxers, and went for a swim. It made me feel better, the water pressing on my body from all sides like a hug, warmer than the air, but not warm. I raised and lowered myself in the water with deep inhalations and exhalations, feeling control and comfort and calm return; after a few minutes of just breathing and floating, I rolled it all out for my inner moron observer.

First, Cynthia had heard that George Roebuck was a drug dealer. She hated the drug culture and all involved in it because of her sister's death as a result of drugs. She noted with increasing suspicion over time that George used the SL Free Library computers with some frequency, despite the fact that he was clearly wealthy enough to buy/own as many computers as he wanted. She began to suspect he was using the library computers to support/enhance his drug business. So, she purchased and installed a net-nanny program suite (*including software called "eBlaster"*) which tracked his online activity (*to an astounding and illegal and unethical and unexpected extent, given my previous judgments about Cynthia's moral boundaries*), including: copies of emails sent and received, screenshots of pages visited, chat logs, searches, uploads/downloads, and more. Using the information gained through the use of the net-nanny software, she figured out that he had cleaned up his act in his own backyard so that he could use the idyllic wilderness surrounding the Tri-Lakes to produce methamphetamine, for delivery and sale to bigger towns ringing the Adirondacks.

I was initially shocked at the volume and quality of information that she had managed to intercept by installing eBlaster on the Library computer: names, places, times and dates ... all were listed in detail. The truth is that people want (*need*) to assume that if they use a throwaway email address and clear the history and cookies of the browser that they're using, that the information disappears as completely as a mess on a kitchen counter; but as soon as his fingers did their walking, either in emails or Google or Facebook or IM or on websites, Cynthia had him. I resolved to work on ways to avoid this form of surveillance as soon as I had finished my business with Cynthia and George and the methamphetamine that he seemed to be making in my home.

From what I could decode, George had four teams of two guys working for him. Each team worked a couple of towns then rotated around to different towns, and into the meth-lab, every week or so. They would connect with buyers for the meth in each town, and make deliveries as they rotated through. By rotating the team, they could work through all of the drugstores in their towns, buying the legal maximum daily amount of pseudoephedrine at each before moving on to the next store. The other supplies and precursor chemicals could apparently be purchased even more easily, according to Cynthia, from Walmart, Home Depot, and a few online sources. Based on the information Cynthia had in her computer on the production of methamphetamine, working at this rate, and assuming a reasonable rate of conversion, they could produce and sell about thirty to forty kilograms of meth each month. Her research seemed to indicate that George would gross somewhere around two to four million dollars per month, less whatever expenses his business incurred.

There were descriptions, and even GPS coordinates of potential locations for their factories, which probably were a couple of trailers and RVs back on clear-cut timberland, leased for next-to-nothing while the forest regrew. There were also some pictures of one site that I think Cynthia must have taken with her digital camera (*this made me shiver, the thought of her sneaking through the woods to take pictures of these people*). I think that she had been trying to build up a supply of evidence against George Roebuck and his cottage meth industry, to dump into my lap to either break up in some way or bring to Frank. My assumption is that she wanted to build a bridge from the factories in the woods to the cash in the cities to George Roebuck, and that she got tripped up or showed her hand at some point along the way, and been kidnapped. The story, as I told it, made sense, fit the facts and information footprint that I had, and seemed plausible. It also left me with a hollow feeling in my stomach as I swam back to the shore of my camp with a giant looming lack of a plan.

She had wanted, had asked for, my help in working this problem; a problem ridiculously outside of her skillset. She was more suited to data-mining or making those silly amuse bouche things she filled her weekends with, than slogging through the woods to spy on drug-dealers and break-up multi-million dollar crime rings. I could have helped, should have helped, would have helped; but the Amish seemed more interesting on the day that she asked, so I put her off. I would have helped her eventually ... today ... but she couldn't wait, and now she was in some serious trouble, and I would have to see what I could do to get her out.

I dried off, cleaned up the campsite a bit, put up a tarp and prepared my gear for the stormy weather that was due to come in the next day or two. The gear and campsite would wait for me if I got delayed in town for as much as a week, and it was nice to know that it was ready; not as nice as a plan, but better than nothing. I grabbed the garbage and my electronics, and headed back into town, still in the dark; stopping on the way to fill up the Element and grab some hot fat and protein at McD's on the way to SmartPig to try and live up to my name.

SmartPig Thneedery, 12:35 a.m., 9/6/2012

I parked in my spot behind the building, and snuck in like
a ninja, using ambient light to find my way upstairs and in
through the door; once I was inside, I switched on a small
working light at the desk I have by the bookshelf. I could
see the end of what I had to do, and was already past the
beginning, but had no clear idea on how to get from
where I was to where I needed to be at the end of the
process; the middle was entirely unknown to me. I knew
what had happened, not with enough certainty to satisfy
the police, but I wasn't the police, so that was okay. I
knew why it had happened, and who had done it (*within
reason ... I didn't know exactly who kidnapped Cynthia, but I
knew who ordered it done*). I didn't care much how they had
done it. I had to find out where they were keeping her,
and how to extricate her. A Coke from the Coke-fridge
helped both chill and improve the function of my brain as
I settled into the different "quiet" of SmartPig at night ...
the hum of the fridges, buzz of the light, pipe noises of
the old building moving heat and water around, the

occasional creak or pop of wood and metal and glass expanding or contracting at different rates.

By the time I finished my second Coke and gotten a third, noting that I should call Alek (*my Canadian Coke Connection*) to see if he could bring a couple more cases the next time he went through town, I had zen-ed down enough, listening to the sounds of the SmartPig building, to have a couple of ideas float through my head; a few bad ones, a few horrible ones, and a few slightly less bad ones. I had to restore balance to my life and world, and doing that would require shifting the balance of other peoples' lives and worlds. I would need to adjust George Roebuck's cost/benefit equation for his life and work in such a way that harming either Cynthia or me was perceived as being more costly than releasing her (*and leaving us alone*). I was not more powerful than him, but I needed to find a way to exert sufficient force over him to force a change in his behavior that went against his previous inclinations. Altering his world, and/or his perception of the world, and/or the way that he interacted with his environment, in such a way that he would choose to release Cynthia and also leave both of us unharmed at the end of the day required either a highly complex or a really simple solution; as always, I tried to work out a simple solution.

At some point in every investigation that I undertake, I get reminded by things that pop up, or that I miss (*and later wish had popped up*), that I don't really understand human emotions and motivations as well as I should (*especially in my line of sometimes dangerous work*). I can track information and actions, and draw conclusions based on what I've seen and heard in the past, but I often end up being surprised by what people do. I don't understand their actions, even when/if they explain it to me later.

People often don't act in their own best interest, and worse still, sometimes they act differently under similar stimuli based on mood or greed or sexual drive or sleep-deprivation or any of a thousand other factors that I don't seem to have installed; or that are installed differently in my operating system than in other people's.

My first idea was to talk to George Roebuck directly, explain what I knew, and that I had no interest in sharing my knowledge with anyone provided he return Cynthia to her (*and my*) life unharmed, and post-haste. On the surface this might seem like a stupid plan, but I think there's an underlying wisdom in the simplicity of a bull in a china shop approach; a lack of subtlety implies a lack of guile, and hopefully the chance for trust and a straightforward resolution to the issue (*hopefully without violence or upset*). I like plans that can be explained to a six year old without graphs and charts and maps; based on the KISS principle (*Keep It Simple Stupid*) ... if something can go wrong, it will, so do what you can to reduce the number of chances for things to go wrong where and whenever possible.

Plan B involved my finding the current locations of George Roebuck's active meth lab(*s*), his four teams of chemists/drivers, and the money that this enterprise was generating, and then alerting the authorities to these facts, along with the warning that he had kidnapped Cynthia to protect all of the above. I wasn't crazy about this option, as it relied on lots of things coming together neatly, including multiple raids by people that I had to (*but didn't*) trust to put Cynthia's safe return ahead of a mediagenic drug bust, complete with perp-walked hoods and tables piled high with baggies of white powder and cash (*and probably guns ... those pictures always had some guns on the tables in front of smiling white cops in tac-gear*). It also seemed unlikely that even if I could give them the package complete with George, they would be able to get everyone and everything without exposing Cynthia to extensive risk in either a "she's seen our faces" body-dump, or a "we want a fueled plane, no cops visible, and the letter P stricken from the English language" hostage scenario ... neither of those appealed to my sense of neatness, but seemed potentially worth the risk, if I couldn't find a better option.

Plans C through K involved variations and combinations of the first two options, and fit somewhere between them on a sliding scale of trickiness and risk and trusting people that I didn't trust to act in Cynthia's best interest. I considered taking things from George: family, drugs, money ... or himself. I thought about approaching one or more of his men/teams with an offer to exchange Cynthia for: their continued freedom from incarceration, money, drugs, not being killed (*I had/have no interest in killing anyone, but this type of person might understand and/or respond to this flavor of threat*). I thought about bringing Frank in to SmartPig for a discussion of the situation and see what he could do with the various ingredients I had at our disposal (*different chefs can make soup or salad from the same stuff, based on their inclination and experience*). I thought about finding/following whoever George Roebuck had entrusted Cynthia with, and affecting her release (*similar to what I had done with Sadie, but likely more complex and risky for everyone involved*). I wrote these options down as a list, drew them on my whiteboard in boxes, with balloons and arrows and squiggly lines, used the growing numbers of empty Coke cans (*marked/named with post-its*) to represent all of the players and places and their relations ... until my head hurt, and then I took a nap on the couch.

When I woke up I knew how to choose the best

course of action, drank a Coke from the Coke-fridge quickly enough to get a cold-headache, and headed out to the TLAS.

Tri-Lakes Animal Shelter, 7:48 a.m., 9/6/2012

The TLAS doesn't open until 10 a.m. on the days that it's
open, but someone on the staff gets there by 7 a.m., or a
few minutes after, each day to start the never-ending
process of feeding and cleaning (*input and output
maintenance*) and exercising and caring for the hundred or
so animals that live there at any given time. I rolled up
and dumped the Element into a parking spot between the
other two cars already there (*one was Dorothy's, I didn't
recognize the other*). I grabbed a box of training treats and
some fleece blankets I'd picked up on sale at Kinney's
recently, and headed in through the back door. I found
Dorothy lining up bowls along a table, measuring varying
amounts of food and pills into each, shook the treats and
blanket at her, and wished her a good morning.

"What, no donuts?" she asked, only partly kidding;
Dorothy runs on donuts like I run on Coke.

"Not this morning, sorry, I didn't think to stop at DD
before coming over," I replied.

"You look good and wired; I can hear you crackling

from here ... you must be working on something ... tricky." She had seen me come in early before, and knew that it usually meant that I had blocky chunks of thought knocking around in my brain, just waiting to get their edges rubbed off so that they could fit together the way that they were supposed to.

"You are correct, Madam. It is quite a three-dog problem, and I beg that you won't speak to me for ninety minutes, while I let your wildest beasts drag me around the woods!" She made the joke the first time, and now I served it up for her every time the situation came up.

Without a word, Dorothy headed back into the isolation suite, a series of rooms and pens for the dogs not suitable, for whatever reason, for life in the main kennel, to get my first partner of the morning. I'm never sure if she has a method for picking out, and ordering, the dogs that she serves up when I come in on these days (*or if it's entirely random*), but it generally works pretty well for me, so I'm not too eager to peak behind the curtain and mess with her system. I could feel the floor shuddering in a series of thumps, like someone rolling a couch down a flight of stairs, as she came back in to the room, smiling at my surprise.

I generally get down on my knees to meet new dogs, to reduce my size and their perception of me as a threat, and allow them to meet me on their terms; in this case it worked too well. I had time to think, "Wow, Great Dane, Saint Bernard cross ... you don't see that every day." before the hairy beast came up on me, and chest-bumped me over and onto my back. Dorothy let him straddle me and give me some kisses, before reining him in with the leash and allowing me to roll out from under him. Back on my knees, and better braced this time, I got a good look at him: black and white longish hair, tall enough that his chin could have rested on the top of my head in our respective position, broad in the chest like a Saint Bernard, bright eyes, loose skin, feet as big as my hands. He was easily the biggest dog that I had ever been next to in my life.

"Tyler, meet Gandhi. Gandhi, meet Tyler," said Dorothy. I laughed, for the first time in days, at the thought of this armored vehicle of a dog being named Gandhi, took the leash, and headed out into the woods with him. We had a spectacular time, once we had worked out some ground rules, and I assured Gandhi that I had enough training treats in my pocket to get us through the woods and back. He ate some logs, dug a canyon, drained the pond by a few inches, and dropped a ten-pound poop. He was able to walk at heel, but preferred to walk a few feet ahead of me; on the way back up the hill to the TLAS, we ran full out, terrifying birds and beasts and, as we broke out into the opening near the shelter, a delivery guy for UPS who must have thought that bigfoot had eaten a bear and was now looking for dessert. We came inside through the back door laughing and smiling and panting, neither of us thinking a bit about Cynthia or drug dealers or doing anything but running and playing with big dogs (*or willing humans, as the case may be*).

The next dog was a Saranac Lake Special ... Rottweiler/Shepard/Pit bull mix, with maybe a bit of lab mixed in somewhere down the line, as it was black as night; Dorothy introduced him as Mike. Mike made funny snoring sounds when he pulled at the leash, which Dorothy explained was because someone had cut his throat before leaving him to bleed out on the road at Cascade Acres in Placid. I feel and react to things differently than other people do, but I choked/gagged a little when I touched the line of scar tissue under the fur on Mike's neck when I reached to scratch him. I reined him in less than I would have with another dog, to let him pull, and also move faster to prevent the collar from pulling on his neck. Way back in the woods, we sat down and looked up at the clouds for a while (*at least I did*). Mike turned to face me, leaned in, and rested his cement-block head on my shoulder and sighed. He apparently found some fleas or some such behind my left ear, because he gave me some gentle nibbles until I bribed him to stop with a handful of training treats. There wasn't much positive training going on between me and Mike, but he didn't hate me for being the same species that cut him, so I figured we were doing okay. We walked back off-trail and snuck up on the shelter through thick woods that smelled like rot, but in a good way. He sat perfectly for me when we got back to the office and gave Dorothy a handful of kisses as she walked him back to his crate.

When she came out again, I was certain that she had either made a mistake, or was messing with me; she was leading, almost dragging, a thirty pound brownish beagle mix. The dog took one look at me and, all at the same time, pee'd and started barking at me, while shivering and pulling to get away.

"This is Hope. She doesn't like anybody, but especially hates men. She mostly acts scared, but sometimes that includes biting, so be careful ... unless you want me to grab one of the other dogs?" This last bit came out somewhat a question.

I took Hope's leash and we walked quietly out into the yard behind the shelter, away from the road and parking lot and door. I sat down on the morning-wet ground, let her go to the end of the long lead, put a couple of training treats in a small pile a couple of feet away, and waited.

Hope stayed as far away from me as she could, and stared at me as though I were to blame ... for everything. She shivered and growled, but wasn't barking now that we had left the shelter, and I wasn't making her do anything or go anywhere. She looked at the treats quickly and then away, careful not to make eye contact with me; I picked up one of the little treats and threw it nearer to her. After a few minutes of just sitting there, with me talking to her occasionally, about the weather or Dorothy or my recipe for bacon-enhanced ratatouille, she moved so slowly towards the snack that it was only noticeable when it disappeared; after which she retreated to the far end again, shivering and giving little barks and grunts under her breath, ashamed with herself for giving in to temptation in the face of such an obvious threat, and vicious bastard as myself. We sat there for another ten minutes, me talking, her listening, until she slid a bit closer and ate the rest of the treats in the pile. I told her that she was a good girl, and offered her a couple in my hand, which set her shivering again, and air-snapping from a few feet away. I kept talking and not hitting her, and she eventually leaned against my outstretched leg while eating a series of treat-bits that I chucked to the ground right in front of her. She never got within reach of my hands, but neither did she bite me and by the end of almost an hour, she wasn't shivering anymore. I got up slowly and walked around her and back towards the door we had used earlier. Dorothy gave me a look when we walked in, and I told her that we'd done okay, but not great.

I love these dogs, and wish sometimes that I was able to provide them with a good, loving and stable home; but I can't, so I resolved, as I always do, to visit more, and to try and help the tough ones find forever homes. I thanked Dorothy and joined her for a Coke that she made a big deal of getting out of her fridge for me, while she had a cup of coffee during her mid-morning break. She asked about what I was working on, and I told her that although I couldn't talk with her about it right now, that I would love to pick her brain about it sometime soon. She asked which dog I was going to take home, and I told her that of the three today, my favorite was Mike; she tilted her head as though that was a meaningful answer.

"Did it work?" she asked me in a hopeful tone.

"Did what work?" I asked, although I knew what she was talking about; I wanted a few seconds to wrack my brain for an answer. I hadn't thought about Cynthia or George Roebuck in nearly two hours, and needed to get my head back in line.

"Did my dogs do your detective work for you, and if so, when do they get paid?" she said.

"You know ... they did. I've got my answer; I know what to do. The next time I come I'll be bringing a pile of my world-famous cookies as big as Hope," I answered.

"Always glad to help," she said with a smile, as she finished her coffee. "I gotta get back to work, tell me about it when you can, and give me a call if you need to, or need me for anything."

George Roebuck's House, 1:23 p.m., 9/6/2012

I went straight back to SmartPig from the animal shelter, guzzled a pair of Cokes (*taking a minute afterwards to load another case into the Coke-fridge*), changed my clothes, and washed the dog off of my face and hands before heading over to George's sandwich place. Once there, I got a ham sub, some chips, and bottled water, and asked for George. I was told that he wasn't in, and that they didn't know when he might be (*not too helpful, really*); but I wasn't thwarted. I'd done a few minutes research before heading out, and knew where to head next. A person working for the Saranac Lake School District offices owed me a favor for some work I had done a few years earlier, and it took them no time at all to find an actual home address for George Roebucks and also his ex-wife's separate address, with junior; although it was deeper in than I would have thought ... P.O. boxes for grades and address of record, but the emergency contact and forms from their pediatrician had a billing address and phone number for George that seemed plausible. I drove the Element out of the Village of Saranac Lake and away from my well-worn mental maps of the area, out into uncharted wilderness of Oseetah Lake (*only a few miles outside of Saranac Lake, but I'd never explored the area much, except for paddling across the lake on my way somewhere else*).

I rang a doorbell, but hearing nothing, knocked on the solid-sounding front door as well. After about twenty seconds I could feel, more than hear, someone moving up to the other side of the door, so I smiled appropriately (*#6, earnest, determined, polite, but not overly friendly*) at the peephole (*the first one I'd noticed in the Adirondacks*), and waited to be let in. The man I had seen at the football practice just the other day with Frank opened the door, and gave me a quick examination: looked in my eyes, at my clothes, for a briefcase, mentally checked my age against someone likely to know his son, tried to place me in his own personal socio/economic/employment framework ... failed, and then simply asked.

"What?"

"Mr. Roebuck? (*although I already knew ... that's just how these things start*) I'd like to talk to you about Cynthia Windmere. More specifically, why she is missing, and what it might have to do with you. More specifically still, how her going missing is related to your involvement in the production and sale of methamphetamine both here and in some towns around the rim of the Adirondack Park." I had decided to drop a bomb like this in the hopes that he would, if not panic, at least give some indication of his guilt that I could use to aid my advance to the next step in the process that I hoped and believed would lead to a return to normalcy and comfort in Cynthia's and my lives.

He gave me a stunned five count and an odd bark of a laugh, before opening his mouth to reply; even then, he stopped himself twice before finally speaking. "Well, I guess you're not from the Witnesses or the Mo's or a lost pizza guy. You're not straight enough for a cop, either local or state; and you're not as slick as one of the letter-feds. I heard from my guys that someone was asking for me at the shop, and seein' as you were good enough to buy a sub, I'll ask you in for a minute; but do me the favor of leaving your jacket and backpack here on the front porch and my boy Justin will check you for recording devices. If any of that bugs you too much, you can leave now, and I'll even give you a coupon for ten percent off your next sub. How's that sound to you------?"

"Tyler, Mr. Roebuck, Tyler Cunningham, and that sounds fine to me; if a bit over the top," I answered.

I left my coat and bag on the front step, and stepped over the threshold, where a guy a few years younger than me was waiting with what looked like the little radio my father used to have in the bathroom to listen to 1010 WINS Radio while he was shaving in the mornings. The house was huge and flashy inside ... lots of light wood and marble and gold fittings and high ceilings. It seemed a little out of place in the Adirondacks, and George seemed a little out of place in it himself; as though he'd seen the whole thing in "Successful Drug Kingpins Quarterly" and ordered it over the phone that night. Justin and the who-knows-what detector didn't like my watch, so I took it off and reached back out the door to drop it on top of my coat. George walked away from me, assuming (*rightly*) that I would follow, so I did; we went back through a long hallway and an archway to a living room twice the size of the entirety of SmartPig, and sat at the far end, at an island in a big empty sea of carpeting, made up of a fancy oval poker table with six chairs around it.

"Tyler, I'm George, especially to people who accuse me of kidnapping and murder and drug-trafficking." He barked out another laugh, this one sounding a bit like a very large fat man clapping his hands ... his voice and heart and mind weren't in it; it was just a place-holder, something to fill space and time. "Sit down and tell Justin here what he can get you while we talk."

"A can of Coke would be great, if you have it, but if not, water would be fine. Thanks."

Justin left the room, and the rug and space and something else, maybe a white noise generator, ate up the noise so effectively that a second later it was the quietest space I'd been in months, maybe ever. I could hear George breathing, he wheezed a bit. I was used to the sounds of wind and water and cars and people and pipes and AC and old buildings settling, and none of that happened in this room; it felt like it was just me and George, maybe in the whole world.

"You got that look, like the quiet is zapping you ... me, I love it. I couldn't believe how noisy it was out here in the woods when I moved up here from the city ... noisy and dark, so dark at night."

I didn't want to start this with him getting on top of me, inside my head, so I tried to turn things around a bit, "I like organic, living sounds. This place sounds dead; I couldn't live here."

"Enough! Let's talk about that shit you said about me, and why I shouldn't sue you or worse for sayin' it? If what you said was true, why don't I just make you disappear? Problem solved."

"Because my coming directly to you is either clever or stupid, and you want to know which, and to what degree. You also want to know what I know, what I could prove, who I've told, and what I want. It's likely occurred to you that making me disappear too could be a bigger problem than it's worth, so you wanted to talk with me to figure out which. Either that, or you wanted to show off your really big, really quiet, living room."

George barked again, "Hawh! Sass, and not scared a lick ... like you said, either smart or stupid ... maybe a bit of both. It seems like even with your stuff out front, I'd be a chump to do much more talking here ... tell me what you think, what you know, what you can prove, and what you want."

"I'm going to do just that George," I said as Justin glided in without a noise, deposited what my nose told me was a bourbon and Coke in front of George, cracked an ice-cold can of Coke for me (*which sounded explosively loud in this room*), put it on a coaster on the table, and left again just as quietly as he had entered.

"I'm going to lay all of my cards on the table, as it were." I made a spreading motion of my hands across the felt surface in front of me. "That being the case, I want you to wait until I'm done before you lose your cool and go all Tony Montana on me ... deal?" I was trying to push his buttons on purpose, hoping to keep him off-kilter, desperate for just enough time to sell my idea, my plan, to him; he nodded, and drank an inch or so off the tall glass of his drink.

"I think that Cynthia, the woman from the library, figured out that you were using the computers to facilitate or further the production and sale of methamphetamine. I think that something she did or said at some point in the last few days tipped you off that she was looking at you and your business, and you felt that the safest thing for you was to kidnap her to protect your interests."

"I know that you're making meth in a number of locations within an hour or so of the Tri-Lakes, and both selling the finished product and replenishing your supply of precursor chemicals in eight to ten cities ringing the Adirondack Park. I know pretty much what you're doing and how you're doing it, and know enough to find out where the labs are, and who you've got working for you if I cared to find out."

"If I wanted to, I bet that I could prove all of it with a bit of legwork on my part, but let's get back to that in a minute. What I want is what you want, to be left alone. In this case, that includes Cynthia, the woman from the library. I want her back at her job, unharmed, immediately. In exchange, I will guarantee that you don't get bothered by her or me ever again, about anything. I don't care about meth or money or what you do outside of my little chunk of the world, and I can convince Cynthia to see things that way too, or I can get her to leave and never come back. That's your first choice, the best option."

"The other option involves massive disruption and hassle for both of us. If Cynthia doesn't get released immediately, or is harmed in any permanent way, I would be forced to interfere. I can make things difficult and costly, and possibly even disrupt and break-up everything that you have built here." I gestured around the room, taking in the house, the land, the sub shop, his drug factories ... everything of his; perhaps a little grandiose, but I had to sell my idea, the first option, as the better choice.

"I'm a clever guy George, cleverer than you or any of the guys that work for you. I didn't come here today hoping that you'd be a nice guy and give me what I want because I asked you nicely. I came here in person to try and convince you to do this the easy way. If you refuse and decide to show me your impression of Leo

O'Bannion, bad things will happen to you even after whatever happens to me."

"You see yourself as a Tom Reagan?" George asked me; this brought me up short for a moment. Maybe he was smarter than I had assumed.

"Nope, I'm not in the movie at all ... it's your movie ... I'm a guy on the sidelines bringing you the best deal you'll get all week. One way, you get to keep all of the toys and keep making gazillions of dollars until the world runs out of people dumb enough to use meth. The other way, you lose everything. The first way is better. You don't know me, but you don't need to worry about me coming back to see you for more ... for anything. That's part of the deal; if either of us comes back at you ... ever ... grind us up and serve us as ham salad on one of your subs."

I took a breath, ready for the finale, and his reaction afterwards. "That's it, unless you have questions, I'm done."

He sat, stone-faced for about fifteen seconds before he spoke, "So, you have a sealed letter with a lawyer or some such?"

"Something like that, but a bit more twenty-first century. Time-delayed emails with everything ready to go all over the place. Messy for you, easy for me."

This was the teetering time; he would decide in the next few seconds. It made sense for him to go my way, but I kept quiet and still anyway. The time for pushing and teasing and manipulations was done; he needed to see it for himself, and know in his heart and head and gut that it was the right way ... the smart way.

He looked up at me and smiled; my heart was in my throat until he said, "Tyler, you're fucking me, but you had enough respect to kiss me first, and tell me you were going to fuck me. I never want to see you again, unless it's to buy a sandwich in my place. Where will you be in ninety minutes? I'll have Justin see what he can do about rounding up that girlfriend of yours." It seemed ungracious to correct him about my relationship with Cynthia in my moment of victory, so I gave him the address of SmartPig, finished my Coke, and started on the long walk out of his living room and back towards my car, and a soon-to-be normalizing world. If I was the kind of guy to smile and whistle a happy tune, that's what I would have done; but I'm not, so I tried to decide which watercolor to bring up to Jacob Hostetler, and whether or not I wanted to visit the superb documents collection at St. Lawrence University while I was up there. Before I got to the end of George's driveway, I had picked the right painting and decided to go visit the documents for a long day of research.

Once I got back to SmartPig, I lay down on the couch, and dropped off to sleep until I heard the knock at my door.

CHAOS

SmartPig Thneedery, 4:37 p.m., 9/6/2012

Nobody except me would have been surprised that it wasn't Cynthia at my door, but Justin, along with a guy nearly the size of Hoboken, and twice as ugly. Later on that evening, while licking my wounds, I tried to convince myself that I had been exaggerating (*even to myself*) about his size, but he had to both stoop *and* turn sideways to get through my door. Justin took my surprise and shock as an invitation, and came in, bumping me backwards and out of his way. The rough beast came slouching in next, closing the door, locking it, and standing in front of it with arms crossed; as if the other two things wouldn't have been enough to stop me leaving if I wanted to try.

"George changed his mind," Justin said, looking as though he thought I might be surprised by the announcement.

"Yeah, I figured that out when I opened the door ... well, shit. Is there anything I can do to change your minds about the upcoming unpleasantness? Can I get you a Coke? That's not my top bribe offer by the way, just some kneejerk courtesy, which in hindsight I now regret ... a bit." I was scared and running at the mouth.

"A Coke would be nice," said Barry White's albino and double-Y chromosome nephew in a voice almost low enough to rattle the windows. He headed over to the non-Coke-fridge, and I pointed him to the big stainless steel Church of Coke. He opened it, took in the lack of anything but Coke in the packed fridge, and grabbed three Cokes easily in his giant left hand.

"Cold!" he said in a pleased voice as he handed them out, first to Justin, then me, saving the last one for himself. He cracked his, took a sip, and his face transformed; I could almost see a happy child that a mother must have loved and hugged (*maybe having to climb a stepladder to do it*). "That's the best fucking Coke I've ever had, how come?"

"I got the special fridge, which keeps them at exactly the right temperature, and a guy I know brings these ones to me from Canada; they have to use real cane sugar by law, not sugar from beets or corn, like in the US, and it's really a lot better than what you can get here." Although surreal, this conversation was helping me to not be so frightened. They had come here, obviously intent on hurting or killing me, but some pointless talk had given me a brief respite, a safe harbor in this storm that I had been shamefully unprepared for; I reminded myself to kick my ass later for my tunnel vision in my "planning" on how to deal with George.

"Enough about the fucking soda! We've got things to do and talk about here ... we can do it the hard ... or the really fucking hard way; it's up to you," Justin roared at the giant, but mostly at me.

"If there's an easy way, that'd be my choice," I offered. "It's clear that I miscalculated here, something I tend to do when I fail to take the human element into account in new situations. My solution made sense to me, so I assumed that it would make sense to George; clearly not the case. I'd like to work this out so nothing bad has to happen to anyone, particularly me, if possible." It was at this point in my semi-shameful groveling that I realized, as if someone had painted it on my walls in neon paint, that Cynthia was dead; the certainty with which I now felt her death made my breath catch and speed up, and my eyes itch a bit. Everything seemed to come into a new level of focus: all of my senses as well as my mental faculties, but of course the flood of adrenalin was useless to me in my current situation. I had as much chance of successful fight or flight as a puppy in a bear trap.

"You left the easy way behind you this afternoon in George's living room ... shamed the man in his own home; now the best you can hope for is painless, or nearly so. Make a pile on this table," Justin gestured at the coffee table near the couch, "of the following items: any computers or hard-drives or storage devices, any notes and maps and other documents pertaining to Cynthia Windmere or methamphetamine or George or any of George's associates, any cash or jewelry or electronics or other valuables that a thief might take. Barry is going to break the pinky finger on your left hand now, before you waste time lying or stalling, so that you believe me when I tell you that we want you to do this quickly and efficiently. If I think that you're dicking around at any point in the process, I'll have Barry (*I giggled at the man-mountain's name, but they must have thought it was a whimper because neither looked at me*) break another finger. If we run out of fingers to break, we can hammer or cut shit off, but I'm hoping to avoid that stuff altogether. Are we clear on what I want? If so, please begin." Justin said this in the bored manner of cops on TV, or in movies, reading the Miranda warning to criminals, which would have freaked me out, if I had any out left to freak.

"Two things, Justin ... if Barry breaks any of my fingers, I'll scream. Not to try and give you away, but I'm just not great at dealing with pain, and I have downstairs neighbors; I don't want them (*or me, when you come right down to it*) involved in this ... also, I have a crap-ton of money cached out in the woods which I'll happily give you two if you will just pretend that I wasn't here when you knocked." I wasn't proud of this last bit, not much help for Cynthia or truth and justice and the American way; but I was scared and didn't want anything broken or hammered or cut off, and if money would make this problem go away, I'd give them all I had, and consider myself lucky.

"Thanks for the heads up on the screaming like a little girl thing, Tyler, that's good to know ... considerate for everyone involved. Barry can gag you before doing the deed. On the other thing ... piss up a rope, although I will take another Coke if you don't mind." I nodded, and Barry got up to grab another handful; he looked at me politely, and I shook my head, so he just grabbed two.

Barry put down his Coke, took out a flattened roll of duct-tape, peeled off about a foot, stuck that on his right sleeve, grabbed a bandana out of a pocket, and came over towards me. "This will go easier if you don't fight it. I'm too big; you'll just pull a muscle or hurt yourself struggling." I believed him, and stood when he gestured, turned when he spun his index finger (*like stirring a drink, I couldn't help thinking*), let him push the dry and pocket-tasting bandana into my mouth, and then fix the tape over my lips to stop me spitting it out. He twisted my right arm behind my back, and in one quick and sure move, that spoke of having done this before, he broke my pinky finger.

I screamed into the bandana, and tears squeezed out of my eyes and rolled down my cheeks. Barry let go of my arm, and I spun around quickly to get away from his awful strength, hitting my hand on the way around, and getting another blinding flash of pain. I sat down on the couch to breathe and curse into the bandana for a minute, while the two guys looked on, slightly embarrassed.

"Okay? All set? Can Barry take the tape off now, or are you gonna cry too loud?" Justin asked, and they both chuckled. I nodded, and Barry came over to take the tape off; I spat out the bandana, and drooled out a dispirited, "Motherfucker."

Barry bristled a bit and started towards me, and I raised my hands, and tried to mollify him, "Not you, specifically, just the situation ... you've got to admit that I'm waist-deep in shit, and can't feel solid ground below me." Barry nodded, and sat back down to work on his second Coke.

"Okay, you can start any time now, Tyler; sooner and quicker would be better all the way around," Justin reminded me.

I took a swig of Coke from the half full can, and held the coldness in my right hand against my pinky finger, which had, in fact, been dislocated at the base, not broken *(although why split hairs)*; but was now seated more or less back where it was supposed to be. I walked over and grabbed my laptop, brought it back to the coffee table, and repeated that for all of the external drives and USB sticks around the office. Next I rounded up any of the of the notebooks and papers and maps that I had printed out or doodled on, including some from the garbage, hoping that the amount would be enough to appease Justin and Barry, and that they wouldn't look too closely and notice that all of the good stuff was missing, cached in the woods. Finally I went around the room gathering electronics and a few hundred dollars from a hollow book; I nearly skipped the box I kept on top of the bookcase with some of my parents' jewelry (*rings and cufflinks and necklaces and a pocket watch and such*). I didn't like the idea of these guys having it, but liked the idea of getting another finger broken even less, so I grabbed it, as well as some coins and stamps that my father and I had noodled around with when I was a kid; not worth too much, but I hoped that the thought would be what counted. By the time I was done gathering the booty and putting it on the coffee table, I had calmed down enough to get the beginnings of an idea; so I sat down and started to cry. Barry shoved everything into a duffel-bag and dropped it by the door.

"Hey now, none of that ... it looks like you did a good job. We need to head out in a bit, and if you're crying like a baby, we might attract the attention of your downstairs neighbors; and that's no good." Justin didn't have a credible caring voice, but that might be because of the path our relationship had followed recently.

"I'll be okay, but could I have another Coke to relax ... it also helps the finger." I asked in my best pathetic voice, which wasn't a big stretch from my actual voice at this point. I added in my #8 smile (*sucking up in an obsequious manner*) hopefully, and it paid off; Barry looked at Justin, got a nod, and grabbed me what might be my final Coke from the Coke-fridge.

"Nothing else of value in this place? Our guy says that you don't have another place ... no shit ... you're like homeless?" I nodded, and he went on. "Fucked up ... never mind ... he said you've never had a background check for any long guns, and no handgun license in New York or any other state ... is that right? Do you have any firearms here, Tyler? From a relative or yard sales or under the table at a gun show?" I shook my head, and they both looked a bit disgusted. "No hunting, no shooting, nothing, huh? Well our guy said you were some sort of half-assed private detective, but I just don't see it ... go figure."

"Final set of questions, keep up the good work, and Barry won't have to break any more fingers, and that may be a record ... nobody tends to act smart in this situation ... but you're doing okay. What did you set up in case you disappear or get hit by a bus? Also, who did you talk to about George and Cynthia Windmere and the meth stuff? I'm looking right in your fucking eyes, and I'll know if you're lying, and Barry here won't get the record for least fingers broke, so think carefully before you answer ... take all the time in the world, as long as it ain't more than five seconds."

I looked at him, and Barry, and pretended to think about it for a couple of seconds. Answering too quickly would be worse than taking too long. "I was lying about the emails if something happened to me; I didn't figure I'd need it because my deal seemed to make so much sense ... at the time ... to me. I didn't tell anyone about George or my suspicions about what happened to Cynthia, except for the dogs."

"What? No wait ... don't bother, I don't care. I believe you, and we don't give a fuck how many dogs you told about George. You're positive you didn't tell Frank Gibson? I hear that you two are close." This gave me pause, and I could feel my face changing, so I bumped my pinky against the table, and the pain provided some cover.

"No, not Frank Gibson, and whoever told you that we're close should take a pay cut and maybe a pinky realignment by Barry, because they're feeding you bad information."

I had about thirty-eight percent of an idea, some pain, some caffeine, some upset about Cynthia, and enough curiosity about who "their guy" was to give me a dash of hope. If my subconscious was making plans for further investigations, it must have thought that I was going to make it through this encounter with Justin and Barry. I wondered who it could be ... not Frank, but someone in the law enforcement community. If I could live through the next few hours, I'd have to try and figure out who it was, and why they told George (*or Justin*) about me. For now, though, I had to focus on not dying; I drank some more Coke and waited for their next move.

Justin shifted gears, nodded to Barry, and turned again to address me. "We need to leave now, and you're coming with us. If you can come peaceably, we can all three walk out the back way and drive away in our car. If you're gonna hassle us, either Barry or I can close your account right here, right now, and Barry waits until four in the fucking morning to tote you down the stairs like we planned, except he'll be all grumpy tomorrow, on account of not sleeping well in a strange place." At this, Barry nodded to himself, and looked plaintively at me, as if for help; I gave him an oddly disturbing thumbs-up, signifying that I'd cooperate.

"Okay, then finish up your Coke, and let's go."

I downed the rest of the can, resisted the urge to ask for a pee-break before we headed out, and walked out and down and drove away from SmartPig with Barry and

Justin; hopefully not for the last time.

Ampersand Bay Boat Launch, Lower Saranac Lake,
6:34 p.m., 9/6/2012

We had piled into Justin's banana-yellow crew-cab pickup truck, with Barry and me stuffed in the back. We made a couple of stops on our way out of town, with Justin getting out and throwing stuff in the truck bed at each time, while Barry kept his fingers squeezed on my neck to exert control. George's sub-shop was the first stop, and here Justin muscled a four foot tall rolling garbage can into the truck-bed. Next he pulled in at Aubuchon Hardware for enough stuff to merit a couple of trips of things sufficiently heavy to make the back of the truck bounce on its springs. The maddening thing was seeing people that I knew and not being able to call or wave or just leave; the tinted windows allowed me to see them, but they couldn't see me, and with Barry's giant sausage fingers around my favorite vertebrae, I wasn't tempted to call out. The powerlessness of my situation was disheartening, I felt dead already. Barry's sheer bulk and dumb strength took any action on my part out of the realm of possibility, and he knew it because I could feel his grip relax (*just a bit*) while we were waiting for Justin.

"I'm sorry about the finger Mr. Cunningham, sorry about all of this ... but it's just the way things worked out." Barry mumbled when he felt me wince after trying to make a fist with my right hand.

"Given the situation Barry, you should probably just call me Tyler. The kidnapper/murderer-victim relationship is such that we can skip over social niceties. Just out of curiosity, if you don't mind ... how much bigger than your parents are you?" I didn't care much about Barry's firsthand experience with the 47-XYY karyotype, but it was something to talk about, and significantly more fun than thinking about the impending end of everything, from my point of view.

"My pop is tiny, about five-six, and Ma is about an inch taller. I was bigger than both of them by the time I was in fifth grade, and outgrew my bed by the end of sixth grade. Do you know about me ... about people like me?" he asked, almost shyly, looking at me sideways, head bent over to fit in the crew cab. "Ma always thought it was because they were so old when they had me."

"It wasn't. Based on what I've read, some in British and Scottish studies, it just happens. It's also possible that you have some issues with the regulation of your pituitary gland, although doctors probably would have picked up on that by this point in your life and growth."

"What's all this then?" Justin's arrival back in the front seat upset the sympathetic mood that had been growing in the backseat in the last few minutes, and Barry literally shook himself free of those thoughts and the mood and renewed his bruising grip on my neck. Barry grumbled something about being bored and wanting to get on with

it, looked guiltily at me, and then turned to look out the
window, as Justin took the back way around town, to the
boat dock at Ampersand Bay, on Lower Saranac Lake.

We pulled around to the boat launch. Justin reversed
the truck so that the rear wheels were in the water and
then went over to the docks to bring around a big
covered pontoon boat. As it was a bit chilly and cloudy
and the sun was about to dip behind the tallest trees,
almost everyone that had been on the water was already
home by this time, or just finishing putting their boats in
the dock slips, or up on their car roofs (*in the case of smaller
boats*). I heard a boat start, catch with a throaty rumble,
seconds later begin to run smoothly, and a minute after
that saw Justin chugging back over towards us.

He nosed the front of the boat right up against the
tailgate and chopped the engine. He nimbly skipped up to
the front of the boat from the control panel in back, and
tied a line from the boat to a knob on the back of the
truck before dropping the tailgate down to make a ramp
between the boat and truck. That done, it took him two
minutes to transfer all of the stuff from the truck to the
boat, including the rolling dumpster filled with some of
the stuff from the hardware store, a bunch of bags of
cement, some of the straps that people use to tie boats to
their cars, and finally ... a cooler. He gave a nod, and
Barry and I climbed out of the rear of the truck, stretched
out the kinks, and climbed up into the boat; me first and
then Barry. Justin stood back a bit, with a hand in his
fleece jacket's pocket holding what I assumed was a gun
to cover me if I had been brave enough to try something
... I wasn't.

He motioned me to sit down, and pulled the small
handgun out a bit, to show me, in case I hadn't figured it
out already. He tossed the truck keys to Barry and told

him to untie the boat and then park the truck. Barry did as he was told, forgetting to raise the tailgate, which clanked a bit when he pulled forward, but probably didn't matter much to anyone except me. I was paying special attention to everything around me, as it might be the last time that I saw any of it. A minute later, Barry walked out into the water and pulled himself up into the boat as though he weighed a quarter of his bulk. The boat bobbed up and down, settling towards him a bit, before Justin started it up again and pulled away. I looked around as we reversed and turned, and couldn't see a soul I knew, much less a rescue on the way. I could feel my way into the future and see myself disappearing beneath the waves out here in a hundred slightly varying futures; but couldn't see one where I somehow made it back to SmartPig for a bowl of oatmeal and a Coke.

I knew from fishing with Frank that one of the deepest spots in the lake was a bit more than a mile west southwest from the boat launch, and it seemed from his heading that Justin knew about it also. It was about fifty feet deep, which was more than enough for what I guessed they were planning for me. The wind and cold and my need to pee all worked together to help focus my mind a bit; after the car ride, I needed to get back in control of myself a little if I was going to be able to try anything.

Justin and Barry seemed so calm, almost bored, and prepared for this trip out on the water, that I had to ask, "Did you guys take Cynthia on this same trip?" I was reasonably sure that I already knew the answer, but wanted, needed, to hear them say it; to make it real, and to help me get angry again instead of just being scared.

"If you're as smart as you're supposed to be, you know that we did. I can walk you through it, if you want, though," Justin offered. "We get out to the deeps, find our mark, a spot almost sixty feet deep, we mix some cement, Barry shuts you down painlessly, load you and your crap and the cement in the roller, and over you go. If you feel like screaming for help, the only difference will be that I shoot you first, and you spend a couple of minutes bleeding and hurting before the end, and maybe you go in the water still alive."

"You're monologuing," Barry said under his breath, which impressed me, until I figured out that he was riffing off of 'The Incredibles'.

"Shut the fuck up, Barry." Justin didn't even look his way before continuing, "Your friend ... she was quiet ... no muss, no fuss. Not a baby like you about the finger or any of this. Don't feel too bad, though, you're not the worst; we had a guy, couple of years ago, that puked on Barry with the finger, and screamed at the launch ... didn't matter, nobody sees, nobody hears ... he spent the ride trying to hold his blood and shit inside himself with his hands and crying like a little girl."

"Not to rush things along, but why not kill me now?" I asked out of stupid curiosity, as if from a distance, feeling my mouth getting dry and lips going tacky from stress and adrenalin.

"George figured this out before Barry and me started; the less time you have a body on the boat, the better. If you can hold out, we'd like to mix the cement and put your things in first, leave you until the end. If you start to lose your shit, like your wobbly knees suggest that you might be, we can change up the order of things ... but we'd prefer not, unless we have to do it." Justin looked up from my legs, and searched my eyes and face, then nodded to himself.

I wanted to scream. I wanted to run. I wanted to

attack them both with my bare hands. But what I did instead was stand and shiver and sweat and not come up with any plan better than screaming or running or attacking the guys barehanded who could crush or shoot me without any difficulty or qualms. The detestable phrase, "if rape is inevitable, relax and enjoy it" went through my head. The thought made me want to throat-punch whoever originally gave tongue to it, and then I segued around a bit and came up with a really crappy plan. If it hadn't been so much better than no plan at all, and significantly better than anything else that had gone through my head in the last hour, I would have laughed or cried. It was not a plan that Spenser or Parker or Travis would have liked, but it was the one I had, so as we slowed down, and Justin turned into the chop, I got ready to put my plan into action.

Barry moved over closer to me, and Justin scooped up a gallon or so of water in a five gallon bucket before pouring in some cement mix. He stirred it around with a length of rebar, added a bit more water, and then stirred it some more before pouring it into the bottom of the rolling garbage can ... he did this several more times as I worked up my nerve to try my idea; I figured that it had about a one in five chance of working without my ending up dead, which, although lousy, was significantly better than any other alternative I could see. Justin threw in my laptop and the rest of the contents of the duffel-bag. I cringed when I saw my parents' valuables go in the cement with a plop, and Barry had his hand on my neck in a quarter second, gripping tightly enough to bring stars to the edges of my vision.

"Barry, no worries, I'm okay ... ish. That stuff belonged to my parents, and that's all I have of them now ... but it occurs to me that I'll be with them forever in a few minutes, so who gives a fuck." I didn't want him to break my neck now, before I had a chance to try my lame idea. "Before you ... do it ... can I pee? Those Cokes are killing me, and I don't want to pee myself at the end." I couldn't tell if that sounded plausible, or hard-boiled, or silly, but I tried to sell it with a number three smile, even though he couldn't see my face.

"Okay, but I'm not letting go of your neck, and if you try to dive over or stomp my foot or anything, I'll hurt you before I kill you ... maybe break your arms." Barry was giving me my chance, and I could feel every muscle, every joint, every inch of me getting ready. I felt myself hyperventilating and starting to get light-headed; so I shuffled, with Barry holding onto my neck like he was ready to pop it off, to the edge of the pontoon boat and unzipped my fly.

At first I couldn't pee, and I was positive that Barry would notice and call me on it, and snap my neck. I strained like I was giving birth, and finally it started, a couple of drips at first, and then a steady stream. As things were winding up, I caught the last bit in my cupped hand and without zipping up or even pausing to tuck myself back in, I threw my secret weapon, a handful of pee, into the spot where I desperately hoped Barry's eyes were. He squealed like a little girl getting her pigtails pulled, and swatted me off to one side in his rush to get both hands to his eyes. I was a bit off balance from spinning around, but my butt hit the rail, and I had a momentary hope that I might get off scot-free.

Justin must have stopped getting the garbage-can ready when he heard Barry and me talking. He had stepped off to one side to keep an eye on the proceedings, with a clear view of me not eclipsed by Barry's bulk. Barry swatting me to one side distracted him for a split-second, but by the time my butt hit the railing of the pontoon boat he had his gun out, and in one of those slow-motion moments generally reserved for dropping whole trays of drinks, I watched him shoot me. I saw what looked like a huge hole in the barrel of the handgun flash from black to white-yellow, and simultaneously felt something poke me hard in the upper chest on my left side. I fought the impulse to keep my balance, and instead I let myself fall (*in what I hoped was a convincingly boneless manner*) over the railing and into the water.

I hit the water, turned around under the surface, opened my eyes and felt for the curved metal of the pontoon. I tried to orient myself by the fading light of the day, as I swam gently back under the boat, trying for as little disturbance as was possible. I came up underneath the boat and was surprised by a third pontoon in the middle; luckily I had my right hand up above me and was able to slow and adjust my course without bonking loudly into the middle pontoon. I kept my nose and an ear above the surface of the water and tried to breathe quietly and listen for what Justin and Barry were doing; if either or both dove in to try and find me, I was probably screwed.

"Fuck you! He threw piss in my fucking eye ... let's see you man-up through that!" shouted Barry.

"Well, I hit him hard and center-mass, and I bet he sank like a fucking stone, in those jeans and boots and jacket," replied Justin.

"The sound of that hand-cannon probably stopped peoples' suppers at camps all over the lake," Barry quipped back.

"Well, what the fuck was I gonna do after you let him go, let him dive in and swim away? Speaking of which,

Barry, I haven't seen him come up for air yet, have you?" asked Justin.

"No ... You sure you hit him? Maybe he's holding his breath or something," suggested Barry.

"I hit him hard ... look, there's his blood on the railing, where he went over. Give me a hand dumping this garbage-roller off the front, then we'll clean up the blood. Nobody can hold their breath that long ... we still don't see him, he's dead for sure. He'll come up in a day or two, but that's a problem for another day ... we need to take care of this shit now!" replied Justin, with a tone of finality in his voice.

I was starting to think that I had run through all of my bad luck and might live to see another day. They couldn't think of the underside of the boat as a place to hide, because in their worldviews, this boat was a flat thing that moved across the water, nothing more; nobody hid under boats. I could feel a spreading warmth inside my jacket, and the stinging in my chest shifting from an ache to a throbbing pain, and wondered how much blood I was losing; I briefly panicked about sharks before I got un-stupid again. The sound of the garbage-can dropping off the front of the boat almost made me shriek, which would have been poor form, but luckily my mouth was below water when it happened, as I was just breathing through my nose to keep as low a profile as was possible.

A minute later, talking quietly enough to themselves that I couldn't hear them clearly, they must have reached some decision, because the engine started. I took a couple of deep breaths and as the boat started moving away in a wide arc back towards the boat landing, I dove down a couple of body lengths to avoid the prop as well as being seen. The negative buoyancy of my clothes and boots made it easy to stay down once I had gone deep enough. I stayed down until my lungs were burning and then another thirty seconds; long and deep enough so that I barely made it back up to the surface with all of the drag from my sodden clothes.

I came up with the top of my head facing the thrum of the motor. I stuck my nose out just enough to suck in some air after blowing out what remained in my lungs on the way up. I hoped that my dark hair and the fading light of dusk would camouflage my head a bit if they were still looking. I kept anticipating the bullet splashing through the water and into my skull, but it didn't come. A few minutes later, I started to sink and sputtered my way to the surface. I couldn't see Justin and Barry, or the boat, at all. I held my breath and curled into a fetal position long enough to lose my boots and socks, took a breath, and then did the same with my pants, and then my shirt and jacket. Once these things fell away from me, I felt less as though some weird gravity at the lake-bottom was dragging me down, but I felt so tired, and my chest was screaming at me, drowning out even the ache of my pinky.

I swam for the nearby-ish north shore of the lake, broke a window in an attractive summer cabin with no discernible remorse or regret, and called Dorothy on the pre-Cambrian rotary-dial phone attached to the wall in the kitchen.

"Hi Dot, remember when you said to call if I needed anything. Well ..."

TLAS, 8:41p.m., 9/6/2012

"Hi Tyler ... well ... shit ... uhhh ... are we going to the hospital?" was how Dorothy greeted me when she pulled up in her little Suzuki SUV on the dirt road leading to the summer cabin I had phoned her from. I had been hiding in the woods, shivering and watching for Justin and Barry until I saw the familiar, narrow configuration of her lights, and stepped out to flag her down. She had laid the passenger seat all the way back, and draped a blanket (*possibly one that I had donated to the shelter*) over it. I settled gratefully on it and thanked her for coming.

"I'm sorry to do this to you Dorothy, but I didn't want to go the ambulance and police route. I haven't bled to death or drowned in blood and I can sort of move, so I think not the hospital, but I might raid your supplies at the shelter if that's okay." I had stolen two dishtowels from the summer cabin, packed them over the wound(*s?*) awkwardly using my right hand which was increasingly ouchy each time I bumped it, and wrapped a twin sheet around my shoulder toga-style to keep it in place. I drank a quart of slightly pond-y tasting water from the kitchen tap that reminded me of summer when I was a kid (*thank goodness for caretakers not shutting camps down until the last minute*). I cleaned up the blood and mess that I could see before turning off the light, closing the door, and heading down the driveway to wait for Dorothy. I honestly believed that I might pass out at any point from the second Dorothy answered her phone until I pulled the door closed, banging my pinky ... again ... in the process.

"What's a friend for, if not to drive a getaway vehicle after you've been shot?" she quipped sarcastically. I thought that, given the circumstances, it would have been rude, and possibly dangerous, to correct her, so I held my tongue.

She drove, as always, slightly too fast for every road and each bump made me want to cry; given the sort of day I'd been having, I gave myself permission to do just that. She looked over and opened her mouth to speak, then thought better of it, maybe out of pity. I don't think Spenser or Travis ever cried when Hawk or Meyer rescued them (*and Parker never needed anyone to rescue him*).

She pulled in to the TLAS parking lot a few minutes later and parked behind the dumpster around back. She came around and helped me out of the car and up the stairs into their clinic area, where she pushed me back onto the wide and short stainless steel table that they use for cleanings and performing minor surgeries. My legs hung over from the knees down, which wasn't uncomfortable enough to prevent me from starting to fall asleep until Dorothy unwrapped the sheet, pulled the dishtowels and cut my shirt off. She made an onomatopoetic yuck sound and poured half a bottle of unreasonably cold Betadine all over me, from neck to nipple and out to the tip of my left shoulder. Then she grabbed me roughly by my hip and neck and turned me halfway around so as to pour the rest of the bottle on my back in the same general area. Then she let me lay back on a puddle of the stuff.

It occurred to me that she was treating me like she does the dogs and cats that come through the shelter like a revolving door; I'd even helped her before, but had never been on this side of her bedside manner during treatment. She gripped my left shoulder and pulled the arm up, and swiveled it around roughly; it hurt because of the torn meat, but I couldn't feel the grating of broken bones. "You're lucky, it's just a flesh wound," she commented. "On T.V. they'd call it a 'through and through', and you'd be doing pull-ups when we came back from commercial."

"If it wasn't a 'flesh-wound', Justin would have missed, in which case I'd feel a whole lot luckier." But she was right ... it seemed as though I had had some luck this night after all.

She put on a camping headlamp, clipped a magnifying lens onto one side of her glasses, and had me sit up while she checked the entry and exit holes. She tweezed out a couple of bits of shirt and algae and such from each side, and then used a big squirt bottle of saline solution to really rinse out both sides of the wound; she seemed okay when I whined, but surprised when I cursed ... not what she expects from the usual guests on her table. She drew the edges of the surprisingly small holes most of the way closed with strips of tape augmented with what smelled like crazy glue, covered it with gauze and more tape, and then moved my arm in a circular motion again; everything held ... and it hurt like hell.

She unlocked and opened the meds cabinet and fridge at the other end of the room. She got out a syringe and a handful of vials of pills and liquids. She loaded the syringe and asked if I was allergic to Penicillin. "What are you using, and no, I'm not allergic to anything that I'm aware of, but will I be barking or meowing at the end of this process?"

"Twin Pen, which is Penicillin G with Benzothine to get a bunch of antibiotics into your system quickly, to head off the creeping crud you must have from swimming in Lower Saranac with two holes in you. After that I'm going to give you some Ultram, which is a post-surgical med we use for pain management; along with some Cephalexin, which is a broad spectrum antibiotic in pill form which you should take for two weeks, assuming you don't try to talk Somali pirates into killing you before the pills run out. I'm guesstimating the dosages a bit, as these are vet-meds, and I don't want to call the actual vet for guidance. As it is, I'm going to have to fudge our books a bit or klutz my way into 'dropping' a bunch of meds tomorrow morning when somebody else is in here to see."

"I'm sorry, Dorothy. I didn't want to get you mixed into this," I mumbled, and then yelped as she stuck me with the needle. She dropped the syringe into a sharps container on the wall, and pulled a Coke out of the little dorm-fridge they kept in this room for people to keep their lunches and snacks. She brought it over to me with two each of two different types of pills; I washed them down gratefully with a swig of Coke.

"Now that I know you're not going to bleed out, or pass out ... and if you're done crying for the moment, I'll take a look at that angry bruise on the end of your right hand, where your pinky used to be. While I'm doing that, maybe you can tell me a little bit about what the 'this' is that you've gotten me mixed up in, 'want to' or not."

She grabbed a roll of tape and a couple of what, in a doctor's office, would be called tongue depressors, but in a shelter were probably called something else. She gently prodded the joint where my pinky joined my right hand, manipulated it back into a slightly more natural position relative to the other fingers, taped it to a neighboring finger, covered both with a cut-down tongue depressor, and taped the stabilizing bit of wood to the fingers. I tried not to moan and whimper while she was doing this, but for the most part failed. I could see her thinking to herself that most kittens were tougher than me.

"Do you want the long or short version? Also, bear in mind that some of what I did, and almost all of what the other guys did, was illegal. You knowing about it probably requires you to tell the police or face prosecution."

"Gimme the short version in nice declarative sentences, but I reserve the right to circle back for additional info as needed," she said.

"George Roebuck has been making methamphetamine locally, for sale less-locally. Cynthia Windmere found out by 'big-brothering' the hell out of his computer usage at the library. She confronted him and his minions grabbed and then killed and dumped her in Lower Saranac Lake. I found out and stupidly confronted him also, with the same effect. I lived, so far, and called you." I finished the Coke and she grabbed another one for me.

"You thought your way out of the problem in a way that didn't work for him, same with Cynthia ... Lord save us from smart people who don't get the way that the rest of us think and act." She smiled at me as she said this, but this was something we'd talked about before ... she called it my 'reality gap'.

"QFMFT!" I replied, using a frequent (*and favorite*) response of hers. "The question is, what do I do now? I like my life here, I've finally managed to install a map of the places and people, and know how to make things work here. I don't want to start over in a new place and re-map, remake, my whole world ... again"

"Are you ignoring, or ignorant of the bigger issue? That motherfucker tried to kill you, and almost succeeded. We need to take him out, burn his house down with him inside it, and piss on the ashes!" She flushed as she said this, not from embarrassment and self-consciousness (*as I would have*), but with feeling, I think.

"Tell me what you really think Dorothy, don't stifle your feelings, it'll eat you up inside. I can't kill him, I'm not an assassin. He might have family or pets with him in the house; I'm not burning it down. I don't want to end up in jail at the end of all of this." She turned and started to say something, but stopped herself when I started up again.

"Besides, I think that with his guys failing to kill me, I can convince him that he made a mistake in trying the first time around, and that my original idea can still work," I said in a reasonable voice.

She goggled at me, as though I was speaking in tongues, and nearly yelled, "Even forgetting the fact that it was fucking idiotic the first time around to tell the drug-dealer that you knew what he was up to, and give him a chance to whack you ... which you seem to be doing *AGAIN* ... moron ... even forgetting all of that ... which I can't ... not even for a second ... he killed Cynthia! Even if there was some valid argument that he would buy into for not killing you ... which by the way, there isn't ... he still killed Cynthia ... your friend ... Cynthia! Did you forget? He can't do that and get away with it. I didn't even like her, and it's not okay with me. In the words of Old Jack Burton, 'son of a bitch must pay'. You talk about balance and logic; you've got to kill him and his guys to bring balance and logic back to the universe."

She took my pensive silence for dumbstruck silence. To be fair, the two look pretty similar when I haven't intentionally assigned my face an expressive position. She snapped her fingers and threw another attempt at persuasion at me. "Those crime books with the guy Parker?"

"The Parker novels, written by Richard Stark, who's agent knew him as Donald Westlake, until he died on New Year's Eve of 2008?" I offered.

"Whatever ... that guy ... what would Parker do? Like those silicone bracelets everyone wore a few years ago, except Parker instead of Jesus?" This last idea made me giggle a bit; I don't always understand the rest of the world's sense of humor, nor is mine often in line with theirs, but this thought struck me as funny. I stopped giggling after a moment though, and stood up/off of the surgical table to stretch and walk and think a bit, it occurred to me that while her argument was needlessly retributive, she was, at least partly, correct.

I had originally hoped to restore order to my world by returning Cynthia to the library and ignoring the issues that had brought about her disappearance. That was now impossible on two separate levels: she was dead, and George knew that I knew about both his business and murdering Cynthia (*either of these was obviously adequate reason for him to kill me*). I therefore couldn't worry about restoring balance in the way that I had originally (*and in hindsight foolishly*) hoped to do. But, I could try to preserve what was left of my world; this had to include preserving my life, both corporeally and the life that I had built for myself in the Adirondacks. I had rewritten my world after my parents died, and although what I had now was not what everyone had, I liked it. I didn't want to start over again in a new place almost as much as I didn't want to die. I had explored my new world, pushed back the unknowns day by day, and person by person, and new place by new place; I had fought for the Adirondacks, and didn't want George to win them from me.

I had to kill George Roebuck, it occurred to me, him and the two thugs who had tried to sink me in the lake next to Cynthia and whomever else had bothered them enough to earn that boat ride over the years. Not for revenge as Dorothy posited, but simply to preserve my place in both the universe and my own little corner of it. I didn't know how I was going to do it, or if it was even possible for me to do it, but I once again (*perhaps overoptimistically*) had a vision of the future. It was of me in SmartPig and the local environs, in a world with no George Roebuck (*or Justin or Barry*) in it.

I turned to Dorothy, nodded once, and said, "Parker would kill them all, and that's what I guess I have to try and do ... in a couple of days ... after you help me get out to my camp and into my hammock to hide out and try to come up with a plan that leaves them dead and me alive, without Frank having to arrest me before I go to his house for dinner next Monday."

Dorothy's face contained an odd mix of impressed and hopeful and grim and biting back laughter; I would have to settle for that as the best that I was going to get.

JAMIE SHEFFIELD

ADJUSTMENT

Lonesome Bay, 3:14 a.m., 9/7/2012

I woke up sore and thinking about a ninety degree wedge of a twelve inch peach pie. Instead of peach pie, I gobbled a handful of Dorothy's dog drugs and downed one of the Gatorades we had stolen from the backroom fridge. We had cleaned out the fridges in the backroom and office, as well as desks and cupboards, of everything edible in the assumption that we shouldn't drive through town or delay my hiding, like a scared and wounded tiny woodland mammal (*which I was*), from the world in general, and George and his thugs in particular. Dorothy filled a garbage bag with everything edible that we found and helped me back into her little SUV for the short drive out to the plow turnaround from where I could walk out to my campsite.

She got me through the woods and we hung all of the food except the Gatorade for morning. I had a pair of tuna sandwiches and a quart container originally labeled for two percent milk that we had filled with a mix of whole milk and half and half from the fridges in the

TLAS. I'm not a big fan of tuna but I figured that my body could use the protein. By the time I finished the sandwiches and the milk/cream, I was full and tired and needed Dorothy's help to get into my sleeping bag and tip back into the waiting hug of my hammock. Dorothy wanted to call in sick, stay and help, obviously certain that I was either going to die in my sleep or drive over to surrender myself to George in the morning. I assured her that I planned to do neither and told her that she needed to stay alive and safe and working for the good of the homeless beasts in the Tri-Lakes area (*and in case I got shot again, and needed more mending*).

I could hear her stomping angrily through the woods away from my camp long after the light from her headlamp had faded away. I was asleep before I heard her car start up to bring her home and to bed. After a restful nap, I woke up and felt like hammered shit, but significantly better than I would have felt in a garbage can on the bottom of the lake. So, after washing down the pills and finishing the Gatorade, I pee'd, checked the dressing for leakage (*none*), hobbled back to bed, and went back to sleep for another five hours. I repeated this process in both a boring and painful manner for the next thirty-six hours or so, waking once when Dorothy came by with some bags of food and drink, and to poke and prod and change the dressing. She said that during another visit, which I don't remember, I had sweat through my clothes and sleeping bag. She had stayed for eight hours slapping on dermal-contact thermometers every thirty minutes until my temp dropped below one hundred . I felt as though I should worry about her car being parked out on the road for all that time, but since we didn't get shot or dumped in a lake, it didn't seem worth it after the fact.

Lonesome Bay, 4:23 p.m., 9/8/2012

I climbed out of the hammock with all of my joints feeling stiff and muscles protesting. My mouth tasted as though a tiny pig had spent the last few days in it, eating chili and cabbage and ex-lax; my sleeping bag smelled like a locker-room. When I stripped off my clothes, the dressing on my shoulder was cleaner than I felt it should have been *(given the state of my body and sleeping bag)* That likely meant I'd had another visit from Dorothy while I slept. I could lift my left arm up to shoulder height before my body yelled at me and things felt as though they might start to fall apart; so I didn't go beyond that point. I hobbled around my campsite, picking up garbage and putting my things back in order. My right pinky was sore, but not throbbing anymore ... it was no worse than if I'd caught it in a door now, so I took the tape and splint off and practiced making a fist.

I snuck down to the lakeshore, terrified that I would

see Justin and Barry on George's pontoon boat either looking, or waiting, for me down in the water. There were a number of boats on the water, but none had the right look, and nobody seemed to pay attention, or even notice, when I eased myself into the water to float around for a while. The cold water felt great all over, except for the wounds on my shoulder, where it stung and felt hot and cold and dead/numb in various places and stages. After floating a bit, I tried gently moving my arms and legs, not really swimming, but moving around a bit. Everything seemed crusty and cranky as though all my joints had been lightly coated with some abrasive material while I wasted two days sleeping. I stopped when the bandage came loose and floated away like a white flag on the dark water. Climbing out of the water, the wind stole all of my residual warmth and strength, and by the time I got back up the hill to my camp, I was shivering and stumbling enough to freak myself out a bit.

Dressed in my warmest layers, and fortified by a ginormous serving of oatmeal, I tried to think about the hole I'd dug for myself in the last few days. It occurred to me that I could just pack everything that would fit into my Element, leave the rest, and drive until I got to the far side of the Rocky Mountains. George wouldn't have sufficient interest in silencing me to reach out across thousands of miles to find me among hundreds of millions of people. Spenser or Travis might have immersed themselves in a grueling montage of workout and rehab and training to prepare themselves for a fair fight with the bad guys assembled against them; I had neither the time, nor the abilities, nor the will to focus on that set of chores (*along with my deeply held belief that fair fights were for idiots*). I needed cash and gear and food to keep living in the woods for a bit longer, while I figured out how to deal with George and the minions *(which sounded like the name of a bad cover band to me for some reason, causing me to painfully snarf a bit of oatmeal)*. As I dug out my GPS and set it up to point me towards my nearest supply cache, I got the beginnings of an idea.

I swallowed a handful of the dog drugs and headed off with the GPS and a hydration pack to find a cache that I had hidden last spring about a mile and a quarter southwest of my campsite on Lonesome Bay. I have a bunch of these caches hidden in the woods around the Tri-Lakes, and a few further out along routes that I've traveled and explored in chunks of wilderness that I've brain-mapped for myself in the last few years. This one *(like most of the others I've put out in the woods)* contained five hundred dollars in mixed bills and a roll of quarters, some oatmeal packets and jerky, water purification tablets, an alcohol stove and a bottle of HEET, a map, a GPS receiver, a headlamp, batteries, a Leatherman, a poncho, socks, a skullcap, gloves, and a book *(this one had a copy of "One Flew Over the Cuckoo's Nest" in it)*. I found it without any trouble. For some reason I seem to always place them near a glacial erratic *(I'm inexplicably drawn to those big rocks dropped by a glaciers during the last ice-age … I can't explic it)*. I checked the GPS and map to see where the next closest cache was, and what the easiest route would be to get from where I was to where I wanted to be, when something clicked and my half-formed idea graduated to fully formed. In an instant, I knew a couple of things that I hadn't even a minute ago. One, I was going to stay in the Adirondacks; two, I knew how I was going to deal with Justin and Barry; and three, I'd be on time for dinner on Monday with Frank and Meg … or I would be dead, if things went badly for me *(in which case being late/absent wouldn't matter)*.

I headed back to camp with most of the contents of the cache stuffed into my hydration pack. I'd left the rest in the now mostly empty fifty-cal ammo can that I'd have to restock if I got through this okay. I got back to camp, fed, watered and medicated myself before climbing back into the hammock to read for a few hours to let my back-brain work out the details of the murders that I planned to commit in the coming days.

TLAS, 11:48 p.m., 9/8/2012

Chief Bromden smothered McMurphy at about 10:15 p.m., and by that point, I knew most of what I had to do. I first read "Cuckoo's Nest" when I was ten, and I get more out of it every time; I tend not to talk too much about my relationship with the book and the characters within it with other people because I relate to them differently than other *(regular?)* people do. In this reading, I found some comfort and guidance in the inevitability of the characters' actions, the victory of chaos, and the cost of that victory.

I called Dorothy and asked her to pick me up for a meet at the shelter at 11 p.m.. I told her to leave all of the lights off except for the one in the internal office, a room in the center of the building with no windows.

We parked a little past the shelter on Algonquin Avenue, a residential street nearby, and walked through the woods to the shelter from behind. I didn't want to expose the TLAS or Dorothy to more risk than was necessary to get my plan in motion, although she seemed to be having fun (*she was humming the theme from, "Mission Impossible" the whole time*).

We spent an hour or so using the shelter's ancient desktop computer, with its slow Internet access and an even slower printer, to lay the groundwork for my plan's implementation. Once everything had been double-checked and printed off, I sent a slightly reluctant and confused Dorothy up Panther Mountain with her headlamp, while I made a quick run to Cynthia's house for a needed item. I was back a few minutes before Dorothy (*Panther is both close and teeny, and she must have jogged up and down it*). Once she had hosed off her head in the shelter's grooming sink to cool down, she blocked the door and forced me to explain my plan to her.

"Give, or you don't get out this door, peewee!" she said as she leaned back against the only exit from the room, air-poking menacingly near my injured shoulder.

"Okay, I can tell you some of it, but there are parts that I have to leave out, and others that will develop once the plan is in motion." This wasn't strictly the truth, but it was hopefully close enough to mollify her, and get me out and moving. If I spent too long thinking about the complex series of events that all had to shake out in the right way in the next eighteen hours, I might just hike to SmartPig and drive away in the Element; and I wouldn't like the way that felt.

"I need to break the bad guys into more manageable units, get them out of their comfort zone, and take them off the game board in a way that won't bounce back on me, and you," I began, looking to see if she was going to move away from the door. She wasn't ... yet. I needed to give her a bit more

"They're comfortable in and around Saranac Lake, Lake Placid, Tupper Lake, and the roads connecting them to each other and the world outside of the Park. We're going to use the GPS and my knowledge of the wild places around here to get them off their personal maps, and onto mine. I'll bounce them from nook to cranny all over the backwoods around here, both to make sure that they don't bring extra guys, and to keep them off-balance. Once we've gotten sufficiently far from prying eyes, I've got a way to insure that they leave me alone once and for all."

"Explain how the Ziploc bag and the note that I hid at the base of that huge rock on the back of Panther fits in to the master plan?"

"This note and a GPS receiver (*that I got out of my cache a few hours ago*) will be going to George in a little while, and then I'll head out to hide a couple more notes in some increasingly wild spots. The GPS will have coordinates for the note up on Panther programmed into it, and once he gets there, the note you left will give him the coordinates to the next note ... and so on. It's like a ransom payoff in reverse ... making sure that we control the bad guys instead of the other way around."

She tilted her head like a dog listening hard to an unexpected and confusing noise, so I tried to continue and expand upon my answer. I now wanted to continue not just to appease Dot sufficiently so that she would let me leave, but also to see if my plan made some sense; my last plan for dealing with George had seemed perfectly reasonable to me, and had failed miserably.

"The note that I wrote to him will be dropped off, with the GPS, and it will lead him on a hunt into the woods. He'll think that he's in a position of power because he has guys and guns, and he thinks I'm injured and alone, which, in fact, I will be; but getting him out of town and away from his internal map of the world will shift the balance of power in my favor, possibly by enough to allow me to win. I plan to strip him of his guys in the early rounds, so that at the end of the game, when just the two of us are left, I've got the upper hand by virtue of my home-court advantage ... does that make sense now?" I finished up hopefully.

"Sorta, except that even with them being uncomfortable in the woods, and all, there are more of them than there are of us, and they have guns." I smiled at the fact that she had included herself on my team; she had already helped me too much though, and I couldn't bring her along on this next stage, even though I desperately wanted to do just that.

"Just me, Dot, just me. And their guns won't matter because I'll be *'a leaf on the wind'.*" Serenity or Firefly references always seem to make her happy, but in this case it didn't work; perhaps it was a poor choice of quotes.

"Yeah, that worked out great for Wash ... 'watch me-SPLUNK!' ... if things go badly, when do I tell Meg's husband?"

"If I don't check back in before dinnertime tomorrow then tell Frank if you want, but think about it before you do ... it won't help me by that point, and could make things difficult for you on a number of levels. If I don't make this work, then you would be best off just forgetting about it to the greatest degree possible, and move forward. There'll be a crap-ton of money coming to the shelter once my will is settled, more if you find a way to tell Frank where to look for Cynthia." I had my money set to split mostly between Cyn and Dot, but with Cynthia provably dead, Dorothy and the shelter would get a bunch more.

"Well, that changes things a bit ... I might sign up for

George's team, so I can stop hustling for kibble and cat-litter. Dorothy smiled at me in a way that let me know exactly what she thought of my chances of seeing her before dinnertime, or ever again. "But how will he know that you want to play?"

"I've got a burner-phone I picked up from Kinney's when all of this started. Paid for it with cash and set it up with no useful information in the activation details, I used the Lake Placid McDonald's Wi-Fi. I'm going to head out and drop the GPS and note to George at his mailbox. As soon as I'm clear, I'll call and text him to let him know that I'm alive and that we need to meet, so that I can talk him out of further attempts to kill me."

"He won't take it at face-value, but might assume that I'm dumb enough to put myself in his crosshairs again, which in some ways is exactly what I'm doing. Either way, he'll have to play my game. I think it's probable that he'll limit himself to bringing along just Justin and Barry, to keep his circle of who knows what as small as possible."

"It sounds like a complex way to commit suicide at the end of a nice hike to me, but you're a pretty smart guy, gunshot wound to the contrary ... so I'm just going to wish you good luck, drop you off at your car, and see you later."

She did just that, nobody seemed to be watching my Element, so I waved goodbye to Dorothy and drove off into darkness.

Tupper Lake, Stewart's Convenience Store, 1:47 a.m.,
9/9/2012

"George, are you awake?" he had taken four rings to
answer his phone, and sounded groggy when he
mumbled something into the phone.

"Who the fuck is this, and how'd you get this
number?" It sounded as though he didn't like being called
on his private cell number.

"It's Tyler, George, the guy you tried to kill a few days
ago, despite some perfectly good reasons not to do just
that." I let that sink in, and waited on the line, listening to
his breath for a few seconds.

"I told those morons that if they didn't see you dead,
you're not dead. But in truth, I figured you probably
drowned or bled to death. Why am I talking to you
instead of a tac-team of State Troopers? Not that I mind,
but it don't make sense."

"I want the same thing now that I wanted before ... to

be left alone and living ... only this time I want some money also." I assumed that he wouldn't believe my motivations this time either, unless I added greed into the mix.

"How much, and why should I leave you alone instead of actually killing you this time?"

"I want fifty thousand dollars in twenties and tens, and you shouldn't kill me because this time I actually did leave a note, and this time I have more than guesswork... I literally know where the bodies are buried."

"Okay, come out to the house tomorrow morning for coffee, and we'll work it out."

"No chance, George. I left a GPS and a note explaining the way we're going to do this in the mailbox at the end of your driveway ... don't tell the post office, it may be illegal ... I want you to follow the GPS to a set of coordinates already programmed into it ... there will be a note in a baggie giving you coordinates to another note, and so on ... I'll be watching at one, or more, of the spots to see that you're not bringing a mob with you, and that you've got the money. After a couple of stops and bounces, I'll meet you at a final set of coordinates down near Old Forge. You give me the money, I go on a short vacation, and when I come back, I'll find someplace else to live, thanks to your relocation funds."

"Sounds mostly okay, except I'm bringing my guys, so you don't ambush me in the woods."

"If by guys, you mean Barry and Justin, that's all right with me, but nobody else ... no new faces."

"Fine, whatever. Do I gotta get going now, or can I sleep until a decent hour?"

"Sleep George, you'll need your rest tomorrow ... wear clothes for hiking, and bring water and snacks for all day."

"Fuck you!"

"Sleep tight." I hung up, figuring that we were done.

I had gassed up and grabbed some food and water at Stewart's (*paying cash so as to leave no trace in case of subsequent inquiries*) and dry-swallowed another round of the dog-meds. I had a short drive to the spot where I was going to hide the second note, with the coordinates in it for the third location. My aim was to take George and the boys on a series of hikes to tire them out and get them used to being alone in the woods, seemingly wasting time. By the time we met up for the exchange later in the day, I wanted them all to be stressed and stretched-thin and ready to be caught unaware for the twist that I had in mind.

Bog River Falls Bridge, 2:31 a.m., 9/9/2012

I have no idea why the bridge up above the Bog River Falls was built, but it looks to have been abandoned before it was ever put to use; I planned to make good use of it tonight and tomorrow. Route 30 is a two-laner, and Route 421 is a tiny road off of that; the bridge was on a tinier road (*really an overgrown Jeep trail now*) off of that, which didn't lead anywhere except to an infinite supply of wilderness. The road leading to the bridge has been mostly reclaimed by the forest, and walking down the cracked pavement mostly by feel in the glow of my headlamp's lowest setting, I was, as always, surprised when the clean and angular lines of the bridge loomed out of the dark.

It stretched more than one hundred feet across the river, and was nearly four lanes wide. I had spent a night hanging underneath the bridge (*from the network of support beams*) the previous winter in my hammock. That underside was my goal now.

On the far side of the bridge, I climbed around and underneath the structure and climbed up and into the girders to hide George's second note where it would be plainly visible when they arrived. I was feeling a bit sore and tired by the time I climbed out from under the bridge and walked slowly back to my car to wait for dawn or a phone call, whichever came first. I checked to make sure that my phone was charged and that I had enough bars to make/receive a call, set my alarm for 5:30 a.m., moved the car a bit down the road *(just in case George and company arrived earlier than expected)*, and washed more doggie-pills down with a Gatorade before going to sleep. Dot was supposed to call me in a bit, but I had an alarm set just in case.

Bog River Falls Outlet, 6:37 a.m., 9/9/2012

"Morning Boss! This is your henchperson, Dorothy, calling to report in on enemy troop movements. Out."

"Dorothy, you're using a cell-phone, not a 'walkie'. You can just talk, no need to use communications jargon ... although I like the idea of having a 'henchperson'. What's going on?"

"First, Boooooo about no comms-jargons! Second, thanks! Third, I was parked at the Bartlett Carry turnoff like you suggested, and a couple of minutes ago saw a single yellow crew-cab truck go by. I pulled out a minute later to follow them down the road. I had to slow down a bit at the Panther Mountain parking lot to avoid two guys, one looked like Justin and the other had to be Barry based on your descriptions. I didn't see George, but he could be letting them climb the mountain while he finishes his first cup of coffee. There were no other cars or trucks with them in convoy or in the parking lot"

143

"Thanks Dorothy! Did they see you?"

"Not likely ... I kept my high-beams on when I passed, and they were focused on finding the trailhead. I made the turn at Wawbeek Corner, and drove back into cell-range down by the Upper Saranac boat launch. They should be back down in a few minutes, do you want me to circle back and report when they are headed your way?"

"Nope, thanks for the offer, but you should go to work and help clean and feed homeless beasts. I feel bad enough that I've involved you to this extent, but I couldn't figure out how to watch them and get done what I needed to do. Now though, you should clock out as henchperson, and clock in at the shelter. I'll talk to you later."

Strangely, I felt as confident as I sounded, although there were probably a nearly infinite number of things that could go wrong from here on out; things were going to get exponentially trickier and riskier until a tipping point sometime around midday when they would resolve themselves in one of only two ways ... that I could see.

"Good luck, and Tyler ... do what you have to do to come home tonight, okay?" I don't think that Dorothy had figured out my endgame yet, but if she had, I'm sure that she would have approved. She sees the world in simplistic terms, and tends not to worry much about what happened yesterday.

"Will do. Remember to drop your phone and SIM-card in two different lakes on your way to work, and give Gandhi a cookie from me. Evil Mastermind over and out." I closed the clamshell phone, walked over to look at the Bog River dumping into the bottom of Tupper Lake, stripping the SIM-card and battery out as I went and chucked the phone and card as far as I could (*tossing the battery into the lower end of Tupper Lake seemed needlessly eco-hostile, and I regretted not mentioning it to Dot, although she would probably forget to ditch the phone altogether).*

I walked to the Element and hopped in, ready to turn it around and get headed towards the end of George's treasure hunt, realizing how much I didn't want a flat-tire or dead alternator right now. The car started up and seemed to run smoothly enough as I pointed it towards Long Lake and points south. I could feel George and Justin and Barry move through a similar arc in time space about one hour and thirty miles behind me.

Hoss's Country Corner, 7:58 a.m., 9/9/2012

I had stopped in Long Lake to top up my gas and get some Cokes and jerky and nuts to keep me going for the day, when the sign at Hoss's grabbed my attention.

Hoss's has grown from a simple country store into a complex of connected buildings and services, offering everything from Adirondack souvenirs to fancy coffee to haircuts to bait to ice cream to internet access ... it was the last that pulled at me, despite the fact that I was in something of a hurry.

I gave the bored kid at the counter a twenty dollar bill, indicating the Coke I had taken from their cooler and an unoccupied computer with the same waving hand gesture. Signing in, and then logging in to my iGoogle page and gmail was a matter of a minute, and gave my significantly-too-crazy day a slight tinge of normalcy; weeding out the hundreds of useless emails to end up with three that I wanted to read took a few minutes though. The first was a robo-email from the TLAS, inviting me to a food-related benefit for the beasts, and I

RSVP'd in a fit of optimism (*hopefully not jinxing myself*).

The second was from Gregory Simmons, saying that Jacob Hostetler had come by with a still warm apple pie and ten pounds of smoked bacon from his farm, begging Mike to pass them on along with Jacob's desperate pleas to come up with a more meaningful way to let him thank me for saving his daughter's life (*that seemed a bit dramatic to me, but with farm-fresh Amish bacon in the equation, I was willing to live with it*).

The third was from Meg, reminding me about dinner tomorrow night, and that I had agreed to bring dessert; I googled tiramisu, found a couple of the best/easiest recipes, and emailed them to myself. I threw all of the emails into a "9/2012" folder, and logged out ... of gmail, igoogle, and Hoss's system ... and eventually, Long Lake.

Out in the Element again, I tried to figure out where Justin and Barry (*and maybe George too*) were at this point; my mental map and timing mechanisms placed them in Tupper, driving prudently (*there are lots of cops on all three roads in and out of Tupper*) with coffee and donuts from Stewart's past the huge swamp where I had seen my first Adirondack moose a few years earlier. They would likely be tromping out to the ghost-bridge in a few minutes and back on the road only a bit after that; I needed to get moving.

I was having more fun than seemed proper or judicious or moral, and had to tell myself not to forget why I was doing this, remembering my not-so-great best-case version of how the day would end; even so, I still felt good, despite the steady ache in my shoulder. I swallowed my next round of pills, a bit early but I might not get a chance later in the day, dropped off another treasure-hunt note at the next site, and drove towards some serious middle of nowhere, to get lost, and hopefully find the solution to my problems.

Deep woods near Tahawus, 9:28 a.m., 9/9/2012

The road up to Tahawus from Newcomb, New York, is like a portal through time. The road ends at a trailhead leading hikers up into the High Peaks Wilderness through a back door that allows them to avoid the crowds that you tend to see when hiking in from the Lake Placid side. Also on the road from Newcomb is a ghost town, the leftovers from a series of mines and mining enterprises over the last 150 years; they have taken lead, silver, garnet, titanium, and iron out of the mountains in unbelievable amounts over the last 150 years. The wild country is a mix of private and public land, but both the public and private lands are generally deserted and abandoned; it was the perfect setting for the scene that I wanted to play out with George and his guys.

I came across my first wilderness mine shaft almost ten years ago, while exploring another chunk of wilderness a bit south and east of this spot, closer to Lake Champlain. I did some online, library and physical research, and found that there were dozens, maybe hundreds, of them scattered throughout the Adirondack Park, some only a few yards from mouth to terminus, some going unbelievably deep into the Earth. Over the years I'd found some, explored a few, mapped more for future exploration, and even thought about building a home or retreat inside one; which prompted more research and learning about caves and the special circumstances and care and procedures for spending time in what I had heretofore considered to be just holes in the ground. It was another example of mapping unknowns to expand my world, in this case into the subterranean. In cataloging and examining my world map, this was the best cave that I could think of for the use that I had for it today.

I didn't think that Barry and Justin were trackers, but even though they would expect to see some sign of my earlier passage, I wanted to minimize my impact on the forest around the mine opening, so that they wouldn't be thinking of me; just a walk in the woods to get another set of coordinates in a colossal waste of time before they could meet, and most likely kill, me. I had parked the Element far enough away (*and on a side road leading away from the coordinates*) so they wouldn't pass or see it when trying to find the closest spot on the road to the coordinates that I had given them. I walked up to the yawning and hungry mouth, dark in the bright woods, carefully picking the spot that each footfall would land, and thinking my way ahead through the next few hours (*equally carefully picking the spot where each future action/reaction would take me*).

I had picked this mine because my memory of it indicated that it would meet my needs perfectly. It was on private land, which would discourage trespassing, but the owner was an Italian mineral exploitation consortium that had been sitting on the property for years. They had fired the property manager years ago when they realized that he cost more per year than any damage done by vandals could possibly amount to over the course of a decade.

The mine opening was big enough that it wouldn't threaten Barry or Justin too much, unless they were severely claustrophobic, in which case I was counting on their allegiance to (*and fear of*) George to keep them moving inside. The opening went into the side of the hill at a few degrees below the horizontal for about twenty feet before it began sprouting smaller side passages to the left and right and came to a T-junction about a hundred feet in.

The tunnel going to the left from the T-junction went about thirty feet before ending in a wall, the one to the right went the same distance before the floor dropped away; as I remember, the pit was roughly a hundred feet deep (*a dropped rock took a touch more than two seconds to splash into the water at the bottom*). The pit was about ten feet across, with a single ancient plank across it making a bridge to the far side where the tunnel continued for another ten feet before a turn in the shaft ended my knowledge of what came next (*I was exploring alone, and had no desire to test the plank's strength after who knows how long in the mine*). I emptied my Gatorade, re-checked my gear, pee'd against a nearby tree, turned on my headlamp, and headed into the mine.

I paid special attention to the floor of the mineshaft as I picked my way in, mostly smooth but with some rocks and sticks in places. I didn't leave footprints so much as disturb the stuff on the floor, and since I couldn't avoid doing that, I decided not to worry about it. When I was most of the way down the shaft, I scouted the remaining side-tunnels, and picked one about twenty feet before the T-junction and put my shoulder bag and gear a few feet in behind a pile of ancient boards and wire. I continued down to the T-junction, cracked a chem-light, placed it gently on the floor, and placed another one eight feet back from the edge of the pit, on top of a Ziploc bag containing the note for George and Barry and Justin. Mission accomplished, I retraced my steps, grabbed my gear, and prepared myself for the next stage of this plan.

I spent a few minutes wondering if I should be concerned about my lack of guilt, or if I should worry about trespassing, or any of the other, more serious, crimes that I was about to commit. I concluded that, while perhaps I should, nobody blames a snake or a pig or a dove for being a snake or a pig or a dove (*certainly not the snake/pig/dove*), and so I wouldn't blame me for being me. This was almost certainly a specious argument, but I had an easy time convincing myself (*which is, at the end of the day, the wonderful thing about specious arguments*). I enjoyed some more philosophical games and riddles, and was able to ignore the wet and cold for a while, until I heard Barry and Justin twig-snapping and huffing and cursing their way through the woods towards me.

Mineshaft, near Tahawus, 10:13 a.m., 9/9/2012

I had kept my mouth slightly open to listen and breathe; it has been my experience that I can hear slightly better this way (*and breathe more quietly to boot*), but it proved unnecessary, as, according to plan, Justin and Barry expected that this was simply another stop along my annoying scavenger hunt route, not our meeting place.

I could hear Barry clomping his way up the hill, puffing and snapping sticks and cursing as branches slapped and poked him, long before I ever heard Justin; but either the shape of the valley that the mine was in, or the preternatural quiet of the mine, helped to focus and deliver the sound to me about five minutes before I heard them step into the mine. I saw their bright lights reflected and dancing on the walls and ceiling of the main tunnel outside the side tunnel that I was crouching in. They seemed to have bought into the plan as well as I could have hoped. They sounded pissed off and tired and anxious to get out of the woods (*and particularly this mineshaft*). They both seemed to notice the chem-light at the end of the tunnel at the same moment. Even if they had not literally been in a tunnel, they had now been programmed (*by me*) to have tunnel vision (*I wanted to smile at this thought, a number fourteen, gently amused at the turn of events, but quelled the altogether inappropriate impulse*).

I had to pee ... all of a sudden, I had to pee more than I had ever needed anything in my life. I started to stand up to unzip and let loose and then nearly giggled at the absurdity of it, but stifled the urge to do both. Instead, I just did my imitation of a rock in the dark (*a rock in the dark that had to pee!*).

I had been lying on the floor of the side-tunnel for long enough that I was cold and stiff. I wanted to stretch and stand and could almost taste a big bowl of piping hot oatmeal (*oddly the maple sugar version instead of my standard, raisins and cinnamon, was what tickled my taste-buds' fancy while I waited for Justin and Barry to make their way down the mineshaft and past me*). The last urge that came and went, as the footsteps got closer and their lights flickered up and down and from side to side, was to check my headlamp and Cynthia's shotgun, both of which would be at least noisy, and possibly deadly (*if either Barry or Justin heard me*). The last of these self-destructive impulses was chased from my brain when one of the guys scuffed a rock and it skittered into my side tunnel.

I can't imagine that it made any difference, but I closed my eyes down to mere slits to try and reduce any possible reflections if they shone their lights down my side-tunnel. I was dressed in dark earthen tones and muddy/dirty from the day I'd been having so far, but if either of them decided to check my tunnel out too carefully, they'd likely see me without too much trouble. I saw Justin first, and then Barry, as they continued shuffling down their tunnel and past me; each with a flashlight in one hand and a hiking pole in the other. They seemed to be alternating between tapping the floor to insure that it was still there and sweeping the ceiling to needlessly ward off spiders that hadn't bothered to set up webs this far into the tunnel (*no insects, apparently*). They were both looking down and ahead, at the point on the floor where I had left the first chem-light ... just as they were supposed to. Once they reached the T-junction, I could hear Barry point out the next and final chem-light to Justin, his voice rumbling oddly in the wet/cold/dark.

It was at this point that I stood as quietly as I could, wincing when my knees popped loudly in the tomb-quiet of the mine as I straightened up. I crept around the corner, and into the main body of the tunnel, using the reflected waste-light from Barry and Justin, as well as the dim glow from the chem-lights to follow/find them, first to the T-junction, and then around the corner to the right. I could see the two guys, standing a few feet from the edge of the pit, reading the detailed note that I had left for them by the light of their flashlights, and mumbling to each other in turn as they tried to figure out my directions to the next stop on the treasure hunt.

The note had coordinates and driving directions and route numbers and suggestions for lunch spots and cautionary warnings about a stream crossing; neither of them had finished the note when I fired the shotgun ... I kept pumping the action and firing the shotgun until Cynthia's 870 was empty, my ears were ringing like the bells at Notre Dame, and nobody was left, standing or otherwise, at the edge of the pit.

Mineshaft, near Tahawus, 10:36 a.m., 9/9/2012

CRAP!

When the reverberations of sound and smell and light died down a bit, it occurred to me that I'd been a colossal dumbass. A microsecond later, I noted that I didn't really feel bad about what I had done, just stupid that I had blown the car keys (*and money*) down into a hole that might as well have been a mile deep.

I could see the scene replaying perfectly in slow motion. My first shot caught Justin lower than I had meant to shoot (*I had estimated him to be a greater threat with a gun, assuming that both had them*), catching him with the hand-sized pattern of double ought buckshot a few inches above his belt. With the next shot, I overcorrected like crazy and it went into the ceiling of the tunnel about halfway between us, peppering them with rock and shot debris. The third shot caught Barry somewhere in his upper torso. My fourth round missed when I swung the barrel right to try and get Justin as he seemed (*to me*) to be reaching for something in his jacket. The fifth shot missed them altogether as Barry had tripped or fallen backwards (*perhaps in an attempt to move away from the noise and light and ouchiness at my end of the tunnel*). The light from the fifth shot caught Justin with pin wheeling arms as he tumbled down into the darkness of the pit before I cycled and fired the last shell. I had fired the last round anyway, amp-ed up and scared and angry, muscles working faster than my brain at that moment. By the time I could hear anything again, they must have already hit bottom, because I never heard a splash. I had a moment of ridiculous terror when I remembered a scene from an Austin Powers movie that I had watched with Cyn, where a somewhat bad guy called from the bottom of a pit that he wasn't dead and needed medical assistance; neither Justin nor Barry survived the fall, or if they did, decided not to call for help.

I reached up and clicked on my headlamp and shuffled up to the edge and looked down into the pit. I could see some dim colors at the bottom, likely from their jackets and packs, but couldn't make out any details. I didn't have any rope or rappelling gear, and wouldn't have the knowledge or skill or desire to use it if I had, so I dropped Cynthia's shotgun down after the guys, walked back down the tunnel, grabbed my gear, and walked out into the midday brightness and colors and bird noise. I looked around for police and/or forest rangers, eager to arrest me for trespassing or illegal discharge of a firearm or murder, but didn't see a thing except trees and rocks, marching off to the horizon in every direction. It was as if the mine, and Barry and Justin, and what had happened only one hundred feet and three minutes ago, had never happened; so I walked down the hill to Justin's truck, to try and figure out what to do about it.

Upper Works Road, County. Route 25, 11:28 a.m.,
9/9/2012

I sat in the woods and watched Justin's truck for a couple
of minutes before moving closer, unable to tell if there
was anyone in the backseat, behind the tinted glass (*George
or another of his guys*). It was sitting in direct sun with all of
the windows up, so it would have to be hot inside if there
was anyone. I threw a pinecone and watched for the truck
to sway on its springs for another minute before I walked
down, listening hard all the way for traffic from either
direction ... I couldn't hear anything mechanical besides a
jet way up and flying north across the sky. I tried the
truck's doors and found them locked; I felt around the
bumpers explored the truck-bed, looking for an extra key
... no luck. I found a good-sized rock and listened again
for traffic, and then broke his passenger-side window,
listened again, and climbed in.

I had no idea how to hotwire a car, and assumed that
if I tried I'd cripple the car permanently, so I looked in

places where I'd seen people leave extra keys before: under the driver's seat, in the ashtray, above the visors, and finally ... in the glove box. I was positive that I would strike out. I found the plastic folder that the Toyota dealer had stuck in when delivering the car to Justin filled with the new paperwork and manuals and ... VALET KEY! I dumped the stuff out onto the floor and the last thing to tumble onto the rubber mat was a valet key for his truck.

It wouldn't have been the end of the world if Justin's truck had to stay here. I could throw sufficient logs and rocks down the mineshaft hole to cover the guys, and safely assume that nobody would ever find them. The truck would likely get towed by the Town of Newcomb in a week or two and eventually sold at auction. I doubt that anyone would file a missing persons report on either of them; drug dealers move and/or go missing, but without a body, nobody would look too hard at the truck.

Since I could now move the truck though, I decided to do just that. I gave a final listen, then started the truck up and drove back along Upper Works Road until I got to a turnoff that lead deeper into the absentee owners' defunct mining facilities. There was a gate across the section of road that turned away from Upper Works Road, but if I didn't mind scraping Justin's truck a bit, which I didn't, I could get around the barrier easily.

Once on the smaller road, I quickly made for a tailing pond that I had seen while exploring a couple of years earlier. An abandoned mine makes for an ugly moonscape when compared to the natural beauty of the rest of the Adirondacks, so not many people get back this way, which would work out fine for me (*I hoped*). The tailing ponds in and around Tahawus had been excavated more than a century ago by various mining concerns that came and went. They were used to dump/contain the liquid or sludge waste and by-products of the mining process; some of the ponds look like regular Adirondack lakes and ponds, others did not.

It was to one of the nastier tailing ponds that I was driving Justin's truck. The pond was an iridescent milky green, roughly two hundred yards across, and there was a cement dock-like jetty that extended out about fifty feet towards the center of the mostly round pond. I stopped short of the jetty, and walked out to inspect it, top and bottom. It looked fine, and I couldn't feel it move or sway when I walked partway out and jumped on it, so I thought it was worth a try.

I opened the door to the truck, got all of my stuff out and left it on the ground next to the truck. Then I got all of the loose junk out of the glove box and map pockets and door slots and put it all in a USPS priority mail envelope I found in the truck (*Tyvek, useful, free ... why not*).

I left the envelope by my gear and climbed back into the truck. I opened all the windows and started rolling the Toyota slowly down the dock. My thinking was that if things got splashy and wet before I wanted them to I could likely swim to shore before the toxic junk in the pond melted me (*or gave me superpowers*). I stopped the truck about halfway down, dropped it into neutral, got out to look and listen for any sign that I wasn't the only human within ten miles (*I'm pretty sure that I was*). I leaned in through the window to move the shifter from N to D, and then pulled back out of the truck as it rolled down the last little bit of the jetty.

The truck made a tremendous splash when it went off the end of the jetty and fell into the water, but in five minutes I couldn't even see any more bubbles coming up, much less the truck. The pond water was deep and opaque, and it was my sincere hope that whatever toxic soup mining companies had chosen to violate this pond with over the years would eat the truck before anyone found it. I felt that there was a pretty good chance of this happening, as I wouldn't have dreamed of swimming in it … it barely qualified as water. Feeling better than I had in days, I got up, grabbed my stuff and Justin's, and walked back toward where my GPS receiver indicated my car was. I walked overland, both for a more direct route, and to distance myself from the yellow truck that had been trespassing and gone swimming a little while ago. I didn't see (*or hear*) a soul the whole way back to my Element, and didn't even pass another car until I was most of the way back to Long Lake. I stopped in Long Lake to gas up, buy and down a couple Cokes, eat a few eerily fresh donuts, and gobble more of Dorothy's dog pills.

Campsite #6, Little Green Pond, 3:18 p.m., 9/9/2012

The drive back to my neck of the woods was both relaxing and nerve-wracking at the same time. I've made the drive from Long Lake to Saranac Lake at least a hundred times, and it is lovely and wooded, and passes lots of lakes and streams, but very few people. It is possible to relax almost into a dream-state on the rolling hills and straight road. I was glad to have some cool (*if slightly too warm, and clearly inferior*) Cokes to give me a sugar and caffeine boost.

I kept expecting a roadblock or pursuit or helicopters to stop me. I kept switching around to the local radio stations (*mostly repeaters of North Country Radio, a public radio station based up in Canton, NY*) anticipating/dreading APBs and descriptions of my crimes. The farther that I drove from the mine and pond up in Tahawus, the further from reality my crimes seemed. I had no physical evidence of the crimes on my person/vehicle, having double-bagged my shoes and the papers from Justin's car, and dropped them into the nasty dumpster behind Stewart's in Long Lake. My only lingering (*and likely pointless*) concern was remaining on one of the "big roads", and I couldn't fix that until the Wawbeek turn at the bottom of Upper Saranac Lake, about halfway between Tupper Lake and Saranac Lake.

Life in the Adirondacks inevitably includes driving, and when you drive, unlike in more populated places, you generally only have one choice of how to get from here to there. To get from Tahawus to Newcomb to Long Lake to Tupper Lake there wasn't a best route, there was only one route, with no choices for scenic or quick. This made for easier trip-planning, but left me feeling a bit exposed on the drive back to my stomping grounds. I remembered how easy it had been for my 'henchperson' to spot Justin this morning, and thought about how similarly easy it would be for George to have a minion keeping an eye out for me anywhere along the road. It made me feel claustrophobic, even at high speed and with miles of wilderness in every direction, with only the occasional cluster/island of houses to break up the green ocean of trees.

I turned off of my only routing option, Route 3, at the first opportunity, and took the smaller and windier Route 30 along the western shore of Upper Saranac Lake, thinking of places to stop and hide and think and nap for a couple of hours. I pulled in at Knapp's, a general store near the state campground at Fish Creek, to gas up and grab some food and Cokes and Gatorade and HEET. I recognized a couple of people, but nobody spoke to me, and I decided that I should head for less crowded woods to hide and chill out for a few hours. On my way out, I dropped some change into the payphone outside the store to call Dorothy (*cell-service, especially for my disposable burner-phones, is spotty outside of the towns in the Adirondacks*).

"Hello?" She picked up on the second ring, which was quick for her; I often had to live with leaving a message and getting a callback a few minutes later.

"Hi Dorothy, it's me," I said. "I'm all right, but bushed. I'm going to find a place to sleep for a few hours."

"Tyler, come back here and sleep at my place or upstairs at the shelter."

"Yuck to both, I'll be fine. I just wanted to check in and tell you that everything seems like it might be all right, although I still have to figure out what to do about the big problem."

"So are those two—" I cut her off, not knowing where she was, who she was near, or even what she was going to say, but no matter where she took that sentence, it couldn't improve things.

"I delivered those two leashes, just like we agreed, but I'm tired, and need a nap before driving the rest of the way." I was only about twenty minutes from any place in Saranac Lake, but it couldn't hurt to obfuscate.

"Okay ... well thanks for calling, and stop by when you get back into town." She sounded both resigned and a little pissed, but relieved enough so that she would probably be able to concentrate on whatever she was doing until the end of her day.

"I will ... talk to you later ... and thanks ... for everything." I couldn't pack enough, either in tone or words, into my thanks yet, but I wanted her to hear that statement as a place-holder for future discussions and thanksgivings.

I hung up the phone and shook like a wet dog, thinking of Little Green Pond and the glorious campsites ringing it. It was only about seven minutes away from my current location. I could see, in my mind's eye, each turn and rise between Knapp's and the trees that I'd hang my backup hammock from when I got there.

Little Green pond is at the end of a lengthy dirt road behind the fish hatchery in Lake Clear, NY. Almost nobody knows about the twelve campsites that are well-spaced around the medium-sized pond, and most of those in the know don't camp there; I don't know why, it's free and convenient and spectacularly pretty. It is a little civilized for me. Most of the time I don't generally like camping with the possibility of neighbors, but on a Sunday, any people that had camped there for the weekend would have likely left, so it wouldn't be crowded. In any case, I was willing to deal with neighbors because I was sore and tired and emotionally empty and tired and felt shaky and was also sore (*I'm aware of the repetition, it was for emphasis*). I drove back to my favorite site, number 6, took a chance by just driving down the offshoot dirt road to the site, and was rewarded by a view of nothing but empty water and a thin ribbon of smoke from a campsite on the far side of the pond (*number 11 or number 12 I guessed, but didn't care*).

I pulled the Element around so that it was facing down the path leading back to the main dirt road, and got out my short-stay-essentials: hammock, stove and fuel, food/drink, clean clothes, small gear bag (*Swiss army knife, headlamp, matches, and book*). I put some water on to boil on my alcohol stove, and walked down to the pond to dunk and scrub and change while the water heated. I dried off with my dirty clothes, wadded them up and threw them into the back of the Element, put on the new clothes, and then made a big serving of oatmeal (*three packets in a freezer-weight Ziploc bag, so I wouldn't have any cleanup later*).

While the oatmeal was rehydrating, I found two suitable trees and hung my backup hammock, a Grand Trunk Double: no mosquito netting, but huge and comfy, and it's big enough to completely wrap myself in (*which was just what I wanted to do in about ten minutes*). I ate my oatmeal and drank a liter of Gatorade, and then tumbled into the hammock to think and sleep for a few hours.

In the few minutes before I closed my eyes and went to sleep, I tried to think about why George wouldn't have come on this morning's treasure-hunt. He must have decided, again, that it made more sense to kill me than make a deal with me (*again*). Even though this was his second time coming to the same conclusion, it still seemed like insane troll logic to me, but I have never understood most of what humans do, much less understand why; minimizing my interface with the difficult ones had always been the best approach. The guys hadn't been visibly armed, but nor had they been visibly carrying a bunch of money for me. But I couldn't know for sure considering they had been shot and dumped in an abandoned mineshaft before they knew what was happening. If they had seen it coming they would have been better prepared, and things might have turned out differently. While his muscle was gone, George was still in the picture, and could conceivably/probably/certainly get more muscle, once he decided that his others weren't coming back. I was just feeling around the edges of what I knew about the present situation for a possible solution, when I fell asleep.

Knapp's General Store, 7:04 p.m., 9/9/2012

I woke up too short a time later for the amount of rest that my body needed, but I had found out years earlier that you end up making do with what you've got. I got up and broke my simple camp, forced down some beef jerky and gummy peaches and two warmish Cokes, and drove back to Knapp's knowing what I was going to do, but not how I would be able to do it ... exactly. I bought a six-pack of Coke, a chipwich, two quarts of 5W-30 motor oil, some fishing lures, two packages of hotdogs and hotdog buns, a big roll of duct-tape, two gallons of Coleman fuel, three huge jars of pickles, a cheap broom, a bottle of laundry detergent, a bottle of Windex and some paper towels, a three-pack of road-flares, and some candy bars ... I paid in cash. Before pulling out of the parking lot, I dropped some change into the payphone again, and talked briefly with my acquaintance up in Canton, Gregory Simmons, and asked/told him to head out and do me a favor before it got to be too much later; I had done him what he considered to be a big favor some time ago, and told him that this made us even, or better.

Hanging up, I drove towards Saranac Lake making two stops along the way to prepare for later in the evening. My first stop was for a cache of dangerous toys that I'd researched, and been interested enough to try after reading a book by Ed Abbey about five years ago. I didn't want to throw them out after making them, but also didn't want to keep them at SmartPig or in my car (*as they might warrant an arrest simply by their presence in my car or office*), so they stayed in a small ammo-can in the woods until I picked them up. My second stop took only a few minutes at a plow-turnaround on the nearly always deserted Forest Home Road (*between the fish hatchery and Saranac Lake*) to quickly rearrange some of my groceries; I ended up leaving a ginormous pile of pickles in the bushes for some hungry wildlife to enjoy (*and then later probably regret*). Saranac Lake on a Sunday night is pretty quiet, but I wanted to wait for a few hours before making my next move, to let things quiet down even further.

I drove around downtown, meandered through some backstreets and cruised the few roads between downtown Saranac Lake and Oseetah Lake. Having cemented the flow of traffic and one-way streets in the lesser-traveled roads of Saranac Lake in my internal maps, I was ready (*-ish*) for the next stage in my evening's plans.

53 Broadway, Saranac Lake, 10:27 p.m., 9/9/2012

I walked around the block again, looking at the building from all sides, and was pleased to see that the spaces above the ground floor looked to be businesses, and at least half of them were sporting "Space Available" signs; I didn't want anyone but George inconvenienced by the trouble that I was about to start. I had parked the Element a few blocks up Olive Street and carried a backpack with the three one-gallon-sized pickle jars through the woods to the door behind the building, easily sticking to the dark side of the street, and ducking out of sight the few times a car came by. I couldn't see a soul on the street and was ready to take my chances that what noise I made wouldn't lead anyone to me before I could be somewhere else.

I had a two-foot wrecking bar hooked over my belt and down the inside of my pants, and pulled a pair of flesh-colored nitrile gloves from my first aid kit over my hands as I moved to the door. I had wiped the wrecking bar and pickle jars and road flares down with Windex soaked paper towels to hopefully avoid leaving fingerprints and/or DNA. With one final look for road or foot traffic, I went over to the back door of the kitchen, shielded a bit by a dumpster, and used the wrecking bar to force the crappy door to open, despite a reasonably good lock. I grabbed the backpack, slipped inside, closed the door, and found my three targets quickly in the light leaking in through the big picture window at the front of the sub-shop. I balanced the jars and road-flares on the counter, put the wrecking bar in the backpack, got it back on my shoulders, and lofted the jars; one by the stove, another by some booths, and one at a wall with chips on display from floor to ceiling. The sound was incredible in the stillness of vacant room, but if anyone heard it from beyond the sub-shop it would have likely sounded like dropped recycling bins. I took the caps off of the flares, lit and threw them; it took barely as much time as it takes to tell. I walked briskly back out the door that I had levered open less than a minute earlier, and disappeared back into the woods leading away from Broadway, up towards Olive Street and my Element. By the time I was fifty yards away, I could hear a smoke alarm; by the time I had started my car and rolled the windows down, I could smell a nasty industrial smoke. As I drove away, I heard a low concussion (*propane or natural gas tanks?*) and the sound of the street front picture window blowing out.

I drove quickly and made it out to the base of George's driveway in just a few minutes. I parked my car out of sight, about thirty feet up a neighbor's driveway; when I had come by earlier the neighbor's house had shown no lights and felt like a summer place, so I hoped that I would be safe parking there for the short time that

I planned on being there. George's driveway twisted and turned a few times during its length, to prevent the house from being visible from the road, and also perhaps to control the speed of people driving up the drive (*or to impress them with the landscaping and views of Oseetah*). I walked back to the first big turn from the road and scattered a couple of handfuls of caltrops across the whole width of the surface.

I read about caltrops as an anti-vehicular device in Edward Abbey's "The Monkeywrench Gang" and was intrigued. They were ridiculously easy to make using heavy gauge chicken wire; simply cut an inch back along each wire from an X weld, and bent so that one arm stood up. They made an effective toy for giving out flat tires. I had spent about two hours making hundreds of them obsessively one afternoon, and now (*finally*) was getting a chance to use them, to see how they worked outside of lab conditions. I walked back into the woods and waited for my test subject.

George drove down his driveway at speed about ten minutes later, probably called by the fire department or somebody else who saw the sub-shop on fire. His Rover hit the patch of caltrops as he rounded the turn at what I guessed was roughly twenty miles per hour, and got at least two, and possibly more explosive flats. His ABS worked perfectly when he squashed the brakes a split-second later, and he came to a controlled skidding stop about ten feet in front of the big white pine tree that I was hiding behind. He sat at the wheel for eight seconds (*I counted*), cursing and breathing hard, and then got out to look at the flat tires. He shook his head and cursed his luck when he saw a driver's side flat, and then knelt to look for the problem. I walked quietly behind him and swung the wrecking bar down and across the back of his head. I swung hard the first time, because I didn't want to have to swing a second time; my understanding from research into the matter a few years ago indicated that a first hit was statistically much less likely to leave spatter evidence behind than multiple swings were.

George fell like a bag of dropped groceries, sprawling on his face in the driveway without time (*or awareness*) enough to put his hands up. I rolled him face-up, and slapped a foot of duct-tape across his mouth and ears, rolled him back over and secured his wrists and ankles to themselves, then joined them to each other; the whole process took me under a minute. I got into his Rover, turned off the lights, and drove it slowly back up the driveway (*a bit of guilty pleasure at the feel of squishy driving on the flats*) to where it had been parked in a turnaround the other day when I had come to see him. I made sure that the dome light was off before I let myself out and walked back down the driveway. He hadn't moved, but I could hear his breath whistling out of his nose like a tea-kettle, so I didn't sweat that detail yet. I grabbed the broom from where it lay, on the ground behind the big white pine tree, and swept all of the caltrops off of his driveway and into the grass at the edge; with luck, they wouldn't be noticed.

I walked down to the end of the driveway and looked for lights, while I listened for car sounds in either direction; the coast seemed clear, so I raced to my Element, drove back to George, levered him in the way back (*with some difficulty*), and threw the wrecking bar and the broom in next to him; all of it on top of a semi-disposable blue tarp from Walmart. I covered everything in the back with a dark blanket, stripped off my gloves, and drove away, mindful of the trap that this single road away from George's house was, watching for car lights both in front and behind until I had made some turns and gotten off of the straight line route from his house to Saranac Lake. I made a point of avoiding all of the best lit parts of town, especially the end of Broadway with his sub-shop and the fire department and police and the group of onlookers that always seems to show up to watch something burning.

I was able to get out of town without driving past any moving cars, or people out strolling. The weather and fire and my carefully chosen route took care of most of that; my luck, which I generally don't believe in, (*and had been conspicuously absent in the last week in any event*), took care of the rest. I pointed the Element northwards, and kept the speed ten mph below the limit; I didn't want to get stopped for speeding, or hit a deer at this point. Once I got north of Paul Smiths College, and made the turn onto Route 458, I pulled over to vomit and shake and cry a bit. Seven minutes later, I grabbed a Coke, a few hot dog buns, and a three musketeers bar, and rallied for the drive up to Jacob's farm. This night (*and my life*) was going to get significantly longer and stranger before it normalized again (*if, indeed, it ever would*).

Route 458, near Santa Clara, 12:07 a.m., 9/10/2012

It's been not quite a week since I was driving these same roads under somewhat similar conditions: semi-conscious passengers who would likely prefer to be somewhere else, scared of me and what was going to happen to them; late-night driving through beautiful wilderness while thinking ugly thoughts about ugly people. The big difference was that six days ago, I was certain that I was the "White Hat", fighting the good fight, nobly standing up for helpless and innocent victims, sneaking around the law simply to keep things simple; now I was uncertain of which hat (*if any*) I wore (*white, black, grey, plaid, or otherwise*). I was scrambling desperately to save myself, and hiding from the law so that I wouldn't go to jail forever (*having committed more felonies in this single day than in the rest of my life to date*). The beauty of the road and night and stars and emptiness was, for once, lost on me.

I was juggling thoughts and doubts and silly wishes,

and trying to balance right and wrong and moral absolutes and my surprisingly well-developed sense of self-preservation; thinking about how different the man making this trip less than a week ago was from the man making it tonight. I had never been in a fight that involved more than shoving and name-calling before a few days ago; and honestly, my first round with Justin and Barry was decidedly one-sided, you couldn't really call it a fight anymore than you could call what happened this morning and evening a fight. It seemed that I was a one-man embodiment of what the talking heads on CNN had been talking about for years; conflict had gone from men and armies standing toe to toe to asymmetrical and asynchronous in the space of a generation. I'm a firm believer that fighting fair is for suckers, proof of that particular concept was taped up and rolling around in the back of my Element every time I took these backcountry turns too tight.

I had offered George and Justin and Barry chances (*even enticements*) to disengage at various points, but they had stubbornly insisted on trying to kill me; the outcome of our conflict was determined by their actions and my reactions. I didn't go into George's house at the beginning of all of this looking to kill him and his minions, it was a regrettable outgrowth of his hostile reaction to my proposals involving Cynthia and re-normalizing my life. I was shocked to find that I felt their deaths regrettable, not because of the violence committed and lives ended, but because of the hassle and risk to myself that they engendered. I found that I had made eye-contact with myself in the rear-view, looking for the new man capable of killing, and was surprised to find scared and sick and sad (*but not remorseful*) eyes staring back at me; I had reasons, but no excuses for the ways that I had behaved in the last few days.

As George and I drove further north, out of the trees and into the fields of farms just outside the Adirondack Park, I thought a bit about the transformation, or metamorphosis, that I had undergone in the last few days; and tried to feel around inside my head or chest for some degree, or hint, of discomfort or disgust or sadness or glee for all of the valid reasons that I might feel any of those things. A dragonfly larvae lives in water for as long as five years, until a complex set of biological and environmental factors signal that it is ready to change; at this point the larvae climbs out of the water, breaks free of its old habitat and skin, spreads a set of wings heretofore hidden, and flies off to explore the world in an entirely new way, as an entirely new being ... essentially unrecognizable as the creature that left the husk behind. I was embarrassed by my own grandiose analogy, but could not dismiss it out of hand; it was too compelling and the fit was too eerily accurate. My environment had changed, and I had altered myself (*or been altered by biological programming*) to adjust to the demands of my new environment; I was not the Tyler Cunningham that Cynthia had asked to help her a week ago.

The change that I felt was worrisome on a number of levels, not the least of which was that I had liked the earlier version of Tyler Cunningham (*pretty well*), and hoped that the new model could interface with the rest of the world without having to relearn everything about humans and human interactions as awkwardly and slowly as before. I had enjoyed my few human contacts and a near-universal love of dogs, and had, like Henry Higgins, grown accustomed to the ins and outs of life with Tyler Cunningham. I was not eager for the new me to prove to be hungry for blood or to see a stolen shotgun as the right tool for every job. Thinking about the shotgun, and who I stole it from, brought me back down to Earth and helped me find my center again.

I had initially acted in response to the abduction of my ... friend ... Cynthia; it was odd to use that word, as I had always been comfortable with the idea that friends, like dogs, were something that other people had, while I just pretended. I had done what I always do, scoop big mouthfuls of information, like a whale with krill, feed my analytical brain/gut, and (*to messily bring the metaphor full circle*) poop out some conclusion. In this case, my conclusion was passable, but my analysis was incompletely digested; I had failed (*miserably*) to account for the human elements involved. Greedy and immoral criminals do not act, and react, in the same way that regular humans do. This fact should have been glaringly obvious to someone who had read as much crime fiction as I have in my life.

Stress can temper or crack, strengthen or weaken the substance upon which it acts. I could feel the changes within me, but I didn't understand what they meant (*yet*), or how they would affect my interactions with the rest of the world at this point. I could not say that I had been changed for the better, or for the worse; all I could say (*and I did, although I think it probably just confused George, who was just starting to wake up, based on the thumps and groans coming from the back of the Element*) was that I was glad to be alive. He started to move around a bit in a more organized way, and I, needing to pee and preferring to do it and to deal with George while we were still out in the boonies, pulled over.

"George, I'm sorry that it came to this, but it did." I had gone into the woods and pee'd, come back and opened up the rear hatch of Element. I was looking down at George, hogtied on the floor, under the wool blanket (*I found myself, for a moment, thinking that it must be itchy under there*). "We both made some mistakes, and things progressed to the point where we can't both continue to live in the overlapping worlds that we inhabit. I must have gotten lucky, because I certainly can't call the way that I approached all of this even remotely smart."

He tossed his head around enough to shrug the blanket off, and made some M-based sounds behind the duct-tape gag; I didn't have to remove the tape to know what he was saying/asking/begging, I had been in his exact position four days ago, and remembered the way it felt and tasted and smelled, to be subject to another man.

"Nope, I'm not going to take off the gag, there's no point. You'd scream for help or you'd curse me until I blushed or you'd ask for a last Coke or meal, and want to get away or kill me or both ... I know that I did. I'm not angry with you for acting as you have towards me and my friend Cynthia. It's in your nature, that's all." He shook all over and arched his back, trying to get closer. He mmm-ed especially emphatically, as if that would change my mind.

"I'm not mad, anymore, but I am more careful now than I might have been a few days ago. I don't blame you anymore than I would a shark for doing what they do, but I won't pet you, and I can't let you swim where I, or the people that I care about, swim." I grabbed his hair, pulled his forehead into my chest, as if to hug him, felt on the back of the neck for the highest gap between vertebrae that I could find, slid the thin blade of my fishing knife into the gap, and felt him jerk as I sliced through his spinal cord.

Everything in him tightened once, and then it all went loose. I had wanted to make it as humane and painless as possible, not needing or wanting to hurt or punish the man. I'm sure that it was essentially painless (*certainly better than what I would have gotten from Barry and Justin*), but it occurred to me that it might be scary for him while his body died around his brain (*assuming that he felt fear*); the lights were on, but his body was closing up house for good. He had taken his last functional breath, and his heart would stop within a few minutes; his brain would shut down from oxygen starvation a few minutes after that. I considered talking to him like I do with the injured (*sometimes dying*) dogs that Dorothy sometimes gets, but it seemed disingenuous to me. It probably wouldn't give George much comfort, to have his killer with him at the end, so I just walked away.

I electronically locked my car ('*bloop, bloop*') and walked back into the field by the side of the road to sit down and look at the stars; the same stars that George might have been seeing through the rear-seat moon-roof of my Element. I had thought, for no logical reason, that there might be some thrashing and/or noise, but of course there wasn't. I drank a warm Coke in the cold night, looking up at the stars, thinking about how many planets were within my field of vision; wondered if there was intelligent life on any of them, and if so, what they would make of life on Earth.

I crushed the can into a hockey puck and stood up, feeling my ass, and to a lesser degree my back, soaked through with cold dew from the grass. My car was still and quiet, and contrary to a side-bet that I had going with myself, didn't smell as though George had evacuated his bowels as my research indicated he likely would. It was only a bit over four miles to Jacob's farm, and if Gregory had been able to see him since my call (*Jacob didn't have a phone in the house which complicated things a bit*), then he'd be waiting up for me. If not, I'd have to do some tap-dancing, but looking down possible timelines, I could see more ways that things would work out than ways that they wouldn't.

Hostetler Farm, 12:41 a.m., 9/10/2012

As I crested the small hill and coasted down into the sheltering valley where Jacob's house and barns were, I could see a light burning in the kitchen, and caught a brief red glow out on the porch, where Jacob must have been enjoying a late night pipe on his swing. I turned off my headlights and pulled up to the house with just my parking lights on, parked, and then turned those off too. He stood up to wave, but then sat back down on his swing, so I killed the dome light, got out, locked the Element, and walked over to join him. There was a rocker next to the swing, and I lowered myself gingerly into the chair, noting for the first time since morning how tired and sore and old I felt ... wrung out.

"Tyler Cunningham, you're moving like I do on the second morning of haying season. Can I get you a glass of my wife's grape wine?" This gave me pause for a second (*but only for a second*) as I wondered what other types of wine Jacob's wife made, but I found that, for once, I didn't really care to learn the answer to that question.

"Thank you, Jacob, I think that I could use a glass of

wine."

"Whatever for?" I was tired, and would have had trouble parsing that out if Jacob hadn't started chuckling at his own joke about my odd word choice (*"use a glass of wine"*). I joined him in laughing at the funny "English" (*part of my research on the Amish had included Netflix-ing the movie "Witness"*).

He gave a low whistle, and fifteen seconds later, Sadie came out carrying a wooden tray with a stopper bottle of wine and two low glasses. She wasn't dressed Amish, plain and austere; she was wearing jeans and a t-shirt, but it was clean and she was showing lots less skin than the last time I had seen her. She handed me a glass after pouring one for her father, and favored me with a shy and happy smile that seemed a thousand miles away from the room/scene that I had taken her from in Lake Placid.

"Hi Sadie, how are things?" I asked, hoping that was bland enough to allow me to avoid much conversation with her.

"I'm well, staying here to help through this week, and then catching a ride to visit some family in Pennsylvania for a while. Before you go, remind Father to give you the bread and preserves I've set aside for you. I've nothing but my voice and our kitchen to thank you for my life, so I hope you like fresh bread; the preserves my Ma and I made this weekend with fruits from the farm."

"I'll be sure to remind him before I go, I live on carbs!" Sadie looked to her dad while I said this, and tittered when he raised his eyebrows at the term 'carbs'. "I was glad to help, and it was the most productive use of my time in months, so thank you."

She topped off our glasses, set the bottle down on the tray, which was resting on a table between the swing and my rocker, and wished us a good night. Jacob looked as though he might hurt himself smiling so hard, and it occurred to me to feel guilty, this was going to be like shooting plain-dressed fish in a barrel completely lacking buttons.

"Jacob, I hope that you'll forgive me, both for the late hour, and for the favor that I must ask of you. My father taught me that to take advantage of a friend's offer of help, especially so soon after it was offered, was a rudeness, but the trouble I am in leaves me no choice."

"Tyler Cunningham, your father's advice was good, but only when the offer is a gesture. I owe you my daughter, so unless you aim to take her back and away from me, anything I can do for you will be done."

"Well ... you know, or can imagine, the sort of men that Sadie was mixed up with in Lake Placid?"

Jacob nodded and looked at the bottom of his wine glass, I could feel his blush and anger from my seat, and went on quickly before he worked himself around to speaking.

"A man like that killed a woman who may be as close as I will ever come to marrying." The emphasis on family and duty and doing the right thing among the Amish would be hard to overstate, based on my research findings.

"He was a man involved in the commerce of drugs and sex, and he took her from me. When I went to speak to the man about what I thought he had done, he shot me,*(more or less)*. "That is why I'm moving like you'll move in twenty years, Jacob; this man put a bullet in me only days after killing my Cynthia." I'd debated about how much to share with Jacob, but felt that his being able to put a name to my loss might help tip the balance in my favor.

Jacob was by now leaning forward and both following

my story and trying to anticipate where it was going; I could feel his empathy and sympathy, even though it was too dark to see his face since Sadie had dimmed the kerosene lanterns in the kitchen. He leaned in to top up his glass and fill mine too, using a time-honored camping trick of holding an index finger a half-inch down the inside of my glass, so it wouldn't slop over; I saw him lick his finger when he leaned back to keep listening to my story ... I was desperate to end it with truth, but also with the right spin to allow him to rationalize helping me.

"After he shot me, I lost my calm, my feeling of place in the world, and my desire to work through things peaceably; in the end our conflict could only end in one of two ways: either he or I would be dead." I paused to take a drink, and look to see the roads my next words would travel.

"I'm here because I've done a great wrong in putting my world to right, and I mean to commit a further sin, with your help. I have this man's body in my car, and I need your help getting rid of it."

Jacob sat back and dug in his jacket pocket for a tobacco pouch. He made, or took advantage of, a lengthy process of inspecting, and loading, and then lighting the pipe he kept in the pouch. The smell took me briefly back a thousand years to morning fishing trips with my father, talking and sitting in the stink of pre-mix boat fuel and fish scales and wood smoke and pipe tobacco; I felt, for a moment, as though my dad was sitting on Jacob's shoulder, urging him to help me (*maybe it was Jacob's grape wine*). I once caught myself with a treble-hook, and Dad's calm manner and strong hands on mine were the only things that saved me from screaming and crying like a little baby; he talked to me using the same voice I had used the other day with Hope (*the scared beagle mix*). He pushed the barbs through the webbing between my left index finger and thumb, and cut them out with the pliers he kept in his tackle box ... I miss him.

Finally done diddling around with his pipe, Jacob turned to me and said, "There's nothing for it, but that he'll have to go to the pigs ... pen four would be best... twenty-four fine boars, more than one hundred-fifty pounds each, and eating near two hundred pounds of grain each day, not to mention what slop they get from the women and children."

My mouth dropped open in surprise. I had been expecting to have to finesse him into the solution that popped into my head as soon as Gregory mentioned the bacon, but he had obviously gotten there before me. I started to answer him, but he cut me off.

"What you're asking is little enough for the life of my girl, Tyler Cunningham. What soul this man had is gone, and what's in your car is nothing, but meat or feed now, good for either compost or the hog trough. When I was a boy, my cousin Zeke broke the neck of a calf by mistake, and to hide what he'd done, we hauled the carcass to the big boar pen, and let them at it ... twenty hungry boars stripped the meat and ate the offal and cracked the bones for marrow, even the thigh bones and skull."

"You can't tell Sadie, or your wife, or anyone," I cautioned, unsure of myself in this portion of the discussion.

"You don't know our ways, being an English, but we confess all our sins. In this case however, I'll not confess at our Sunday meeting, but in a private confession, with my brother William, an elder of the community, and Sadie's Uncle. He'll understand what must be done to men such as those who would harm our Sadie, and then I'll take his confession for hiding the crime himself. As long as it gets spoken aloud, we can be forgiven all our sins. I worry about your soul, but can do naught for it in any case."

"It may be beyond saving," I offered lamely, just to fill the momentary quiet.

"No such thing, you'll come up sometime, and see our church, when Sadie comes back from Jed's farm in Pennsylvania; see her cleansed of a year or two of Rumspringa in a morning."

"Now, to your bad man in the car ... back up to the big barn yonder, and we'll cut him out of his clothes ... it would do no good to choke my boars on zippers and fancy belt buckles." He surprised me by chuckling at his own (*slightly morbid*) joke.

I pulled the Element around to the barn that Jacob had pointed to, and he was already there waiting. We cut the clothes off of George, dropped the shreds on the blue tarp, along with the blanket and gloves and strips of tape and broom and bags and receipts and backpack and everything left over from my stop at Knapp's; then we wrapped it tightly in the tarp and threw it back of the Element. We wrestled George, who hadn't had time to stiffen yet, into an odd hybrid between cart and wheelbarrow, to trundle him over to the fourth pen, which was filled with snuffling pigs happy to see Jacob (*and likely also happy to see George*). The two of us lifted him up and over the fence, and into the main trough a few feet inside the pen.

"I'm guessing that I don't want to slip and bump my head and fall in here, Jacob?"

"Too right, Tyler Cunningham, the pigs would be full for days after eating the two of you ... Ha!" His laugh rang out strangely like George's, which gave me a momentary chill.

We went back out of the covered pen and he pointed out another building, this one low and long, and met me (*and the Element*) over there. It was his sugaring house, where they boiled maple sap down into syrup. He got the huge wood-fired furnace going, and we lofted the blue tarp, including all of its contents, into the flames. He had a long stick to stir the flames and evidence around, and within thirty minutes (*and another glass of wine from a bottle and tin cups he pulled out of his coat*), nothing was left except for a few hunks of melted and unidentifiable metal which he swore would fall out and into the ash-trench when he cleaned it next.

We went back over to the barn, me driving and Jacob walking (*he refused my offer of a lift, and I didn't press the issue*), to check in on the pigs. I could see a few bone fragments and some nasty stuff that might have been intestines still in the trough, but couldn't swear that they hadn't been there when we dropped George in. Jacob scattered a five-gallon bucket of grain all over the area where the boars had eaten most of George, waited and talked about the winter up here as opposed to down in the Tri-Lakes, blowing cold versus more snow; the boars attacked the area until it looked entirely picked over and clean (*except for the pig shit and hay and mud ... so not really clean*). The whole process had taken less than an hour.

"Some of his teeth might make it through them boars, but they'll most likely dissolve in the manure lagoon before they end up on our fields a year or two from now."

"So I guess he's really gone," I said stupidly.

"Yes, he's certainly gone Tyler Cunningham. He'll not hurt you or Sadie or anyone again." I think that he had needed or wanted to do something, to lash out at those who had hurt his daughter, and helping me had given him the chance. When we got back to his house, me driving, him walking, Jacob loaded the back of the Element with the bread and preserves from Sadie, added a few bottles of wine (*he didn't say what types, but smiled when I jokingly asked*), and threw in a ginormous side of bacon with a wink and a chuckle. Once the car was loaded, he clapped me on the shoulder, the left one, and I cried out like a kitten that got its tail stepped on. He looked over and shrugged, "Sorry boy, but around here, if you're not bleeding to death, you get back to work after the women tend to your hurt, and forget it by dinner." Having made me feel like a wimp for not being better already, Jacob shook my hand, turned, and headed into the house without another word.

I was too tired to make it all the way home, but didn't want to have Jacob's whole community wake up to see my Element in the morning. I decided to drive part way back to a place where I could just tilt the seat back for a few hours and take a nap. I drove slowly east for a few miles. Once I got past the farmland and back into the low woods and bogs, I threw the fishing knife and wrecking bar into one of the dark ponds on the side of the road. I eventually passed a sign that let me know that I had crossed into the Bombay State Forest, a chunk of nearly 23,000 acres of reforested land (*this fact leapt unbidden into my head, letting me know that I was starting my return to normalcy*) where I could sleep undisturbed. I pulled over at the edge of a bog smelling of rot and mud (*but in a good, natural, way*). I edged all the way into the plow turnaround, cranked the seat back to sleep for a few hours, and dreamed of the fantastic tiramisu that I would learn how to make (*and claim was an old family recipe*) for dinner the following night with Meg and Frank.

EQUILIBRIUM

Bombay State Forest, 10:16 a.m., 9/10/2012

I woke up roasting hot from the mid-morning sun slicing in through the front window (*turning my car into a greenhouse*), stiff all over from almost eight hours of sleep in the car seat, and with my shoulder and pinky throbbing from abuse and neglect that I had bought on credit with adrenalin yesterday (*and would apparently pay for today*).

I stretched and shook out some of the stiffness while I pee'd and put the last of my bottled water into a pot on an alky-stove for a bowl of oatmeal. I walked down to the nearby no-name pond to wash a bit and let my gravity filter make the water drinkable. Once a half-gallon finished dripping through the filter, I slammed a much needed liter of water, thinking, as I often do, that I can still taste pond even at the far end of the filtering process.

I grabbed the last Coke in the six-pack ring plastic, to wash the pond and oatmeal down, and feed my starving caffeine addiction. I had a bit of a headache, perhaps from the wine last night, perhaps from the day that preceded the wine; I added some Tylenol and Advil to the antibiotics and pain-meds that Dorothy had given me, and planned my day.

I stopped off at the Price Chopper in Malone to do some shopping (*based on my recipe research down in Long Lake for tiramisu*) before heading south on Route 30, back into the Adirondack Park and whatever my life would be: post-Cynthia, post-gunshot, post-Tahawus, post-George, post-pigs. I called Dorothy on my way out of town, stopping at the top of the rise above the valley that the city crouches in, about 1000 yards shy of the place where I would lose cell-service for most of the ride back down to home. I asked her if I could use her kitchen this afternoon, and if she wanted to come to dinner with me. She laughed and said that she'd leave right now to meet me at her place, but I told her that I was an hour out, so she could take her time.

I love the drive from Malone to Paul Smiths, it's different than lots of the other drives in my repertoire ... more agrarian and with wider shoulders, so I don't worry as much about smacking into a deer; the only downside is that it only leads to Malone.

Dorothy's apartment, Saranac Lake, 1:32 p.m. 9/10/2012

It smelled like an Italian bakery and café, savory and sweet and sharp; also a bit like brunch in a saloon with a cat box in a back room; Dorothy's apartment always smelled a bit of cat: cat food, cat shit, catnip, and just ... cat. The tiramisu was coming together nicely, which contributed to the cacophony of olfactory input.

I had Googled and analyzed and read through dozens of recipes to pull together the common elements, ingredients and preparation techniques, and had come up with a good generic recipe. The trick in selling the food as an 'old family recipe' is to make it your own with some carefully selected alterations in ingredients that will make your version stand out, and if possible, please your audience at the same time (*without seeming to suck up*). I feel that I had been able to do just that with the recipe that I made: bourbon and maple syrup made it into my recipe, bacon felt like a "Bridge Too Far", so I left it out *(this time)*.

The three cats that live with Dorothy provide an ongoing undertone of cat-funk (*both in terms of smell and attitude, Dorothy would insist*), and are always brutally conflicted the entire time that I am cooking; they love cheese and egg and cream, and hate me (*as all cats seem to do*). I tried to bribe them with the egg white in a bowl, but they took turns (*one lapping while the other two watched for sneak attacks with concealed chainsaws*) and started yelling at Dorothy to move the bowl into the living room (*which she did*). Dorothy has a tougher time believing that all cats hate me than she does that all dogs love me for some reason; I think that both are related to my somewhat dysfunctional human affect, although I can find no research to support the dog/cat dichotomy end of this theory. Most of the time when I come to Dorothy's apartment, the cats flee before me, and spend my entire visit complaining from the safety of the bathroom; shocked and appalled if I have to inconvenience them by actually using the bathroom. I've asked Dorothy why she doesn't have dogs instead of, or in addition to, the cats, and her answer is always centered around cats being able to thrive on neglect for days at a time, whereas dogs need care and the outdoors multiple times each day; this is quite similar to my reason for not living with a dog, except without cats entering the picture/discussion.

With Grandma's Tiramisu chilling in the fridge, the cats in exile in the bathroom, and Dorothy sitting at her kitchen table, we talked while I cleaned a seemingly endless supply of bowls and the things useful for mixing and mashing ingredients in those same bowls (*enough bowls and stuff that I spent a minute inventorying the piles of dirty stuff to see if Dorothy had slipped in some extra dishes for me to do as some form of facility-use fee*). All of the bowls and mixing things seemed to be coated with the appropriate amounts of goo, so I let it go short of accusations. Once everything was clean and lying out on kitchen towels (*I refuse to dry dishes, it just seems wrong when they will dry on their own, given time*), I grabbed a Coke out of her 'everything-fridge', as Dorothy calls it when mocking me, sat down and said, "Go ahead ... ask ... you've been very patient. I was going to hold some stuff back originally, but we're eating dinner with a cop tonight, and you probably have to know the truth in order to avoid it effectively enough to keep me out of the clink up in Dannemora."

"Well, I saw the two guys pull in to climb Panther, looking for the Tyler-cache that I hid under the big rock down past the summit. Then I talked to you, and chucked my phone into Upper Saranac Lake. That was yesterday morning ... Now, tell me everything that's happened to, near, or because of you, since then."

I did, up to and including my perfidious (*aka Grandma's*) tiramisu recipe this afternoon. She waited until I was done and then laughed and told me flat out that there was no way she was coming to dinner at Frank and Meg's place.

"I'm really not worried about George and certainly not about Justin and Barry coming up in a dinner conversation with Frank and Meg; I do, however, have concerns about Cynthia coming up as she was the one Frank originally told me to bring. We need to come up with something simple to move us past talk about Cynthia."

"We could tell them that we're engaged," Dorothy mumbled.

"Dorothy, unless you mean you and Cynthia, nobody's going to believe it; and Cynthia was demonstrably heterosexual, so that's probably out too."

"I meant us, asshole. I had a boyfriend in high

school."

"... and I bet that he knew you were gay before you did."

"Yeah, maybe ..." she answered, tilting her head in the direction of the memory. "Anyway, I think we should stick with Boss Ben's presumption of a death in the family, that we haven't heard from her in a week, and don't know where she is ... none of that is an out and out lie, and anything more specific or tricky ends up being difficult."

"Agreed."

And that's what we went with for the dinner ... that and my world-famous tiramisu.

Frank and Meg Gibson's House, Saranac Lake, 6:08 p.m., 9/10/2012

Dorothy and I arrived a bit before the announced 6 p.m. invitation time, and Frank's face fell immediately when he saw Dorothy instead of the expected (*hoped for?*) Cynthia. Frank and Dorothy get along well enough, but she and Meg are very close and tend to talk around him in a conversation; Dorothy had predicted this response and brought a growler of UBU Ale from the Lake Placid Craft Brewery (*a half gallon bottle drawn straight from the keg for local consumption*) to help things run more smoothly. Meg made yummy noises in anticipation of the tiramisu, and I was almost knocked down by Toby, the new foster dog that was living with them. When I stumbled and recovered, both Meg and Frank noted how stiffly I moved, and that I looked tired.

"I had a hammock suspension line let go the other night, and it dumped me on my left shoulder pretty hard

... on a pointy rock too." I answered, by way of explanation, hoping that the wimpy-sounding excuse would suffice to move us along to greener conversational pastures.

"Hard to fall out of a tent," Frank mocked me, as always, for my bizarre hammock-camping. Frank and Meg and I had gone canoe camping last summer, and he never missed an opportunity to try and convince me to come back to tents from the weirdness of hammocks.

"True, Frank, but on most nights, I get a better sleep in my hammock than I ever did sleeping on the ground. There's supposed to be a frost tonight, and I can't wait to climb into bed and rock myself to sleep; if it's clear enough, I may lose the tarp overhead and watch the stars."

You've been out on Lonesome Bay for some time now, haven't you? Did you find a nice spot out there?" Frank doesn't really care if I stay longer than the three days I'm supposed to at any one backcountry spot, but he likes to poke. Still, though, he had seen my Element out that way on and off over the last week.

"Yup, but also a couple of nights down in Tupper and one up near Rainbow Falls. It is about time to move though, I've been thinking about some of the state land on Kiwassa Lake ... I haven't been out that way much and it might be nice at this time of year. I've also been thinking about heading out for a week to paddle around the shore of Cranberry Lake, camping as I go ... a little vacation."

"Vacation from what? The toughest thing you face day-to-day is falling out of your hammock. It'd be great if you could find a way to use your backcountry skills and knowledge for something socially useful, you know ... make a difference while you walk the Earth like Kane."

Frank paused, and Meg started to say something, but he cut her off, continuing. "There are things happening in the woods around here that I'm not happy about ... I hear about them without knowing enough to do anything about it, and I'd like to change that ... more to the point, Tyler, I'd like to ask you about a couple of things that you might know about, or be able to help me with."

I looked over at Frank, nodding and drinking a sip of the nearly frozen Coke that Meg handed me. *(Once she found out about my fondness for really cold Coke, she started filling a cooler with ice and salt to lower the temperature of the Cokes that she offers me each time I'm over for dinner; while they are sometimes crunchy, I appreciate the caring that the effort shows, and even somewhat like the salty taste on the rim of her chilled Cokes.)* I had picked up a weird vibe running between him and Meg earlier, when Dorothy and I had just walked in; Frank had started to talk a few times and she'd shaken her head minutely. It had worked for a bit, but Frank had something on his mind; it remained to be seen what it was, and how much he knew, or suspected, about how I'd spent my last week.

In the brief respite that guzzling half the Coke gave me, I darted my eyes around the room as subtly as I could, hoping for a signal in somebody's eyes. Frank looked serious and ready to talk turkey. Meg looked nervous and scared and a bit sad. Dorothy had a relaxed smile, but the smile didn't reach her eyes, and she felt ... brittle, as if she might dive out a window and run off into the night if someone yelled "BOO!". Luckily nobody yelled boo, and a quarter second later I got a cold headache, which offered my face something else to do but talk for another few seconds, while I tried to decide if my forehead was going to split open. I used the time to try and see ahead, around some conversational curves, to where he could possibly be going with this; I could feel Dorothy tensing and looking at me as she picked up on the weirdness too. I tried to imagine what Travis or Spenser or Parker would have done in this situation, but I couldn't remember it ever coming up, so I did the only thing I could think of; it was, in fact inevitable given the situation ... I burped ... loud and long.

"Well ... I ... uh ... what?" I handled the initial response phase like a pro.

Dorothy looked to be edging towards the open window as a result of my response, and Meg jumped in before Frank could answer, "Frank Gibson, these people are guests in your house, and Tyler is not a police officer, and won't be involved in something that might be dangerous for him. Hammock-camping is plenty dangerous enough for him, clearly."

Dorothy processed what Meg had said, and relaxed a bit, as did I. It was obvious that they had spoken about something before we had arrived, and that it did not involve my being a 'person of interest' in multiple murders; it sounded like he actually might need my help.

Meg thought of me as a dog-lover and artist and trust-fund orphan (*all true*), and ignored the other things that I occasionally did that crossed over into Frank's world. I was, in general, happy for our relationship to function on that basis, as I'm sure was Frank. In this particular instance, I was ecstatic that she still felt that way, because it meant that Frank hadn't given her reason to think otherwise (*either by what he did or didn't say, or the way that he had acted around her*). This probably meant that I was safe with Frank, or at least that I wasn't in imminent danger of leaving their house in cuffs.

"Dammit Meg, he's not the guy you think he is ... or want to think he is. He's not a cop, but he's also not just a *'trust-afarian'*. I was gonna do all this after dinner, but since we started, I might as well grab him now, if we've got time before the lasagna's ready." Meg looked a little put out, but not actually angry or scared; she grabbed the covered tiramisu and told Frank that he could have ten minutes.

"Dorothy and I have stuff we can talk about, since you don't seem to want us here for your little talk ... no, you stay, we'll go. Do you want me to take Toby?"

"No Hon, we'll take him out back. Let me grab a mug from that growler, and we'll get gone." He took the big bottle from Dorothy and disappeared into the kitchen to pour himself a mug. He was back in forty-five seconds with a huge mug of the dark beer for himself and a freezing Coke for me. We took Toby and went out into their fenced backyard for our talk.

Gibson Backyard, 6:17 p.m., 9/10/2012

Meg and Frank lived on an acre. Their lot was roughly 40 by 120 yards, and they had fenced in about a quarter of the lot for the dog run. Over the years that I'd known them, they have taken in a series of foster dogs, in addition to whatever dog was living with them permanently (*currently, an old golden retriever named Chester*). Toby ran out the back door ahead of us and bounced over to fill Chester in on the excitement in the house (*food-smells, visitors, Mom/Dad stress, etc.*). Chester padded slowly over for a rub and thump from me, and one of the treats that Frank always had in his pockets when he was at home (*and maybe at work too, although I had no way of knowing that*). Frank motioned with his beer towards the picnic table, sat down, and started talking without waiting for me.

"I've been thinking about you some this week, actually wanted to catch up with you earlier, but kept missing you

at your 'Thneedery' ... also out at your campsite ... bad
luck I guess. That thing with Hostetler's daughter ... no,
no, don't say anything Tyler, let me talk a bit ... that
business was a nastiness avoided in a pretty clean way ...
although I'm pretty sure that I'm happier not knowing too
much about ... whatever." He took a swallow of beer, and
didn't bother to wipe the slight foam mustache away,
either unaware of it, or unworried.

"Gregory Simmons is a good guy, and a good man ...
we do some hunting together, maybe you didn't know ...
we both grew up in Canton before I moved down here
for work. Your name came up in a conversation about
hunting out at his parents' this fall, and he got quiet and a
bit sly, and said that he owed you, big, but wouldn't talk
about it. I've seen the same sly smile from a couple
people that I've talked to about you over the years ... not
often, most people don't know you, or think you're a dot-
com bazillionaire living like Walden in the woods." Living
like Thoreau in the woods, I thought, but didn't say. I was
nearly breathless with fear, wondering where this was
going.

"But there's a small group of people, people you've
helped with tricky stuff, or people who know those
people, and they smile tricky little knowing smiles, and get
defensive and angry with me if I hint around at you
sticking your nose where you oughtn't, or operating as a
detective without a license. People I've known longer
than you've been up here, lecturing me on how you're
their friend, just doing another friend a favor. It doesn't
seem like money changes hands exactly, but I've seen
those pictures you paint or your photos on some walls
around the North Country, and there's a photograph in
your office of you at Mona Krieder's house in Key West.
I asked, and she said your stay was a gift, but she had a

203

shit-eating grin on her face when she said it, so I figure that you did her a 'favor' at some time before she gifted you with a week at her place in the Keys."

"Frank, nothing you've said is wrong, and nothing you've said is illegal or immoral; so if you're going somewhere with this ... get there quicker." I was trying to balance nonchalance and slightly pissed, but it felt as though a hefty percentage of scared was leaking through into my delivery.

"Sorry Tyler, no offense intended, I'm working my way around to it sorta slow-like, because it's fourteen kinds of awkward for me. You're a friend of Meg's, but you and me, we're not really friends. I'm an officer of the law, and I'm not convinced that some of your favors don't break the law sometimes, which, even in a good cause, for a good reason, is still breaking the law. I find myself in the odd position of wanting to ask you for a favor, but I can't pay you or buy a painting of a sunset on a lake or loan you my hunting lodge. If you say no, we can head back in, and I'll never bring it up again." It was getting dark in the backyard, with the tall screen blocking the setting sun, but it looked as though he was blushing a bit.

"Just ask, Frank, and we'll see what I say." I was starting to get significantly less nervous about leaving here in cuffs; this seemed an overly roundabout approach to wringing a murder confession out of me.

"I've been connecting the dots on and off for a week ... you and the Hostetler girl, drugs, crime, George Roebuck, the backcountry, a fire at the sub-shop, and way too much goddamn money." Frank took his beer down to half, and licked some foam off of his upper lip this time.

"Um ... I must do dots differently ... can you explain a

bit, and get to the part that includes me ... and a favor?" I asked.

"I'm getting there, give me a sec ... You might have heard about a fire at the sub shop in town, belongs to George Roebuck ... might not have though, if you were camping. It wasn't a huge deal, cosmetic more than structural ... the fire department is about 300 yards away, and they got it out quick and easy, nobody hurt."

"Good news. How'd it start? Kitchen fire, electrical, vandals, dumbassery?" I felt as though I had to ask.

"The official report's not in yet, but it seems like multiple ignition points, so maybe vandals, but let me get back to that in a minute. When the firemen were tearing out a wall to make sure that they'd killed the fire ... that it wasn't back behind the drywall and smoldering up to the office spaces on the next floor ... they found a bunch of vacuum-sealed bricks of cash money."

"No shit? How much?" Cynthia's research had indicated that he'd be pulling in ridiculous amounts of money, but not knowing his expenses and overhead, it was hard to know how much would end up laundered back through the sub shop, and how much would have to be hidden; not to mention where he'd end up hiding it. I couldn't help asking, but it didn't seem as though it would be an unusual question.

"The short answer is a fuck-load ... excuse my French, Tyler. I was gonna say a crap-ton, but it's considerably more than that. Once they found it, and the fire guys were sure nothing was gonna burn down, we had to freeze the scene until we could get a pair of staties over from Raybrook to watch our guys watching the fire guys pulling it out, and then moving it all into the van, and then moving it over to the secure storage facility in Raybrook. The pile was just a bit smaller than the box my big-ass TV up in the house came in, and until we hear back from the bean-counters, the best we could do was count and weigh the bundles ... sixteen bundles weighing a total of two-hundred-forty-one pounds. They looked to be mostly twenty dollar bills, but I saw some hundreds and some tens in two of the packets ... best guess by the department geek is ..." he paused dramatically, looking at me with eyebrows raised, a question and challenge implicit.

"A bit over two-million, probably not more than two point five. Four-hundred-fifty-four new bills in a pound, times two-hundred-forty-one pounds, times twenty dollar average bill value, less a bit for greasy bills and plastic wrap, comes in around two-million, probably a little better. Does Saranac Lake get to keep it?"

"Ha! That's awesome ... no, we do not get to keep it, although we sure could use it ... nope, it'll go down to Albany, and vanish into the system, some here, some in DC ... who knows. But a bunch of us stood up in our best work uniforms for a photo-op today with the money spread out on a table. I won't make that much working my whole life, and that earwig has it in the walls of his shitty sandwich shop."

"Cheap though, and pretty fast, if you time it right," I added. "The subs, I mean."

"Yeah, way quicker than McD's around lunchtime ... anyway, I've gone off target ... but that much money is pretty cool to see all in one place ... I got a back-ache from toting it around last night and today ... imagine that ... a back-ache from money."

"Okay, so what is on target?" I prompted, hoping that I'd already figured it at least partway out, and trying not to release my newly minted #19 smile (*shit-eating, wow have I been lucky, I'm getting away with murder ... in this case literally*) while he continued.

"Nobody makes that kind of money with a sub shop, or even one-hundred of 'em ... George has been making money selling drugs, but not around here ... at least not on that scale. You're gonna have to take my word on that, but his slice off the small-time action in the Tri-Lakes wouldn't do more than inflate his shops' income figures a bit which is exactly what our forensic accountants think is the case." Frank paused for a second here to look at me; I nodded him on, indicating that I knew about forensic accounting. He brought the beer in his mug down to within an inch of its life and went on.

"That much money gives us PC *(probable cause, I nodded at him to continue)* to bring in George for a talk, and maybe even search his house, but when we get over to his place, George is gone. One of the volunteer firemen called him when they got the call about the sub shop, but if George made it to the scene, nobody saw him. His cell phone pings off the towers in a way that places it in, or near, his house. I think he's gone ... taken off with the rest of his money." I had to work hard not to dazzle Frank with my #19 ... this was perfect!

"More than that, I have an idea about how he made all of that money, and I'd like you to help me prove it," he added.

"How could I do that Frank, as you've pointed out before, I'm not a cop. I don't ..."

"Stop it," Frank interrupted. "I think we can both agree that while I don't know exactly what you are, we can also agree that you've got a brain that works differently than mine and other cops. You know the country around here, and seem to have a knack for doing the right thing to help good people. What I want is your help in finding out where..."

"George's production facilities are," I interrupted. "It stands to reason that he's making ... or growing" I added quickly, not wanting to show my hand/knowledge too much, or too quickly, "drugs here in the park, in the backcountry, since that's what we have plenty of around here."

"If he's not selling in the area, he must be selling outside of the park ... to the dealers, or more likely to the regional managers of the drug trade around here, because the people in charge in Syracuse and Albany wouldn't let George take this kind of money out of their cities from dealing on the street level; so he must be supplying them at a wholesale level," Frank observed.

"Astrometry," I muttered.

"Gesundheit!" said Frank, and smiled a bit. "What did you say?"

"Deductive astrometry. It's how astronomers find hard, or impossible to see items in deep space."

Frank looked at me as though I was speaking Dutch, but the smile stayed on his face as it dawned on him that I was doing my 'brain that works differently' thing.

"Astronomers watch the things that they can see, and note irregularities in the way that they move or behave. From irregularities in a star's movements, they can figure out the sizes and orbital paths of planets, or other objects, that they can't see; and they locate black holes in a similar way." He looked as though he sort of understood what I was talking about, but not quite. "Come on inside, and I'll show you before dinner," I said.

He started to speak, and I cut him off, "Your beer's warm, my Coke is gone, the dogs are scratching at the door, and I'll help you find where George is making his drugs ... now come inside so I can show you what I'm talking about. Grab me a big unfitted sheet, a marble, two heavy fridge magnets, a cup of laundry soap, and eight thumbtacks. Then meet me in the living room."

He grabbed his empty mug, and now equally empty growler, and headed inside for the items I'd assigned him; my happiness and relief and excitement was hard to contain, and I stopped trying as he turned away from me.

For the seventh time in my life, I was aware of a genuine smile creasing my face. I was, to some degree, responsible for Cynthia's death through my stalling when she needed my help with George. I wanted to find, or perform, some form of penance for my neglect. I had removed the man ultimately responsible for her death, and his minions who had actually done the dirty work, but, while this would seem a fitting revenge for her murder, revenge is not my thing; it's a waste of time and energy. I had killed George and Barry and Justin to protect my life and my self-interests, I wasn't capable of the self-deception necessary to fool myself into thinking that it had been for Cynthia. Cynthia was dead ... irrevocably ... nothing I could do would bring her back or make her happy *(or sad, for that matter)* or undo my failure to aid and/or protect her; but I could finish what she had started.

By dismantling George's methamphetamine enterprise, I could complete the journey that she had started but been unable to finish. She had begun her own war on drugs in our corner of the Adirondacks, for her own reasons, and I would do what I could to finish it, for my own reasons; the fact that I would be helping Frank just legitimized my tidying up the leftovers of Cynthia's war on George.

Meg and Frank's Living Room, 6:38 p.m., 9/10/2012

We were standing in the living room facing four kitchen chairs in a rectangular formation with a sheet stretched tightly between them tacked to the chairs at the corners of the sheet. Meg and Frank did not to have a marble anywhere in the house, so I stole the most spherical cherry tomato that I could find out of Meg's salad, with a promise not to stain their sheet.

"Okay class, George and I were talking about applying a technique astronomers use for locating unseen heavenly bodies, to locate unseen things here on Earth ... So, Deductive Astrometry 101, in five minutes," I promised.

"More like seven," Meg answered, holding a kitchen timer that was counting down the seconds until we could take the lasagna out.

"Better still," I said (*thinking 'because seven is a 'Double Mersenne Prime', but not saying that for fear they might chuck me out before I could eat some of Meg's lasagna*). Partly this show was because I love sharing nerdery with people willing to listen and learn, and the other part was to help push George into asking for my help in dismantling George's drug business.

"The sheet represents a distant star system, suspected of having some planets; or based on my talk with Frank, it's a system that we don't understand. The cherry tomato represents a star in the first case, and a known quantity or person in the second case. When we drop it into the sheet, where will it go?"

Dorothy raised her hand, blushed, and then said, "Right in the center."

"Why?" I quizzed.

"Because, it'll be pulled down by gravity and settle at the lowest/easiest point, which is in the middle."

"Good. That's right, because objects with mass tend to react the same way every time to the gravitation of a nearby massive object. In this case, the Earth pulling on the tomato towards the lowest point in the sheet. For the distant star system, the object with mass is a star all by itself in its system; in the unknown system here on Earth, it's a known quantity or person doing what we expect. Okay Dorothy, drop it ... gently ... onto the sheet." I handed Dorothy the tomato, and let her place it on the sheet, where it rolled down and into the center.

"Now Meg, scoot under the sheet and mark it with a spot of detergent on your finger."

She crawled under the sheet that was suspended like a child's fort, a yard or so above the floor, and the dogs went too, all three having fun, mostly because they knew it would be a short lecture; Meg marked the tomato's position with a dot of laundry soap.

"Now everyone close your eyes, don't open them until I tell you to, and when I do, try to figure out what is different and why."

I reached and placed one of the two white fridge magnets *(those satisfyingly solid metal disks that can hold a calendar on the fridge door)* a bit off center and toward the back of the sheet, then crawled underneath and put the second one near enough that their attraction took over and they locked together.

"Open your eyes, watch where the tomato ends up, and tell me why."

I let the tomato go from about the same spot as Dorothy, and it rolled *(happily for my little lesson)* to a spot a few inches behind the initial soap spot, and roughly halfway between the marked spot and the magnet.

Frank got it. "It was affected by the weight of the magnets, and the system adjusts to compensate."

"Bravo, you get to mark this one Frank." He crawled under, again with the dogs accompanying, and marked the sheet in the spot where the tomato stopped this time.

"Last time, and then lasagna, followed by my grandmother's 'Tiramisu Fantastique' for anyone who still has room ... close your eyes." I quietly put a few books under each of the legs of one of the chairs.

"For six bonus points! Open your eyes, watch where the tomato ends up, and tell me why."

I let the tomato go from about the same spot as the last time, and it rolled to a spot a few inches behind the last soap spot and away from the raised chair.

Dorothy clapped and raised her hand. "This time the whole system was altered, and the balance point was shifted away from the change-agent."

"Nicely done young lady! So what have we learned about how scientists use deductive astrometry to study and explain and predict the characteristics of distant stars, and possibly planetary, systems?" I asked.

Frank started, "Items with sufficient mass change the balance of a system. So ... scientists can tell how big the item is, and where it is, even if they can't see or study it directly, by seeing the effect that it has on what can be seen—the observable object, or objects, in the system."

Meg picked up from there, "Also ... an entire system can be affected by some force acting upon it, and even if that force can't be seen or studied directly, the force can be analyzed in terms of origin and magnitude by measuring the effect that it has on the observable objects in the system."

"Okay..." Frank said nodding, obviously putting the pieces together to apply to his own current puzzle. Slowly he looked up at me with the intense stare of someone who has just fit the last piece into a complex puzzle, when the picture becomes clear. "So, to find an unknown system or operation, look for evidence that the system has adjusted or compensated for the new variable in the mix ... if we look at the known system, the Park, we should be able to note changes in the way things are working that will allow us, you/me/others, to find out what George has been doing and where he has been doing it for the last few years."

"A plus, Frank ... for all of you, you've all earned ginormous servings of both lasagna and tiramisu for dinner."

Frank gave me a 'you may not be a worthless cupcake after all' look, and mouthed 'after supper' in a way that made me feel reasonably confident that I'd be hunting down George's drug factories not only with Frank's blessing, but possibly with his support.

It was a great lasagna, and Grandma's Tiramisu was the best (*first*) I'd ever had!

Dorothy's Driveway, 9:34 p.m., 9/10/2012

Dinner was entirely taken up with chewing and completely non-threatening talk about camping and dogs and hunting and dogs and dessert (*Frank asked Meg to ask for the recipe*), and more talk about dogs. The Gibson family dog, who was getting stiff with arthritis, and the visitor dog Toby, who we all agreed was young and obnoxious, seemed to be good for each other. We all thought that young dogs keep old dogs going for a variety of reasons that we couldn't agree upon.

After dinner, we adjourned to the living room where they all had coffee, and I grabbed a last Coke out of the cooler that Meg had set up for me; it wasn't Canadian, and I believed that I could taste the fake sugar, but the intense cold and slightly salty tang on the rim and can was a nice change from what I'd been dealing with for much of the past week. At about 9 p.m., I unconsciously reached for the bottle of pills that had been my constant companion, which reminded me that I was hurting; Dorothy saw the move and made noises about having to check in on a sick dog on her way home, to get us moving towards the door.

While Meg hustled the last remnants of dinner into the kitchen, and Dorothy played with Toby by the front door (*hosing him down with a few minutes of training and love*), I pulled Frank aside for a minute. We stepped into the narrow hallway that ran between the entryway and the living room, and talked briefly about the astrometry demonstration, and how it might relate to George and his drug production.

I kicked things off to start and steer them in the best possible direction. "If you think George has taken off to avoid issues about the money you found in the sub-shop, then he must have had more money stored someplace. If he is out of the way, now is a great time for me to do some poking for his production facilities, if they're still in operation."

"I think that they're making too much money for anyone left in his 'management team' to walk away from it ... my bet is that someone will try and take it over and keep things going, at least for a while," Frank opined.

"Agreed, and as the saying goes, 'nature hates a vacuum'. The great thing about that truism is that most vacuums are imperfect, and collapse over time." He looked at me as though I was speaking Navajo (*something I had actually tried out on him once, while learning about code-talkers*), so I continued. "Whatever nature uses to fill the void left by George probably won't do it as well as he did, and will leave more and bigger openings for you boys in blue to exploit, if I can point you in the right direction. Point of order, though, what if George's absence is because he's on vacation to Vegas or pursuing his lifelong dream of seeing Graceland?" I had to probe this avenue carefully, to see how committed Frank, and I assumed the rest of the law enforcement community, were to George being a bad guy on the lamb.

"Nah ... it's a distant possibility, but not likely. He pissed someone off and/or someone was trying to move on him, and the fire was a symptom. I think he got close enough on the night of the fire to see that we'd find the money he had hidden inside the wall, as well as the writing on the metaphorical wall." He pushed up his glasses with his middle finger when he saw me raise my eyebrows at his use of the word 'metaphorical', "George decided to drop everything, and hit the road with what he had, before his choices were prison or a pine box."

It was a relief to see that I wasn't the only one who could draw incorrect conclusions from data and jump in the wrong direction based on those conclusions. The good news was that the lack of information and leads that they would find about George in the future would only serve to reinforce their misapprehensions.

"Cool. I've got some ideas about where the labs or farms might be, and I'll check them out in the next couple of days. If I find something, I'll give you a call." Frank nodded happily, as I had thought that he might.

"I've always got my cell on me, and that may be the easiest way to reach me." He clapped me on the back and started the two of us towards the door. I wasn't exactly going to be working for, or with, him, but Frank had invited me inside his investigation of George, and given me tacit approval to poke around looking for the labs (*which was exactly what I wanted as well ... for my own reasons*). He had gotten the business portion of the visit out of the way, along with getting us fed, and now he was ready for us to go, so he could walk around the house in his boxers and eat some leftover tiramisu.

Dorothy was waiting in the front hall for us, and we did kisses and handshakes all around, and congratulated ourselves on a perfectly wonderful evening (*which it certainly was, as Frank had not arrested me for the three murders I'd committed in the last twenty-four hours*). We walked out and climbed into my Element, and I aimed the car towards Dorothy's apartment.

"Nope, to the shelter," she said.

"There really is a dog that you need to check on?" I had figured that that was an excuse to help ease me out of the house before my shoulder fell off.

"Yeah, and he's sitting right next to me. I'll check the shoulder, and see if I need to add some more or different antibiotics to the mix. Have the pain meds been okay?" She looked over at me.

"Sure they've been okay. I sometimes felt a little spacey or queasy, but I figured that could have been getting shot or having to feed the bad guy to hungry pigs."

"Boars," she corrected, "male pigs are called boars, and female pigs are sows. The ones raised for meat are always boars because they eat and convert feed to meat faster and more efficiently than the sows do."

I giggled and thanked her for the information. We pulled into the shelter and around to the back, where we wouldn't be seen by people driving by on the road. There was no need for that level of care anymore, but it had very quickly become a habit, and might take a week or two to lose again. We got inside and Dorothy actually did check on a couple of dogs with minor health issues before she gave the cold steel table a spray and wipe-down with the blue sterilizing/antiseptic stuff they seem to use on everything, and I undid my shirt, pulled it off, and hopped up to give her a look under the bright overheads and her headlamp.

She grunted and whistled and poked and squeezed and had me move my left arm in a big windmill, noting the points where I slowed, or made a noise, or my circle wavered. At the end of the exam, she made a happy noise, and affixed a pair of much smaller bandages, big Band-Aids almost, after smearing them with some triple-antibiotic goo. She went away for a minute, and came back with more of the same antibiotics that I had been taking, enough to take the course through three weeks.

"I'm going to talk to a friend of mine about range of motion issues in your shoulder. Your bones were unaffected, but a chunk of muscle got torn out by the bullet; it may heal and regrow, but you might benefit from some PT. At some point a physical therapist or your doctor is going to see that you were shot, but if you can put it off for six months or a year, it'll be less of an issue ... so you've got to balance those things against each other."

"So give me the good news, bad news spread in twenty-five words or less."

"The bad news is that you're gonna die ... the good news is that it's not likely to happen for forty to fifty years."

"I can live with that."

"So, having gotten through dinner tonight without anything awkward coming up, what do we do in the time between now and when you, and I, do eventually die? I mean, Cynthia being gone is certainly going to come up; same with George and maybe his minions, Jason and Barney." Another of the thirteen things that I like about Dorothy is her directness; her ability to cut away conversational fluff, leaving only the important things.

Her inability to remember names is not one of the thirteen things that I like about Dot.

"Justin and Barry ... I don't think that they'll come up; there's no reason that we should know them, much less where they are, even if someone does report them missing. I think that George is going to go away even more effectively; the police have an answer that they like, and they'll make the information that they already have, and that which they accrue as time goes by, fit that answer. Cynthia ..." I took a deep breath, and sighed it out while I put my shirt back on, and slid off the exam table.

"Cynthia is an entirely different matter. She is missing, and more to the point, will be missed. Ben will report her to the police before long if I don't ... and if I'm not the one to report her missing, it'd look weird because we're close ... were close... in a way that doesn't fit into a neat box, and people may assume 'boyfriend' or some analogous descriptor. The good news is that I already grabbed everything that I could find that linked her to George. The creepy net-nanny program is still running at the library, but the logs aren't going anywhere, or to anyone, so nobody's privacy is actually being invaded. I should go to her house and check on her fish tank." I was starting to run down, and trying to distract myself from the shittiness of admitting that Cynthia was gone, and it didn't really make a difference in the world, except to me. She had disappeared, and it didn't ... matter.

"What about the bodies?" Dorothy asked. I'd worked at forgetting about the bodies, who knew how many, in that deep spot in Lower Saranac Lake, only about a mile and a quarter from my campsite on Lonesome Bay.

"I was thinking that I might take scuba lessons at Paul Smith's College or NCCC this winter, and see if I can find

Cynthia in the spring. The others don't bother me much, to paraphrase Josey Wales, 'fish got to eat, same as worms'. But Cynthia had ideas about being in the Earth after she was dead, and I know a great spot. There's an abandoned old cemetery, back in the woods down south a bit, with trees growing up in and amongst the tombstones; I went there once with Cyn while I was trying to get her into geocaching, and she loved the spot."

"I'd like to come, if that's okay. Cynthia and I weren't friends, but she loved you, and that counts for a lot; she deserves more than one mourner."

"I'd like that, Dorothy, and I think she would too, although she said that you always smelled like wet dog and cat litter." I smiled at the end, and hugged it out with Dorothy, because I knew that's how she saw the world working. I dropped her at her apartment, and went over to SmartPig, with the idea of feeding and topping up my fish tank, but the couch looked so good that after a perfect Coke from the Coke fridge, I went to sleep, still fully dressed, and with my shoes on.

SmartPig Thneedery, 2:46 a.m., 9/11/2012

I woke up in darkness, except for my saltwater tank; I'd turned on the tank lights when I'd come in after dropping Dorothy off (*despite it being a weird hour and potentially messing up the circadian rhythms of all the beasties contained within*). My twenty gallon saltwater tank has timers on the lights, but I sometimes override them when feeding the beasties during off-hours or as a kind of night light (*with the blue LEDs lighting the tank*). It's nice to sit in the dark, watching the shrimp doing their custodian schtick all over the tank in the soft blue light, checking for food, cleaning the coral and anemone and algae, and exploring their world ... continuously mapping the changes as well as the stuff that stays the same.

I had originally started keeping a saltwater tank because it was different and difficult, and I was at a stage in my life when being noticeably contrary seemed like a good idea. I have stayed with it over the years because I find the beasties and ecosystems and relationships much more interesting than I did in the freshwater tanks that I used to keep.

My clownfish, Pennywise and Poundfoolish, have an amazing habit of grabbing chunks of my homemade tank food that are too big for them to eat, and hauling it back to feed the anemone in which they live ... home improvement and maintenance. The corals and anemones are complex cities/colonies of plants and animals that are symbiotic to a degree that is unheard of on land or in freshwater. I keep a number of shrimp and crabs and snails and starfish and a sea cucumber (*who reminds me of an Arrakeen sandworm*) as custodians of the tank, and they work ceaselessly keeping the streets and neighborhoods clean. I change twenty percent of the water monthly, top it off every couple of days, and my biological filtration system takes care of the excess nutrients (*from poop and overfeeding*) by growing algae under lights in one of those hang-on-the-back filters; the main hassle is figuring out what to do with all of the algae that my filter grows (*I don't know of any other saltwater tank owners or pet stores within an hour of the Tri-Lakes, or I'd give it away ... as it is, I end up chucking a tennis ball sized lump every month, and feeling guilty about it*).

I like to watch and think about the creatures and colonies and systems living together and getting along (*mostly*) in a volume of water smaller than a bathtub. I sometimes (*the last week for example*) have trouble living in a six million acre park with less than 150,000 people, mostly because of boundary and behavior issues and rules that I don't understand, or don't have hardwired like other people and the things in my tank do. Seeing complex systems work in my tank gives me hope for my being able to come to terms with the rest of my world, for at least some flavor of grudging truce or co-existence, if not an actual series of alliances. Other times, I just see it as a tank of salty water with a handful of critters from around the world just getting by, sometimes eating each other for fun or profit (*which felt a bit like this last week*).

I stretched and noted that my shoes were still on, which was odd, and immediately I found them to be wildly uncomfortable despite my having slept nearly five hours in them. I grabbed a Coke from the Coke-fridge, and ripped off a hunk of Sadie-bread, dipping it in some blueberry preserves from a huge mason jar. I had a few things running through my head, none of them likely to involve anyone killing me or vice-versa, which was a welcome relief.

I needed to retrieve the research on George's operation and figure out how/when/where to scout them and/or find other/new production spots; or determine if, in fact, they had just closed up shop and gone to work for someone else when George vanished.

I needed to move my gear to a new camping spot, and start switching out summer gear for the heavier stuff for winter (*fall would take care of itself, as it always does in the Adirondacks … quickly*).

I needed to report Cynthia missing, or get someone else to do it, in a way that didn't garner me any negative attention, distract Frank from his misapprehensions about George, or help connect the dots in a way that made things more complicated.

I needed to do some trading of fragments of life from my saltwater tank in exchange for new/different fragments from other saltwater hobbyists in New York State before we lost our hospitable temperature window (*it is possible to ship them cheaply/effectively using the USPS Priority boxes, but only during a period of a few weeks in the spring*

223

and fall when the temperatures are balanced between too hot and too cold to sit in trucks and on loading docks and in mailboxes). These four projects would keep me happily busy and hopping for the next week or two, which was about as far ahead as I liked to plan.

I noticed in my planning that I was not gripped by the lethargizing (*yup, totally made up that word*) sadness that September 11th has brought me the last ten years, and felt around inside my head for possible reasons. I miss and love my parents as much as I did on that morning; they drank coffee while I slurped a slightly too warm Coke, and we made plans for dinner ... Chinese, mainly dumplings, from Noodles on 28th. I can see both of their faces; I check from time to time, worried by the idea that if I forget, there might not be anyone on Earth who knows, or remembers, what they looked like. It occurred to me that something about the last week's trials had forced significant changes to happen to my person and my worldview, in some way solidifying the map in my head of the people and places in my life. It may have changed the Adirondacks from a place into HOME in a way that eleven years of explorations had not, and could not. I was no longer living in the psychological shadow cast by the events of that day; it was history, not forgotten, but not actively informing my day to day existence to the same degree that it had for the last decade. I had turned the page and started a new chapter.

My 'map of the world' had changed in all sorts of ways in the last week. There were new warnings and markings in places like Tahawus and Jacob's hog-barn and that stretch of Lower Saranac, which until recently had only seemed like a nice place to hunt for deep-water fish. Beyond that though, I had made those, and other chunks of the Park mine; not through purchase (*which was just money, after all*), but by choosing to stay and fight (*even if I didn't fight fair*). My parents had made New York City theirs and then given it to me, but with them gone it was no longer mine; so I'd had to head north and find a new place to make my own. The trouble was that I never had to earn my world until last week; it had all been given to me too easily, which was fine (*in its way*) when parents do it for their children, but lacked a certain ooomph for an adult.

Tons of summer people with too much money drop a chunk of their millions to build McMansions on Lake Placid or Upper Saranac Lake, but it's not a part of them, just a bed with a pretty view, until/if they have to earn it in some way. I wouldn't have chosen to lose Cynthia or get shot, or kill Justin and Barry and George, to make this place my home (*one certainly hopes that there are easier ways*), but that's how it had shaken out, and the Park and I now had a different relationship. Last night with Frank, I'd agreed to help him for the same reason that I generally helped the others that I'd gotten involved with through the years of my tenure in the Adirondacks: it seemed like it might be a fun and interesting way to explore and learn and expand my world a bit. This morning though, I found that I wanted to help because the idea of those people using my wilderness to make their poison, useful only for creating money and misery, bothered me. It was like watching someone come into SmartPig, piss on the wall, and leave.

I'd planned to wait until first light to go out and get the cache containing both Cynthia's and my notes and maps, but suddenly I was ready to go ... NOW. I stuffed my GPS and headlamp, some spare batteries and snacks, a trio of Cokes from the Coke-fridge, and a fleecy hat into a largish pack, and headed out with a bounce in my step that had nothing to do with my longish nap. I was still sore and stiff and tired and recuperating, but I had a goal. I was motivated, and everything in SmartPig and the world outside seemed a bit more sharply focused, a bit more lovely, and a bit more mine.

The wall clock clicked over to 3:14 a.m. just as I was crossing the threshold, which I took as an auspicious launch as well as a hint from the world to stop for pie at the Kwik-E-Mart on my way out of town.

Woods near Second Pond, 4:24 a.m., 9/11/2012

The woods were dark and quiet and cold and damp, and there wasn't another human for miles. The moon was waning, with less than a quarter remaining, so not much light filtered through the trees, and first light was two hours away; it was my favorite time in the woods. Night beasts were just starting to wrap things up, and the daylight beasts were starting to move and call and get ready; I could hear them all.

The first few minutes out of my car and into the woods, I reverse-stalked myself to listen for people following; I'd take a bearing with the GPS, jog for 300 yards with my headlamp on, shut the light off and wait for five minutes before repeating the process. There wasn't anyone there, but I hadn't quite lost the scared/paranoid feeling that the previous week had engendered, and it seemed a habit worth holding on to, at least for a bit.

At the end of the fourth such cycle at the end of the waiting time, I noticed that I could see pretty well through the open/mature forest; I was in a huge tract of red pines that had been planted the last time someone had clearcut the woods here. The trees had been planted in lines, if not rows, and I could take a bearing and check every few minutes, making adequate progress with much less light-pollution (*and human footprint*) in the woods.

Walking in near darkness requires focus and care, but is not actually difficult. You need to lift your feet a bit higher, and place them as if the ground is fragile. Your walking speed should be reduced, but once you get into the pattern, you can still cover a fair amount of ground. I walk with my mouth open and turning my head slowly from side to side; I don't claim echolocation, but the scuffing of my shoes over the needles and twigs sounds a little different whether there is a bush or a rock-wall in front of me. If you let your body try, the lizard-bits at the back of your brain know quite a bit about the natural world that we try to forget because at heart we're scared of the dark. My hands out in front of me, I ran into less trees and bushes than would seem statistically probable, and I avoided a couple of huge glacial erratics more by feel than by the dim light filtering down through the tree canopy.

My trip took longer than it would have in daylight, or even with my headlamp on the whole way, but it was sort of cool to fade into the night a bit. During my run and wait cycles, I had heard nothing in the woods, until more than four minutes into each wait; at which point animals all around me would 'forget' that I had stomped through, and upset their world with light and sound. Once I started dark-walking, the forest sounds came up pretty quickly; I was walking slowing and quietly, and not advertising my position with the light. The tenor of my interactions with the night, and its animals, changed. Instead of scaring them, I was surprising them; sometimes getting to within yards before I would hear them scamper or bound or fly off in a hurry.

I reached the ginormous rock that the cache I was looking for lived under, and poked into the dog-sized hole with a long stick before reaching in. I had once been scared most of the way to death while geocaching, when I reached into a hollow stump and grabbed a garter snake instead of the Tupperware container that I was hoping for. We were both equally scared, but I was bigger, so the snake bit me and also let loose with its nasty-smelling musk. Since then, I poke/rattle sticks into dark places before I put my fleshy bits inside them. In this case, it was wasted energy and time, but I don't begrudge the delay; I still have a tiny scar on my hand from the bite, which got infected. I grabbed the ammo-can, pulled it out, and moved back a bit to open it and transfer the papers and notebooks to my backpack before putting the cache back in place for future use.

I snacked up with some jerky-enhanced GORP, drank a slightly shaken and warm Coke, and leaned back into the hill to doze a bit until the sun lit the woods for my walk out. I was working on a few ideas to incorporate the information that I already had on George's Meth-production (*from Cynthia's snooping*) with some investigation of my own, involving a combination of time spent in the backwoods, on the computer or phone, and maybe mooching some law enforcement resources from Frank (*since I was, to some degree, on his dime*). By the time I woke up, and could see my way through the forest back towards my Element, I had some solid plans on how to spend my day.

SmartPig Thneedery, 9:29 a.m., 9/11/2012

On my walk out from the info-cache near Second Pond, I thought about what criteria George and his chemists would likely use in site selection for their meth-labs. I had Cyn's info, and my notes from last week in my pack, but I wanted to give my brain free-rein with the problem now, and compare that to her info later.

He'd want (*would have wanted*) big chunks of public or private land far away from the few population centers that we have in the Park, but still serviced by passable roads, to allow for the passage of supplies in and drugs out. Thinking of Tri-Lakes as the epicenter of their activity, I would avoid land to the north, northeast, southeast, and south, as generally being too populous for what they wanted to use it for, especially when compared to the big tracts of empty public and private (*mostly timber company*) wilderness to the southwest, west, and northwest of George's base in the Tri-Lakes.

There are only thirty-eight forest rangers in the whole Adirondack Park, and they mostly patrol the places where lots of people go; so if you could get deep into the backcountry, away from the touristy hotspots, and pull a tree down across your access point once you were in and supplied for a production-run, you could work hassle-free for weeks (*maybe even months*) before moving. When they had to move they could just back up a resupply truck to the downed tree, and pass food and propane and other supplies to the other truck across a tailgate bridge. Alternately, there were plenty of huge private landholdings (*paper companies, Rockefellers and their ilk, mining companies, the Nature Conservancy, etc.*) that didn't use or visit their land for years at a time, and you'd be free from worry about rangers bothering you; if the land was managed by a local for the owner, they'd likely be happy to lease a few acres to you for 'hunting or camping' for a couple hundred or thousand dollars a year.

I reached my Element with a picture of the Adirondack Park in my head, all of the land with major tourism or cities marked off, the same with entirely roadless areas; it left a lot of ground to cover, but some phone work later in the morning would hopefully give me some leads, and then I could hit the road, hunting for meth-labs (*be vewwy, vewwy quiet!*).

The McDonald's Sausage McMuffin, two for three dollar deal, is an incredible bargain if you're in the market for a ginormous dose of fat and protein and carbs, which I was. I got four of them at the drive-through on my way to SmartPig to look at GoogleMaps and GoogleEarth, and read Cynthia's notes again.

Cynthia had identified spots where she thought the meth labs could be. George's guys had done a pretty good job of site selection, but they (*or Cynthia*) had missed some sweet spots that I would have chosen over a couple of theirs, so I printed some maps, marked them up and waited for businesses to open in waves; first at 9 a.m., and then at 10 a.m. To supplement Cynthia's list I focused on areas I thought would be good locations and then called towing services and garages in or near my favorite spots (*thanks Google*), looking for people who had paid for tows or off-road type repairs/upgrades (*broken axles, knobbly ties, etc.*) with cash since April (*since the backcountry meth season was likely limited to April through October*). I got a couple of hits, and marked the service location or garage on my maps. I also called restaurants and camping gear stores in the tiny towns I thought that George's people might pass through for frequent or outsized cash purchases. George's crew would be paying for everything in cash, which would keep them below the law enforcement radar, but might be memorable in tiny, poor towns in those parts of the Adirondacks.

I got a few more possibles after dozens of phone calls, and marked the second tier places on the maps where I should look if all of my primary leads didn't pan out (*and just before I started driving around with my head out the window calling out, "Yoo Hoo, Meth-Labs!"*). By the time I was done, I had a list of possibles, in a probable descending order of likely payoff starting with the list from Cynthia's notes and supplemented with my list of promising sites.

I wanted to start checking them out as soon as I grabbed a quick nap and could load my weeklong tripping gear into the Element. I called Frank, made a lunch date with him at Tail o' the Pup in Raybrook to talk shop a bit, then I put together the stuff that I would need for a week of car-camping (*sleeping setup, cooking setup, gear bag, electronics and chargers and inverter, clothes for twenty degrees, dehydrated food for a week, and two cases of Canadian Coke from my strategic reserve in the basement of the SmartPig building).* I hoped that I wouldn't be out that long, but didn't want run out or have to resupply. I lay down on the couch, excited and nervous and happy at the prospect of the next few days; thought of one final tweak, called Dorothy to arrange it, and went to sleep with an alarm set to wake me in time for the late-lunch meeting with Frank and to eat some fried pickles at Tail o' the Pup on the SLPD's dime if I was lucky.

It was a great lunch, I let Frank know that I'd be out of town for a few days, snooping around the Park a bit; then I stopped off to see Dot at the TLAS.

Washboard, Tupper Lake, 3:04 p.m., 9/11/2012

I throw dirty clothes in my car almost every time I drive through Tupper Lake so that I can stop at the Washboard, my third favorite multi-business in the world. The Washboard offers laundry machines, and full or self-service laundry, as well as homemade donuts that you can watch being fried (*and spread with the best maple cream on Earth, if you'll let them*), and Native American Art (*including paintings and jewelry and carvings and rugs*).

I ran in and waved at Gert, the ancient woman who has been in the Washboard every single time I've stopped in no matter what day or time. I threw two loads into the huge machines on the end; one a pair of sleeping bags that I was probably done with for the season, the other with three weeks of clothes (*I don't own clothes that need dry cleaning or separating*).

"Hi, Tyson!" Gert screeched. "Get you a box of maple creams?"

"Hi Gert," I have no idea why she thinks my name is Tyson, but after about eight tries at clearing up the mystery of my name, it didn't seem to be a point worth pushing on. "Yup, sounds good, but you better make it four maple creams and two plain."

Gert gave me a funny look, but nodded and waddled off to make my donuts. She looks to be a thousand years old, and as though a light breeze would blow her off her feet and break her, but she barehands the donuts out of the oil and into the flat box that holds six; holding the box always burns my hands on the way out to my car (*although I try not to let her see it hurting me*).

By the time I had loaded and soaped and quartered my machines, she came back with a box that was hot enough to blister stone, and, as always, I traded her a box for a twenty dollar bill and told her to keep it, but asked if she'd move my stuff into the dryers if the wash finished before I got back (*it would, I timed it so that it always did ... it was a thing that we did*). I waved on my way out, concentrating hard, so as not to whine or cry from the pain of carrying the box before I got out the main door. I got back into the Element to explain the rest of my road trip rules to my new passenger (*and partner in crime fighting*).

FLASHBACK, TLAS, 2:03 p.m., 9/11/2012

Hope had been visibly terrified of me when I picked her up from Dorothy at the shelter, and I almost called the whole thing off, but was talked out of it by Dorothy.

"Nah, she seems to like you more than any of us, and it will do her good to get out of here and away from the noise and stress ... speaking of which, can I come along?" She was only half joking, and I could both see and hear some concern in her.

"This isn't gonna be like that other stuff is it?" she asked looking over her shoulder at the nearby shelter staff members. "You're going to bring her back in one piece, right? She doesn't need to get more messed up, and neither do you."

"Nope, she'll be fine. I will seem more like a vacationer and less like a cop if I have a dog like Hope with me. We'll have a fun time. She'll eat some human food, maybe some raw fish if I can catch anything, and she'll help me navigate, like dogs are supposed to ... it'll be great!"

"Just you remember that neither of you is named Turner or Hooch or Thelma or Louise ... come back and tell me all about it." She had leaned over and surprised both Hope and me with kisses on the tops of our heads, before turning quickly and heading back into the depths of the shelter to take care of some important work.

Hope and I headed out to the Element with a bag of food, a pair of bowls, and a fleece blanket wrapped around a couple of toys and some chewies. I put the food and bowls in the way back with my gear, and arranged her blanket and toys on the front passenger seat. She let me lift her into the Element without snapping, but I could feel her shaking all over until I put her down; she rolled into a tight ball with her nose tucked under her back legs and eyes facing away from me as we headed south to Tupper and the closest of the dots (*Cynthia's precise locations*) and the larger circles (*my hunches, backed by paid-in-cash garage calls and/or large cash expenditures*) on my map.

Route 30 S, 3:37 p.m., 9/11/2012

I balanced the box of donuts on the dashboard, made a few cop jokes about myself, took one of the ones with maple cream spread on it, and waited. Hope was doing her best imitation of a grumpy round rock, but she wasn't made of stone, and the smell of the hot dough and oil got to her before long. She groaned and grunted and rotated and adjusted her balled up shape so that her head was now resting on her butt, facing me. I could see her small brown eyes watching my right hand bring the donut up to my mouth for each bite, and after a few times, she swallowed loudly, then sighed delicately. I finished my first donut, and reached into the box for one of the plain ones. I felt it to make sure that it wasn't magma hot, and then broke off half and put it on the edge of her blanket (*and the passenger seat*), as far as was possible from her balled up form.

She was concentrating so intently on the donut that

she didn't have time to react when I reached down and put it on the chair. After the fact, she seemed to want to move, but the donut was already there and my hand was back on the wheel. She watched the donut and sniffed it hard, either in an attempt to draw it closer by vacuum power, or to detect whatever subtle poisons I had clearly loaded the Trojan donut with.

A minute later, when I grabbed my next maple cream donut, and with my other hand full of steering wheel, she felt confident enough to stretch her neck out, until she could pick her donut up gently with just the tips of her teeth. She dropped it again in the center of the ball that she had made of herself, and appraised the thing for five long seconds, before inhaling it. When she was done, she looked back towards me and sighed contentedly, but with hunger and desire, not the hatred and fear that her looks had contained before. I tried not to let the gloating reach my eyes or mouth, and handed her the next half donut.

By the time we had reached the turnoff at Rock Island Bay, to head off the big road and onto a series of bumpy little ones, Hope had finished both of her donuts, and was licking the maple cream off of a piece of one of mine.

We bounced and jounced around a half-assed gate that might stop people from Massachusetts from getting their Priuses back onto the old logging trails, but barely slowed down Hope and me in the nimble Element. We could hear some branches scratching along both sides; I made a mental note to ask Frank about reimbursement, and then made a further note reminding myself that this was fun, and that I didn't care about the scratches.

When we went by a small pond dotted with geese chattering at each other, and sounding for all the world like a cocktail party where everyone had had too much to drink, Hope sat up nice and tall to check out the birds, and gave a couple of off-duty woofs. We drove away from the road and around Mt. Morris, towards Little Simon Pond, closing in on Cynthia's first set of coordinates minute by minute.

I passed the tiny, almost invisible, side road heading up beside a creek that came down off the back of Mt. Morris, and while I couldn't see a trailer, I could see reasonably fresh tire tracks leading both up and down the steep, but passable, jeep trail. I recognized the approach and jeep-trail heading uphill from the meth-camp pictures that Cynthia had foolishly shot. I kept driving along the road for a few hundred more yards until I had made a couple of turns along the shore of Little Simon Pond, to a pull-off next to the water, looking out at the single island on this backcountry pond. I grabbed the donuts off the dashboard, and a couple Cokes and my un-serious fishing gear, then went around to let Hope jump down and walked her *(via the long lead)* down to the water's edge.

I clipped a carabineer to her leash and to a belt loop on my shorts and let go of her. I put the donuts in my tackle-box, cracked a Coke, and walked out into the water to do a bit of casting into some weeds a ways down the shore from Hope and me, where a tiny creek dumped into the pond by some boulders. Hope turned a few circles and lay down to watch.

Over the next hour, I got a few bites, and hooked a couple of nice bass, which we would enjoy for dinner later; along with a feisty sunfish that swallowed my treble-hook so completely that I injured it removing the hooks; so I decided to give it to Hope to snack on. Once I'd ripped the hooks out of the poor fish, I chucked it up on shore near Hope. She sniffed at it until it jumped, scaring her mightily; she then scooped it up and gave a quick crunch to kill it, before spending the next fifteen minutes eating it and making happy noises behind me while I kept fishing as the sun moved further and further behind me, lengthening my shadow across the water.

Hope and I were enjoying the fading afternoon, together, but each in our own way; I'd say something to her every few minutes; she'd ignore me. When I went back to grab a Coke and a donut, I gave her the maple cream one that she'd started back on Route 30 S (*she didn't wag or smile, but it was a close call*). Around 5:10 p.m., I heard a truck high-center and clang off of a rock down about where the creek-trail to Mt. Morris must have been (*Cynthia's closest marked point on the map*). I forced myself not to turn around, even when I heard the truck slow to swing out around the Element.

Hope growled and stood up to bark a few times, which grated my nerves, but made for perfect 'hide in plain site' cover. The truck kept going to a wide spot further down the pond, and then turned around to return to their hiding place; I heard it clang off the same spot going back up the hill, and fished for another forty minutes before packing it in for the night, reasonably certain that the truck belonged to George's drug-production machinery.

As the sun was dipping behind Mt. Morris, I drove straight through on the road to Simon Pond, so that Hope and I didn't have to double back past the meth-lab (*I hadn't seen any meth, but it was exactly where emails between George and one of his guys had said that it would be, so I wasn't much in doubt, and certainly didn't want to check it out more closely*). We swung around and pointed the Element back into town to pick up my laundry, thanking Gert, and heading back out and mostly northwest, towards Canton and Potsdam. I found a nice spot to pull off into a chunk of State Forest Preserve just north of the Piercefield

Flow, where Hope and I could enjoy the sound of running water, and set up camp.

I hung a hammock and threw my bag inside it, cooked both bass in foil with butter and a spice premix that I make once a year in a huge batch from sea salt, cracked-peppercorns, dried/minced garlic, and a bit of brown sugar; Hope loved it!

The night sounds and dark and cool seemed to make her a little uncomfortable. She balanced her diminishing fear of me with her growing fear of the woods at night, and curled up between my feet and the stones of the fire pit as I sat cross-legged. When it was time for bed, she protested being left alone in the nest I'd made in the back of the Element (*I'd taken the rear seats out for this trip*) for so long that I eventually caved in, and joined her, trading a comfy night's sleep for a quiet one. She made a warm pressure behind my knees and at some point in the night was scared by loons on the Flow. She whimpered her way into the opening of my bag and crawled down to sleep by/on/amongst my feet at the closed end. I fell asleep smiling (*no number, this one was actually mine*).

Piercefield Flow, 4:45 a.m., 9/12/2012

Sleeping on someone else's pattern and schedule was a
new experience for me, and when Hope started tunneling
up from the bottom of my sleeping bag, I woke with a
start; her faced poked through the opening, right by my
face, a second later, and she gave me a casual/
embarrassed/'say nothing' look that let me know that
what happens in Piercefield Flow, stays in Piercefield
Flow.

We had gotten up a few times during the night, either
she or I initiating it, but in each case we'd both head out
to pee and walk the perimeter of our camp to look and
listen and smell. There was enough light spread by the
dome light of my Element to move around and get some
breakfast started for both of us. I cranked up my alky-
stove on the tailgate of the Honda so that Hope wouldn't
knock it over and burn the Park, put her on a super-long
lead to explore a bit, took down my mostly un-used

hammock, and was just setting up our food when the water started to steam in the way that it does just before boiling.

I made a big bowl of oatmeal for myself, and enjoyed it with a Coke; Hope had a bowl of kibble that I gravified with some leftover hot water, and lapped some cool water from the Flow. I talked about my plans for the day with Hope, she wasn't listening very hard, but I normally talk things over with a parallel (*and fully non-corporeal*) me, so the occasional eye contact and sigh or burp provided a nice counterpoint to my discourse. With her (*imagined*) guiding questions and responses, I tightened up our schedule a bit, worked through some possible bumps in the road ahead, and improved the plan for how I was going to inform Frank about the positives and the possibles.

We were close enough to Tupper Lake still for Hope's sad eyes to make a convincing argument for going back and waiting for Gert to get to the Washboard and make us some donuts. But I used my veto power, and we headed northwest and away from Tupper, stopping at the gas station at Sevey Corners to fill up my gas tank, and load up on some crappy road food for the two of us.

Sevey Corners, 5:58 a.m., 9/12/2012

From Sevey Corners we had to drive north on Route 56 for a bit until we got to a wide spot in the road called Stark.

Stark is most notable for a sign announcing it to be Stark. It is also known *(by me ... now)* for a gravel track that leads away from the road to the north, above and behind the Stark Falls and Crary Falls Reservoirs. This track breaks off into a series of less and less serious/navigable tracks. I kept one eye on the GPS *(for direction of travel only, it didn't show anything but blank green screen where we were driving)* and one eye on the graveled tire ruts that we were following; they weren't nearly big enough for names or to make it onto Garmin's mapping software, but could eat my muffler for lunch if I wasn't careful in straddling the biggest ruts.

Hope sat up as tall as she could, and was just barely able to see over the dashboard, loving the view and smells and bounces. Around one turn we surprised a pair of young deer that showed no reaction to our presence beyond briefly lifting, and then returning, their heads to some sweet clover they were enjoying. Hope assumed, or pretended, that they were big dogs, and did nothing more than wag and give a near-silent woof in their direction.

I took about two dozen turns on the way in and was incredibly glad that I'd marked the point where we had left the road with my GPS leaving an electronic trail of breadcrumbs that we could follow back to Route 56. I couldn't have told you with any certainty whether or not we were on public or private land by the time we got to the blocked road, but we hadn't passed a camp or cabin for a while.

We were exploring this area for a few reasons: first, it seemed the perfect spot for George to hide one of his labs, based on isolation and empty space and few attractions for tourists; second, I'd talked to a trio of businesses that each remembered having recent cash dealings that were enough outside of the ordinary to be notable (*a cargo van needing a tow, a huge purchase of propane and supplies every few weeks by the same guys, and weekly blow-out dinners at a tiny locals' only diner*), all within a few miles of where I was driving right now; third, Cynthia had emails mentioning Stark as a place; fourth, it was the closest likely circle on my map to where Hope and I had camped last night. I was exploring my way through a fair amount of gas and dirt-road miles, hoping not to be wasting my time, when I drove around a turn and saw a downed tree blocking the road. I had to force myself not to nudge Hope and point, with an 'I told you so'.

There was a big pine down and across the road, with some evidence of recent truck traffic on both sides of the trunk. In my mind's eye, I could see supplies of all sorts being slid from the truck on my side to the truck on the inside of the blockade. I looked for, and found, the marks where a chain had been attached to the tree to pull it down and across the road. My GPS indicated that Whitney Pond was just back through the woods a few hundred yards.

I looked over at Hope, who seemed excited to get to work after the bumpy drive, but I wasn't sure that the things that had made her perfect for yesterday's subterfuge wouldn't work against us today. In fact, I was nearly certain that she'd bark and sink us in the spy business (*and I had no desire to get shot again*), so I turned around, took a nearby T-junction turn, and headed down and away from the downed tree, following a track leading south that I hoped would lead to what my paper map called Thirty-Five Pond.

I found a smaller track off the already tiny trail that looked as though it would curve up to the pond I wanted to find. I took it and was rewarded by a pretty little body of water that looked worth returning to for fishing and camping sometime (*despite the fact that I was reasonably sure that I was on the private holding of some massive paper company*).

Hope and I got out to stretch and pee, and sniff around the clearing by the water; it appeared not to have been visited in a year or more, judging by the grass in the fire pit. I backed the truck most of the way down to the water, tied the extra-long lead to the bumper, and got out my fishing pole.

I had two reasons to do this: first, I wanted to spend a bit of time with Hope in this new spot before heading out and leaving her, and second, I wanted to establish some cover if anybody up at the presumed drug-lab had heard/seen us go by and followed us down. I didn't think it very likely that anyone had noted our passing; but it was a pretty morning, and I had fun fishing while Hope chased frogs and grasshoppers along the shore. I caught a couple of sunnies and a perch for her to gnaw on while I was gone (*I killed them first this time; she seemed to like them as well as the live one yesterday afternoon, and I felt better about it*).

Whitney Pond, 8:42 a.m., 9/12/2012

I walked north from the oddly named Thirty-Five Pond, leaving Hope close enough to the pond to drink, with adequate fish to stuff her belly, and shade under the truck if the day got hot. I debated walking a straight line between her and where I assumed a drug lab was hidden up at Whitney Pond (*using my handheld GPS, it'd be easy*) but I figured that it would be quicker and quieter sticking to the road.

I walked at a good pace, stopping to listen for a full minute every two-hundred to three-hundred yards. I couldn't hear a thing beside bugs and birds until I was almost to the downed tree across the Whitney Pond offshoot. I stopped at the log to drink from my hydration pack's hose, and eat a handful of GORP; the sound was a fairly constant buzz, punctuated every minute or two by a thunk or clunk. I tried to place it, and eventually got an image of a handsaw and a growing woodpile; nights must be getting cold up in 'meth-camp' for the chemists, and they were supplementing whatever heat they had with wood.

I listened for another five minutes before heading up into the woods, eschewing the road at this point in case I was unlucky enough to be there when a re-supply meet-up was scheduled. I worried briefly about a lookout, but after stalking and listening through the woods like a ninja for a bit, I reasoned that even if they had posted a sentry at first, months of nothing happening would make it hard to maintain discipline. I bet myself that if there was a lookout, he had fallen back to the camp months ago.

I crept through the woods, keeping it slow and stealthy enough that the birds and squirrels didn't stop their workdays to worry about, or scold, me. Once I got close to the camp, I could hear a radio from inside the trailer, but didn't sweat it (*although I still tried to keep my noise down and stay low*). They, and their camp, looked exactly as I had thought they would, and it occurred to me that I didn't need to go closer. I had confirmed their location, and the fact that they were secreted behind a blockade was enough for me to draw conclusions about what was going on in the trailer.

I thought about Hope, waiting for me down at the oddly named pond, and Dorothy and Frank, and Cynthia's spirit, languishing in the lake; I turned around and crept back down through the woods towards safety. I had been having fun being clever and stealthy and wood-crafty, but it wasn't necessary for the completion of my appointed task, and in fact it might prove dangerous and hinder or halt my investigations (*and/or life*). Dorothy and Frank would be okay if I didn't make it back, and would likely be motivated to find and persecute (*if not prosecute*) the people that had hurt me, but Hope was tied to my bumper, and suddenly the image of her stranded there, alone in the woods, made me sad and homesick for Thirty-Five Pond.

I walked a bit faster as I got away from what I was starting to think of as 'meth-camp B'. I let me feet do their thing while my brain worked on retooling my mission protocol to more effectively minimize risk and maximize effect. In addition to re-writing my mission orders, I distracted myself from the foolish desire to hurry through the last bit of my journey by playing with the number thirty-five in my head; the silly pond name bothered me on some level.

Thirty-five is the product of two primes, the highest that one can count on their fingers in a base-six system, and the fifth pentagonal number. I ended up assuming that the surveyor had only been capable of coming up with thirty-four creative pond names before the Adirondacks' endless supply of bodies of water had exasperated him.

By the time I was down the road and closing in on Thirty-Five Pond (*cutting one leg off of the triangle by bushwhacking a bit*), I had some ideas about closing down my end of the investigation more quickly (*and safely*). I got to the clearing, saw Hope sleeping in the sun by the truck, and lay down with her by the water after shedding my pack. She woke up and came over to share two careful fishy kisses on my right ear before curling up along my side, settling down with an exaggerated sigh.

Sevey Corners, 12:53 p.m., 9/12/2012

We swung up past the downed tree and meth-camp as we were leaving; and I had a tense few seconds as we confronted a big truck, with two hard looking guys in it, driving towards us.

They pulled half-off and I did the same, so we could pass each other, single lane fashion. I had no way of knowing if they were coming back from a supply run for the meth-camp, or just looking for a spot to fish and drink some beers. The occupants were staring at me and Hope (*who had climbed into my lap to give me driving advice and growl a bit of trash-talk and stay safe from the uglies in the red truck*), perhaps because my Element was not the kind of vehicle generally seen on these back roads.

When Hope paused for a second in her low toned growling and woofing, my nerves got in the way, and I couldn't help commenting, "I don't know. Fly casual." I drove past them at a distance of about eighteen inches, and then it was over. I watched them recede in my rearview (*without anyone tapping brakes*) until Hope and I rounded a turn, at which point I drove thirteen percent faster than was absolutely safe to get us back to the main road.

With the GPS breadcrumb trail, it was about seventeen times easier finding our way back to the main road from Thirty-Five Pond than it had been finding our way in. Once we were back on Route 5, heading south, we stopped in at the 'Gas 'n' Sip' at Sevey Corners, again, to top up the tank (*I've never worried that I had too much gas in my vehicle*).

When I went in to pay, I grabbed four questionable hotdogs off of the roller, loaded all of them with chili and cheese, and went out to feast at the picnic table with Hope. She gobbled both of hers down, once they had cooled, as though they were the best chili-cheese dogs she'd ever had. I opened a liter of water, pouring half into Hope's bowl, to help us wash down the roadside perfection. The sun was shining, we were eating junk food in the only place with lights and electricity for miles around, and we were setting up bad guys operating in my backyard for a fall ... for things to be any better, I'd have to be in my hammock eating bacon and drinking an ice-cold Coke.

I used walking Hope as an excuse to walk out of view of the gas station windows to pee at the border where the Gas 'n' Sip parking lot stopped fighting the wilderness; ten feet from the edge of the pavement were deer paths that men had never walked. It made me happy to think that the Park would swallow this place whole in about fifty years if mankind disappeared.

We headed westwards on Route 3, towards Watertown, with the sun slightly behind and to our left, burning the arm I hung out the driver's side window in a pleasant way. Once we left Sevey Corners, there were only trees on both sides of the road until we got a bit past Cranberry Lake; at which point we headed back off of the main road, to look for a nice place to spend the afternoon and evening; hopefully finishing up the meth-hunt tomorrow.

Wanakena, 2:47 p.m., 9/12/2012

We drove past Cranberry Lake, turned off Route 3 and down towards the tiny group of houses that make up the town of Wanakena; which grew up around logging, and nowadays has a symbiotic relationship with the ranger school run by the State University of New York. There's no gas station in town, but they have a general store on River Street which multi-tasks as post office, town offices and the 'tourism' center.

Hope walked in with me after I got the nod from the old man behind the counter, and we picked up some stew meat, root veggies, a stick of butter, and as a reward for hard work (*someone, somewhere, must have done some*) a pint of Perry's coffee ice cream. We grabbed our goodies and drove down to the end of Main Street, which abruptly changes into a hiking trail, with a turnaround to let people looking for the rest of town (*which doesn't exist*) get back out to the main road. I parked off the shoulder and left

Hope in the passenger seat while I loaded my pack with what we'd need for the night. Before heading out, we split the pint of ice cream; dessert-first makes sense when lacking a freezer.

We walked about five-hundred yards down the path and found a perfect spot near the bottom (*or top, depending on where you started*) of a lake formed by a beaver dammed (*and possibly damned*) creek. There was a campsite that was well-kept by the rangers-in-training, so I took a risk and let Hope off her lead for a bit while I set up my hammock and found some firewood. She seemed happy to be free and went for a swim, and then wandered off into the woods after all of the things that beagles smell and chase. She kept coming back to check on me from time to time, and I gave her treats and praise and an ear-rub each time. When the afternoon sounds started changing into the precursors of the Adirondack night songs, I remembered/worried about how she had reacted to night sounds the previous evening, and during one of her check-ins, I re-attached her to the long lead and got started on our supper.

I had enough wood for about an hour of campfire, and got it going while I prepared our suppers. I put unfair halves (*meaning I got more*) of the stew meat cubes onto the foil, rough chopped the root veggies, cut up half the butter on top of each, then dusted the mixture with the same seasoning premix I had used the night before. Next, I folded the packets closed and wrapped another layer of foil around each, then laid it over the fire using the grill someone had left next to the fire pit (*it looked like a rack from a refrigerator, but it worked fine*). After about five minutes of sizzling and tantalizing smells, I flipped the packets over and gave it another five minutes before pulling them off (*and onto the ground for Hope*) and onto a log for me, using a Leatherman to grip the hot foil.

I slit open the top of Hope's and warned her to wait, but she had to test it and gave herself a little burn (*like I do every time in restaurants when they warn me about hot plates*). The foil stew was great, and by the time we were done, we both had full bellies and grease all the way back to our ears. I was ready for a swim and some serious thinking and map work; Hope joined me for the swim, but then just took a nap while I worked.

I got the headlamp out of my pack, along with my map and notes, and thought about shutting down George's operation for good. I wanted to give Frank the directions to as many functioning meth-camps as possible. I figured four to six camps would allow him (*and me*) to be reasonably certain that those running the operation wouldn't shut down or get away before the cops could grab them up; and with a bunch of arrested felons, there was a good chance of getting one or more to give up the locations of any other camps for reduced prison-time. I already had one definite location, identified by Cynthia, and confirmed by me during my earlier fishing trip; now I had a second location. I hoped to find as many as four additional camps in the next day or two.

Looking at, and plotting, the distribution of possible meth-camps on my big map of the Park gave me a mental picture of a rough semi-circle of camps with the Tri-Lakes at the center(*ish*); the meth-camp near Tupper Lake, Cynthia's find, was too close to a city to fit in with the rest of the pattern, so I took a leap, and assumed that it had been the first meth-camp, and that later iterations had been planned further into the backcountry (*small camps in the back of beyond made for lower profile meth production, or so I assumed George had figured*). Sticking to my idea that George (*or whoever worked the maps for him*) wouldn't have gone north, northeast or east, that still left some huge tracts of land (*both public and private*) in which he could have set up a couple more meth-camps. The place I found today fit that pattern, so I looked at the empty spots on the map, trying to get a feel for the pattern of the meth-camps so far; using the occurrences of unusual/repeated cash outlays close to appetizing chunks of wilderness gave me a couple more ideas about where to look, as long as Hope and I were in this part of the Park. Looking at an optimized mental map, I envisioned a total of eight meth camps, spread throughout the quieter places in the Park.

It looked as though if I continued to the west, towards Watertown on Route 3, I could get near a possible third location mentioned in some emails between George and his minions. I liked the looks of this one because a gas station at nearby Bear Lake had sold the same, non-local, guy new truck tires on two separate occasions, both for cash, and filled numerous propane tanks for him every week or two, also for cash. After checking out the spot near Bear Lake, I would loop around south, and head homewards via Old Forge (*on Route 28*), where there was a nice confluence of open/empty space and a few instances of large cash payments that were enough to make me suspicious, all pointing to a space a few miles north of Old Forge.

At this point, I noticed that I was stiff and cold and straining to see in the failing afternoon light; Hope was twitching in her sleep, thinking about squirrels, or maybe those rednecks we'd seen earlier in the day. I stood up, and made enough noise doing it to wake Hope, so we took a little walk around the perimeter of our camp, straightening stuff and hanging a bear-bag, before getting ready for bed.

I had laid her fleece blanket (*folded and scrunched into a nest of sorts, I'm not a beast*) below my hammock, and climbed into bed above Hope. For a while I could hear her turning around and then whimpering a bit as the sound and light finished the change from day to night. She stood up and bumped my butt with her nose and gave a little woof up at me. I looked over the edge and started to ask her if she wanted to join me, (*making the 'up' gesture*) and before I got the words out, she was on top of me, making happy noises and turning around in dog circles. I reached down and groped around for her fleece, laid it on top of her, and we fell asleep like that. The only downside was that the pressure on my mid-section hastened my late-night pee wake-up call (*an issue with hammock-camping anyway*) ... we managed to settle back down again for a few hours after that, with me reading, using Hope for a bookrest.

Wanakena, 4:22 a.m., 9/13/2012

It was going to be dark for a while, but both Hope and I woke up agitated, and couldn't get back to sleep, so I made some oatmeal for myself, and kibble with some gravy (*thanks again to the miracle of leftover hot water*) for Hope. We both enjoyed our breakfasts, watching the light from the sliver of moon dance on the rippling water, thanks to some bird or beast ruffling the otherwise smooth surface of the little pond, which seemed to lack a name on all of my maps.

I broke camp while giving Hope the chance to explore off-lead a bit, and was paid off with a big splash and some barking as she surprised and upset and then swam after a duck for thirty yards towards the center of the pond. Neither Hope nor the duck seemed to take it too seriously, and a good time was had by all. Hope came back up and had shaken or rolled off most of the water by the time I was ready to hike out to the car, aided by my headlamp.

Dry Timber Lake, 6:14 a.m., 9/13/2012

Hope and I left Wanakena in out rearview mirror long before sunrise, topped up and grabbed some appropriate road food at the Nice 'n Easy gas station and grocery store in Star Lake, a few miles further to the west, and were exploring the back roads south of Fine, NY as the sun peeked and then crept over some of the shorter trees. Hope snored and farted in the passenger seat next to me as we drove, waking up every once in a while, over a bump or when I would reach over to stroke her back. Although her system had not yet adjusted to the rigors of road food, she seemed to be handling the trip pretty well, so far.

I didn't often get this far west in the Park, and I could feel the difference, in the types of trees that grew, and the lights on the horizon (*from Fort Drum I suppose*), and the sensation of 'edge'; we were about to fall off the rim of the Park and into a more civilized world. I was eager to turn around and get back into the woods, but needed to check out this set of solid coordinates.

We bumped and bounced our way to a narrow track that should have lead back to Dry Timber Lake, but it was blocked about seventy-five yards down by the ubiquitous fallen tree. I had to back and pull a W-turn to get out of the cul-de-sac, and felt oddly exposed while engaged in the forward and back movement in the Element. Hope woke, either from the starting and stopping motion, or by picking up on my tension; she stood and looked out the window and gave a single woof at the woods before curling back up into a ball.

On our drive out, I saw a pickup truck in the distance that rang a bell, possibly the hard-eyed rednecks from the previous day. I took a random turn at speed and raced down the dirt track and around a turn so that whoever it was wouldn't get a chance (*or another chance*) to see me and Hope up close and personal.

I did another W-turn after rounding a few bends, and sat facing back the way that we had come from for a full ten minutes, talking to Hope, rubbing her ears, trying to calm one of us down (*hard to say which*). I had visions of armed legions of rednecks coming down my side road, blocking my escape with their truck(*s*) and dumping Hope and me into shallow graves. I strained my ears for the sound of a truck engine coming closer, and for a minute could hear the dull growl of a diesel engine, and crackle of gravel under a heavy vehicle, but then it faded again, as they continued on their way to the meth-camp (*or fishing spot or family barbeque or swimmin' hole ... who knows?*). I felt okay marking that spot down on my map as 'positive' for meth-camp status. I drove too fast on the way back out to Route 3.

Old Forge, 10:08 a.m., 9/13/2012

Hope and I pointed the truck south from Fine, and headed down Route 812 to Lowville and Boonville, before looping back north on Route 28 towards Old Forge. We stopped in Old Forge for breakfast at the Five Corners Café , and to make a few follow-up phone calls *(including one to Frank to tell him that I was making progress)*, before heading up to explore the backcountry north of Old Forge.

I'd had an interesting conversation with a tow-truck operator who had helped to jack/tow a trailer back up onto a dirt road between Cranberry Pond and Woods Lake. I'd also talked to a guy working at Old Forge Hardware, who'd had a cash customer for multiple grill-sized propane tanks every week since snowmelt, and more recently for hundreds of dollars of cold-weather clothing. It seemed likely, at least to me, that George had another meth-camp up in the woods north of Old Forge.

I pointed the Element out of town on Big Moose Road, and once I got up within a few miles of where the tow-truck had helped pull the trailer out of a ditch, I began taking random turns, trying to wander in circles that generally took me back towards (*and around*) Cranberry Pond and Woods Lake. I stopped towards noon up at Big Burnt Lake (*a slight detour from my back road looping*) to go for a swim and do some fishing. I hung a hammock near the water and, after getting a few bites and catching a snack for Hope, took a nap. I tied Hope's long lead to one of the trees that my hammock was hung from, and she eventually settled underneath me, dreaming of something that made her twitch and cry a bit.

Eventually, we struggled out of nap-mode, and spent a few more hours, unsuccessfully, exploring the woods and roads north of Old Forge, looking for signs of the missing meth-camp. I found some great paddling-trip access points, and determined to explore the connected series of lakes and rivers and reservoirs up there before snow flew, but never did see anything that confirmed my hunch that George had set up one of his production labs in the area.

I was headed back down through a slightly different network of tiny tracks and jeep trails than we'd taken on the way in, when Hope and I took a blind turn in the road and passed those same cold-eyed rednecks in their pickup for what must have been one too many times. I thought that I saw a second of recognition in the passenger's eyes as they drove past. It was confirmed a second later in my rearview, when I saw the brake lights flare, the truck skid into a turn, back up and maneuver through a 180 degree turn on the blessedly narrow track prior to chasing me (*and Hope*) down.

North of Old Forge, 3:22 p.m., 9/13/2012

I stomped hard on the gas and felt the Element strain against the gravel road, spitting a few stones before gripping and accelerating down the road. I could see the bad guys' truck in my rearview as it completed a seventeen-point turn and came after me (*I took a microsecond to appreciate having the kind of life that allowed me to use the words 'bad guy' and mean it, before coming to my senses*). I had a significant lead on the truck, but two things occurred to me with the kind of perfect clarity that one achieves only after fucking up. First, I had admitted to them that something was up by shifting into getaway mode and stomping on my gas. Second, I was driving fast down a road that quite likely ended before long because they had a tree down to stop vehicles (*like ... mine*). I couldn't do anything to change either of those facts by slowing down, so I kept my foot pressed to the floor until the truck began to shimmy on the roadbed surface at just under 80mph. I tried to think about what I was going to do when I ran out of road, or they caught up to us, but I kept coming up with negatives: no cell-service, no road out (*but this one*), no caltrops, no cops, no gun, no wings.

I looked over at Hope, who had woken up when we started speeding up and bouncing exponentially more. She whined and got wide-eyed in fear, something I hadn't seen in days from her; I knew exactly how she felt. I had been treating this like a vacation, ignoring the fact (*again*) that these were dangerous people, capable of doing whatever they felt necessary to safeguard their money and livelihood and freedom. I flicked my eyes to the rearview for a second, and was uselessly angry that the following truck was noticeably closer than it had been ten seconds ago. They had a faster truck or a better driver, it didn't matter which, but I could feel my breath hitching and see my eyes clouding with angry tears at the unfairness of it. I was happy and safe and healthy and enjoying my road-trip with Hope. I didn't want another Justin and Barry session, and I really didn't want Hope getting hurt or abandoned out here.

Like a switch had flipped, I suddenly got angry (*an extreme rarity in my life*). I felt the useless fear and edginess recede, and the adrenalin flooding my heart and limbs and brain seemed now to steady my hands on the wheel. It brought a quiet clarity to my thoughts, and a focus to my vision that hadn't been present a moment before; this was the way that my endocrine system was supposed to work when in crisis. My options and choices weren't any better than they had been a minute ago, but I could look at them more clearly now that I wasn't going to waste what time I had left (*before the literal end of the road*) crying or whining about it.

I grabbed the map I'd printed out of the area with my

right hand, and held it up at 12 o'clock above the steering wheel to check it out, and remind myself of the physical layout of the road ahead of me.

We would reach a transition to public, then private, then public land again in about two miles. It seemed likely (*given the presence of the truck currently chasing me*) that one of the upcoming transitions would be blocked by a big tree. Before the likely blockade, about a mile away from us (*in roughly forty-three seconds my brain chimed in, unbidden*), there was a ninety degree turn off to the left leading to a tiny boat-launch and fishing access point onto some tiny pond that I couldn't see the name of at the moment (*which bothered me more than it should have, given the givens*). If I took that turn, I crossed a bridge over a little creek, made one more turn, and then entered the slight widening of the road that would serve as parking lot for the boat-launch. I had an idea, and so accelerated beyond the speed that I felt safe driving on this road in the blind hope of getting around the turns with a few seconds to give my bare-bones plan a prayer of working.

I roared into the left hand turn, showering the side of the road with gravel and banging the side of the Element into support rails of the bridge; shedding speed so fast that I almost stalled as I downshifted to try and gain back some speed and time before the chase-truck caught up.

I limped around the next turn, and down the last stretch of road into the parking lot before the boat ramp and water of Mud Lake (*I was as disappointed as you to find out the name of the pond from a sign at the top of the parking lot as I sped by*). I skidded to a stop, flung the door open, and ten seconds later, the other truck slowed to a stop at the top end of the parking lot.

They were stopped at an angle, so that their truck blocked the whole width of the way out of the parking lot, passenger side closer to the water; their growling diesel was much noisier than the Element's purring engine. I hoped that the open driver's side door and lack of my head visible in the rear window would lead them to believe that I had run into the woods; as, indeed, I had very badly wanted to do. After the longest five seconds of my life, I heard a door open and feet hit the ground and start walking across the thirty or so yards towards where I was parked.

"We just wanna talk, come on outta the woods and we can settle this without any hassle ... we just wanna know who you're working for, and what they want." It was entirely possible that he was telling the truth, but I wouldn't have any of the right answers for him, nor could I convincingly make them up.

I reached down and patted Hope, then sat up, shifting into reverse as I did so. I had waited to do this until now because I thought the reverse indicator light might give him a hint, even subconsciously, that I was there and I wanted to jealously guard every possible advantage. I stomped the gas to the floor and tried to keep the Element aimed at the front of their truck as all of the wheels struggled to grab and maintain traction on the gravel of the parking lot.

The passenger who had been walking my way jumped to the side after shooting at the back of the Element looming in his vision. I could see the driver, unprepared for this option, take too long to come to a decision before scrambling to get his truck into reverse. I ran the right rear side of the Element into their truck at a hair over 20mph, crunching in their radiator partway, pushing them back off of the roadway into the parking lot drainage ditch, and moving them out of my way (*all in all, a better outcome than I had any right to hope for*).

I jammed the shifter into first for a half second to pull forward a couple of feet, hoping not to be hung up from the collision, and then reversed down the road until the bridge turn, at which point I swung the wheel down to the left, shifted back into first, and roared across the bridge and away; my engine whining from the high RPMs.

I pulled over a half mile down the road, at the first big, dead, and leaning tree I saw standing next to the road. I listened for pursuit, heard none, and jumped out to grab the tow rope out of the back. I stole a page out of their book, threw the rope around a branch about twelve feet up (*years of bear-bagging finally paying off!*), tied it to the trailer hitch (*which I'd never used before today*) in a way that seemed sure to be bad for the Element, and pulled the tree down across the road. It cracked and creaked, and on the second pull the whole rear end of my Element lifted off of the ground, but on the third try, the tree came crashing down across the road.

Given the thick stems and limbs and trunk, I was sure that their truck, even in good shape (*which I didn't think it was*) couldn't drive across. I cut the tow-rope in a couple of places with my knife (*so they couldn't use it to free themselves*), threw the pieces I could grab into the back, and drove off cackling like a madman; Hope sitting in my lap, whining and kissing my face and peeing a little bit (*don't worry, Hope, I second those emotions!*).

Old Forge, 4:18 p.m., 9/13/2012

I kept checking for reception on my cell phone. I was almost all the way in town and on my way to the Public Library (*which I'd stopped at to steal WiFi on occasion*) before I was able to connect and dial Frank. I pulled into the parking lot, the only space available was reserved for people with a handicap sticker, so I pulled into that slot (*I'd move if someone else came, but for now, my need was significant*). I grabbed and powered up my laptop while his phone was ringing.

"FRANK! I'll be done talking in two minutes. As soon as I'm done call your guys at the State Police or DEA with the coordinates I'm about to send you via email. I got attacked in the woods just now by some of the drug dealers, but I got away, so now they know that I know. It's possible that they think I'm a competitor, but you should still get your guys to hit all of the places that I send you coordinates for as soon as is humanly possible.

The bad guys that I ran into probably won't be able to call their drug-lab phone-tree for a couple of hours, but no more than that. FUCK! ... sorry." I was rattled and trying to keep calm enough to give him all he needed to know to get busy catching bad guys.

"Tyler, are you sure ... ?" he started to interrupt.

"Frank, shut the fuck up and listen. The first three sets of coordinates are one-hundred percent. The one I refer to as site A is just a bit outside of Tupper, and can be approached in only two directions so you can bottle them in with cars. Site B has so many roads going in and out that if you can possibly get a helicopter you should use it for site B to supplement cars. Site C has only one access point, so it can be hit hard and fast, by your sloppiest team. Site D is the weakest set of coordinates; being the spot where the red truck guys attacked me, but it should be within a mile of the coordinates; if you can bottle up the roads north of Old Forge, all around that set of coords, it should work." I stopped to breathe, and Frank jumped in before I could start up again.

"Tyler, calm down, slow down, there's no way I'm gonna remember all of this, and we need to get this right."

"You're right Frank ... let me finish talking through it, and I'll send a copy of everything to your email ... okay?"

"Good ... go on."

"I think that there are three to five more meth-labs, but we don't have time to find them, so you have to go with what I'm sending, and you can try to squeeze more info out of the guys you catch. I have some ideas, but nothing concrete. I'll send rough coordinates for those ones, but they're essentially guesses at this point, although I'm pretty sure they're out there ... within a mile or five of the rough coordinates I'll send."

"Is that it?" Frank asked, when I'd stopped talking for a few seconds. "Four definites that we have to move on right now, this afternoon, and four-ish maybes that we can push anyone we pick up to ID, or just search for after this stuff shakes out."

I may have underestimated Frank, or just not seen him operating in his element before; he was calm and helped me deal with the stress and adrenalin better than I would have otherwise, through his manner and questions.

"Yup, but make sure your guys go in ready for guns, or with overwhelming numbers, or both. These guys don't fool around." I was out of breath, as though I'd been running.

"Neither do we. Send the emails, keep your cell on, and get somewhere very public, with Wi-Fi if possible, while I get things going. I'm assuming that I can use your name in a complaint report to help move things along at speed if needed"

"Yeah, no problem, although I'd just as soon not be in papers or on TV if possible ... ok ... start calling people, you should see both emails in a minute or so. I'll talk to you later."

"Thanks, Tyler, you did a great job, although Meg'll kill me for putting you in harm's way. This is incredible. Call me on my cell in one hour and I should have news." He hung up, and then so did I.

I had written most of the email at the end of each segment of my road trip over the last two days. I included the coordinates and some details about the location and approach to each of the three positive meth-labs/camps, along with the rough guess for Site D (*based on where I'd run into the meth truck*). I hoped that the email, in combination with Frank's word on my being attacked, would be enough to get them moving before lunch. I said that I thought there were probably four more additional labs in the woods, and included a G-map with shaded areas to indicate my possibles. I also mentioned that, if they had the extra manpower, sending a crew of local PD or Staties out to the final set of coordinates that I had given him to pick up the guys who had chased me would be a good investment in time and resources, although I wondered how he could scoop them up if they insisted that they were simply asking for directions. I finished up the email, pushed send, breathed a sigh of relief, and took Hope for a walk on the library's manicured lawn.

Stewart's, Long Lake, 5:33 p.m., 9/13/2012

"Hi, there's no cell-service here, so I'm calling from a land line in Stewart's, as such my answers may lack detail." Frank had picked up quickly; he must have been waiting for my call.

"Long Lake, huh ... welcome to the '80s. It's slow going, getting the response we were hoping for, but it may improve as the night goes by."

"That sounds like bad news Frank ... what's up? They didn't buy it?" I could see in my mind's eye how the whole day was supposed to go. Coordinated teams moving in on the primary sites and the truck guys, and wiping the whole thing clean by dinnertime. It had been too much to hope for, so I waited nervously to hear the extent of the bad news.

"The trouble is in moving that many chess pieces around a big board like the Park ... getting different locales to coordinate their efforts, and making things

274

happen at the same time."

"Ugh ... how bad? Are they all going to walk?"

"No, I don't think so. I called in a complaint to the Old Forge PD and State Troopers about shots fired and reckless driving and drug use/paraphernalia at the boat launch. My thinking is they'll get out there pretty quick and scoop up your bad guys, and there'll be something wrong with them or their truck ... they're bad guys after all."

"Nice ..." I said, and meant it. With a bit of luck the truck guys might even think that they were just unlucky, and not call in an alarm when they got their phone call.

"I got the tate guys in Raybrook and some Feds in Albany to agree to raid your Site A, in Tupper. It's the easiest to get the heavy team from Raybrook to, and costs the least if it's a waste of time, which you and I know it isn't, but they don't. We're killing the nearby cell towers from the time we roll on the lab until we have them. Once we have them, dropping on the other two positive sites should be an easy sell, and we should be able to hold the guys without charges for the time it takes to hit the other sites, even your 'soft coordinate' site. My hope is that once we get some of these guys looking at years inside, one of them will give up the locations of the other labs, if they're out there."

"They are Frank, I can feel them."

"I believe you, but who knows ... maybe we can get a plane to overfly your hunch zones and find them that way, if we can't squeeze someone from the first four sites. So ... what do you think ... not what we'd hoped for, I know, but ..."

"Frank, it's super, I think it'll work ... thanks, and good job!"

"Tyler, I'll talk to you later, but I owe you for this ...

you made this happen, and I'm going to come out of it looking good." Cynthia and I made it happen, I thought, but didn't say.

"Tell me how grateful you are after you see my poor Element tonight."

"Wait a second ... how messed up is it? Can you drive it back to Saranac Lake?"

"No problem. The rear lights are busted on the right side, the bumper is thrashed, but not dragging, and all of the glass on the back end is cracked or gone, but I 'fixed' it with lots of duct tape and cardboard."

"What the hell did you ... never mind ... you're in Long Lake and heading home now right?"

"Yup."

I'll put in a call that my wife's car was stolen and crashed and is being returned to my garage by a dealer. I can get the guys between Long Lake and Saranac, and the Troopers, to look the other way on the lights and such, so long as you don't speed ... okay?"

"Awesome. I'll keep it five below the limit the whole time, especially in Tupper." Lots of people joke about getting pulled over in Tupper Lake, but I actually was one time, for doing thirty-seven in a thirty-five zone.

"Sounds good, Tyler. Drive safe, call me when you hit town, leave the Element at Evergreen Auto, and I'll give you a lift home. I'll be gone and busy for days, thanks to you."

He might get some credit for all of this, but he'd also be going along to kick in a trailer door or two, and likely have to fill out a few pounds of paperwork in the next weeks. I didn't envy him the next week or two.

I wished him well, hung up, bought a mess of hotdogs for the road. I headed home with a song in my heart (*and head ... and mouth*) and Hope in my copilot's seat.

EPILOG

SmartPig Thneedery, 7:18 a.m., 11/8/2012

Stories don't end neatly, at least not real ones ... or maybe just not mine. There are threads that stick out in all directions, even when everything should be all neat and tied together, and it can irritate the hell out of you (*somewhat like the unfortunate fall/winter a few years ago when SmartPig Thneedery produced wool mittens and socks and hats that were uncannily itchy*). As time passed, and things refused to resolve in the ways that I would have liked them to, I found, as had always worked in the past, that adding small servings of Marcus Aurelius to my reading diet helped everything feel better (*even if it wasn't actually better*).

The raids and arrests at George's meth-camps were considered a huge victory in the war on drugs in Northern New York. Site A and the people working there, and a sizable quantity of methamphetamine and precursor chemicals, were surrounded and scooped up intact. Sites B and C were raided after varying degrees of delay, and with less unmitigated success: at B, the trailer and precursors were found, but the people and meth got away due to a lack of coordination in the raid; at C, a standoff between law enforcement officers and the meth-camp counselors (*and the delay of materials seizure*) resulted in a fire that destroyed most of the evidence. Site D was a surprise, given the lack of perfect directions; the team working that area found the camp without any problem, and seized a huge amount of guns and drugs (*they surmise that it may have been the meth truck's base of operations*). The state and federal authorities were able to work out deals with one or more of the meth-camp employees (*making deals with people who cook up death for a living is never popular, so the details weren't released, even to Frank*), which resulted in finding two more meth-camps; one outside of Indian Lake, and another to the north of Cranberry Lake, both of which were raided successfully.

I can still feel the ones that got away as ragged holes in my conscience; two meth-camp counselors and a crap-ton of meth from B, a pair of camps that we never found (*but that I'm certain existed/exist near Newcomb*), and the truck guys. The truck guys were released (*rightly I would have to admit*) owing to lack of grounds or evidence for holding them. If they had guns or drugs in their truck or on their persons, they had dumped them in the water or woods by the time the troopers snagged them.

I find some solace in the fact that we eviscerated the meth-camp program, the cops and me; there was even some spillover outside of the Park, with guys that the cops had busted in the meth-camps giving up distributors in the cities ringing the Park. Since the program had been such a success, I have no doubt that it will come back again. As long as drugs cost less to produce than people will pay for them, someone will keep making them. I try to feel bad about that, about not ending meth production in my Park forever, but I can't. We did what we could, I did what I could, and it was a lot.

Frank got a commendation and gets loaned out as a liaison to state and federal agencies as a drug guy in the Park now and then. He barely saw Meg for a couple of weeks, just coming home to sleep once in a while, or to rest his writing hand; but still thanked me when he saw me next. I made sure to wait a bit to let the impact of the damage to my Element sink in and mingle with the glory of the arrests and disruptions to the meth production and distribution apparatus of New York State. Within a week, he found me, and gave me a form to fill out in octuplicate that helped to cover some of the damage to my Element by smooshing the damage into part of the cost of making the busts; with me as an informant and victim of the criminal apparatus. I didn't sell Frank any of my artwork, but neither did he arrest me for what he knew I'd done (*and worse, what he probably suspected I'd done*); he also greeted me with a bit less apprehension when we ran into each other around town, as we do in the course of our daily lives.

I gave Dorothy the full details of my road trip, although she was much more interested in the details of Hope's camping adventures than my brave and glorious dealings with evil hordes of meth-zombies. She raised an eyebrow when I let slip some of the dietary oddities that Hope had enjoyed along the way, but laughed and clapped like a kid when I mentioned the two of us sleeping in the hammock together, smiled at a story of coyotes challenging us from the woods near Wanakena, and went to get me a pair of icy Cokes when I told her about the getaway near Old Forge (*with me holding Hope pinned to the seat with an arm, to stop her getting thrown around*).

She asked if I couldn't have just run into the woods at the end of Cedar River Road, and when I said, "Yeah, but ..." and looked over at Hope ... Dot gasped and smiled and bent over to kiss the top of my head; she seemed to care more about that than anything else (*except possibly my not getting killed*) that had happened in the last two weeks.

It was no surprise to anyone but me that Hope and I stayed together. When I sheepishly mentioned to Dorothy that I would like to bring Hope home on a trial basis, she smacked me on the head, called me a muttonhead, and told me that she had filled out all of the adoption paperwork when I'd initially picked her up for my camping trip. Hope is sleeping on my feet as I type this up in the SmartPig office, paying me back every few minutes for sharing some Chinese food with her last night. We've been back over some of the same ground that we covered on our road trip, this time just for fun; I hope she likes exploring the outdoors in winter as well, I've been looking into fleece and booties and a backpack for her for a trip up Marcy this February.

Cynthia was declared missing when her boss, Ben, and I went in to file a missing person's report together on September 18th (*after she'd been absent from work for two weeks*). They've had no luck tracking her down by credit-card, and her bank accounts haven't been touched since the end of August. I helped her parents go through her stuff and shut the house up after the report was filed; her fish went to live with a co-worker at the library. It was both awkward and horrible lying to her parents about where I thought she might be, but I think it's always horrible in those instances; even if you're only thinking, rather than knowing, the worst, and trying to keep it from people's loved ones. I miss her every day, and while it hasn't shut my life down, it also doesn't seem to get any better with the passage of time.

I learned some things about myself during those ten days in September; some good, some bad, all of it interesting. I had assumed that my seeing things from a different perspective meant that I didn't miss important information, or leap to wrong conclusions, like other people do; I do, just in different ways. I never went to prom, never had a girlfriend, never loved anyone or anything like "normal" people do, and assumed that I never would; but I have a dog now, and people that I care about, and while I'm certain that it's different than what other people feel or mean when they talk about love, it's what I have. I like living at the edge of the map, I like working on expanding and improving my personal map, and I like picking at the nasty/dangerous/scary stuff around the edges; but I've learned the hard way that there are monsters here, that poking them can make them angry and snappy, and that I'm no Spenser or Parker or Travis ... I'm just Tyler.

I have twice felt as though my world was stolen from me, and twice been shown that this was not the case. The events of 9/11 that took my parents (*and New York City*) from me when I was a child forced me to relocate and redraw my world; bending to the will of those stronger than me, like the inhabitants of a felled tree giving in to the inevitability of a forced displacement. The loss of Cynthia, and George's subsequent assault on me and my place/security in the Adirondacks, this time as an adult, required that I learn the lesson of standing my ground, and fighting to protect my space in the world; a lesson that I could/should have learned from the Mantis Shrimp in my saltwater tank. I wish that I believed that the world (*and life*) had no more painful lessons to teach me, but feel that I've been tested by life's storms, and stand ready to face what comes next.

Later today, I've been summoned to lunch out at one of the fancy Great Camps on Upper Saint Regis Lake. Their Chris Craft will be dispatched to pick me up at noon; the details of the meeting (*case?*) sound interesting from what I could glean from the owner's personal secretary (*both what he said, and what he didn't, in our brief conversation*). I know a guy that did some work out there repairing the foundations on some of the outbuildings, and he said that they have a Stickley dining table that seats forty; I would like to see the table, and also see what use that kind of money has for a guy with my particular skill-set (*and skill-deficits*). Hopefully something scary, silly, interesting, and requiring research into arcane branches of lore (*Adirondack and otherwise*) that I've never even imagined.

Tyler Cunningham

Grandma's Tiramisu

5 egg yolks
½ cup maple syrup
½ cup bourbon
1 pound mascarpone cheese
1 cup heavy whipping cream
1 dash vanilla extract
40 ladyfinger cookies
12 ounces espresso
3T bourbon
2T sugar in the raw
2T cocoa powder

1) Beat the egg yolks in a heatproof bowl
2) Add maple syrup and the ½ cup of bourbon, wisk until blended
3) Put yolk/syrup/bourbon mix over heat in a double boiler, mix until smooth and just beginning to bubble, set aside to cool
4) Whip heavy cream and vanilla extract to soft peaks in another bowl
5) Mash/whisk the mascarpone until smooth in another bowl
6) Pour yolk/syrup/bourbon custard over mascarpone and mix until smooth
7) Fold in the whipped cream with a spatula
8) Mix espresso, sugar, and 3T of bourbon in another bowl
9) Dip one ladyfinger at a time into the coffee mix and arrange them fairly tightly packed across the bottom of a 11"X7" (*or volumetrically similar*) dish
10) When the bottom of the dish is covered in dipped ladyfingers, spread half of the yolk/mascarpone/cream mix over the cookies
11) Repeat step #9
12) Repeat step #10
13) Sift the cocoa powder over the top
14) Chill covered for 4 hours before eating

The maple syrup and bourbon serve to make it mine, make it Adirondack-y (*for Meg*), and make it a little less tricky (*for Frank*).

ACKNOWLEDGMENTS

Writing this book has been a goal of mine for the last thirty years; accomplishing this goal without a crap-ton of help would have been impossible. I had the help of family and friends and complete strangers alike, in a hundred different ways; everything had to work perfectly, and thanks to having the best support on the planet, it did. "Here Be Monsters" is the product of a perfect storm of love and help and information and inspiration.

The folks at National Novel Writing Month (NaNoWriMo) provided me with a time and organizational framework that allowed me to write the first draft in a fabulous and hectic month (August 2012). Amazon's self-publishing services, through CreateSpace and Kindle Desktop Publishing (KDP) provided me with not only the means to publish this book, but also an abundance of useful information and resources that made it much easier to do so.

The Adirondack Park is both an inspiration for, and a character in, this book. The natural beauty and empty space and peace that the Park, and especially the Tri-Lakes Region, provide make a perfect setting for my life and for Tyler's.

The Tri-Lakes Humane Society (TLHS) is a massive force for good in the Adirondack Park, and an inspiration to me as a writer and a human being. The Tri-Lakes Animal Shelter (TLAS) in the novel is loosely based on them … everything good about it is true, the illegal activities were entirely made up. We've brought four dogs home from the TLHS to live with us, and all of them were instrumental in helping me write the book in one way or another.

The students that I have had the opportunity to work with, and learn from, over the years at Lake Placid Middle/High School have helped me to celebrate our differences, and explore some of the various ways that there are to see the world.

Friends and family have inspired and supported me throughout the writing and editing process, and I can't thank them enough. My parents (Jim and Jill Sheffield), sister (Sarah Sheffield), wonderful son (Ben), and wife (Gail Gibson Sheffield) all gave me the time and space that I needed to follow this dream, and their bottomless love gave me the courage to try. Rick Schott, Bryce Fortran, Derek Murawsky, Kevin Curdgel, and Stephen Carvalho have helped me expand my map of the world through their friendship while camping in all conditions. Countless other friends have also offered encouragement, especially Jonathan Webber and Gail Bennett Schott who have given me unending support and positive vibes during the writing and editing process.

A big shout out to the entire staff at SmartPig Publishing for their tireless efforts throughout the process ... thanks Gail!

While I couldn't have done it without any of you, any errors or omissions are all mine.

ABOUT THE AUTHOR

Jamie Sheffield lives in the Adirondack Park with his wife and son and two dogs, Miles and Puck. When he's not writing mysteries, he's probably camping or exploring the last great wilderness in the Northeast. He has been a Special Education Teacher in the Lake Placid Central School District for the last fifteen years. Besides writing, Jamie loves cooking and reading and dogs and all manner of outdoor pursuits.

"Here Be Monsters" is his debut novel.

Follow the ongoing adventures of Tyler Cunningham
and read other works by the author.

Visit Jamie Sheffield's website:

www.jamiesheffield.com